SPECIAL MESSAGE

KT-500-622

THE ULVERSCROFT FOUNDATION
(registered UK charity number 264873)
was established in 1972 to provide funds for
research, diagnosis and treatment of eye diseases.
Examples of major projects funded by
the Ulverscroft Foundation are:-

- The Children's Eye Unit at Moorfields Eye Hospital, London
- The Ulverscroft Children's Eye Unit at Great Ormond Street Hospital for Sick Children
- Funding research into eye diseases and treatment at the Department of Ophthalmology, University of Leicester
- The Ulverscroft Vision Research Group, Institute of Child Health
- Twin operating theatres at the Western Ophthalmic Hospital, London
- The Chair of Ophthalmology at the Royal Australian College of Ophthalmologists

You can help further the work of the Foundation
by making a donation or leaving a legacy.
Every contribution is gratefully received. If you
would like to help support the Foundation or
require further information, please contact:

THE ULVERSCROFT FOUNDATION
The Green, Bradgate Road, Anstey
Leicester LE7 7FU, England
Tel: (0116) 236 4325

website: www.ulverscroft-foundation.org.uk

Jim Kelly was born in 1957 and is the son of a Scotland Yard detective. He went to university in Sheffield, later training and working as a journalist on publications including the *Financial Times*. He has been shortlisted for the John Creasey Award, and has since won a CWA Dagger in the Library and the New Angle Prize for Literature. He lives in Ely.

You can discover more about the author at jim-kelly.co.uk

THE MATHEMATICAL BRIDGE

Cambridge, 1940: It is the first winter of the war and snow is falling thick and fast. When a college porter hears a child's cries for help coming from the river below the ancient Mathematical Bridge, Detective Inspector Eden Brooke is summoned. Despite his desperate attempts at rescue, the flood carries the child's body into the night. The boy was Sean Flynn, part of a group of Irish Catholic children evacuated from a poor London parish. When a local electronics factory is attacked and an Irish Republican slogan left at the scene, Brooke questions whether there could be a connection between the two events. As more riddles come to light, he begins to close in on a killer, but there is one last twist: it seems that Sean Flynn had his own startling secret.

JIM KELLY

◆

THE MATHEMATICAL BRIDGE

Complete and Unabridged

CHARNWOOD
Leicester

First published in Great Britain in 2019 by
Allison & Busby Limited
London

First Charnwood Edition
published 2020
by arrangement with
Allison & Busby Limited
London

A catalogue record for this book is available
from the British Library.

ISBN 978–1–4448–4454–2

Published by
Ulverscroft Limited
Anstey, Leicestershire

Set by Words & Graphics Ltd.
Anstey, Leicestershire
Printed and bound in Great Britain by
T. J. International Ltd., Padstow, Cornwall

This book is printed on acid-free paper

To Steve and Gabrielle Bennett
for a friendship that stretches from Dryden,
to Shaw, to Brooke

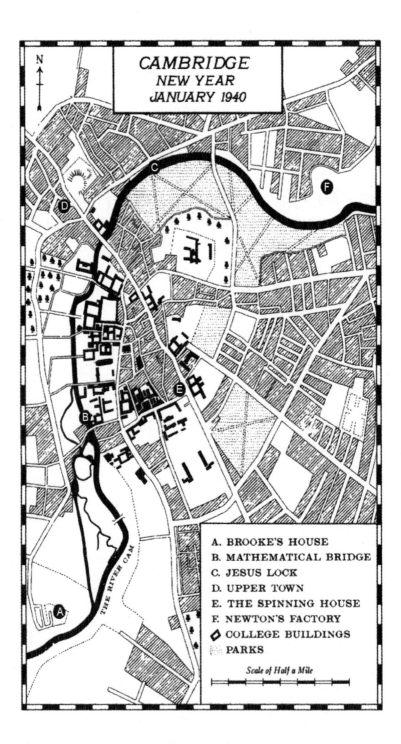

CAMBRIDGE
NEW YEAR
JANUARY 1940

A. BROOKE'S HOUSE
B. MATHEMATICAL BRIDGE
C. JESUS LOCK
D. UPPER TOWN
E. THE SPINNING HOUSE
F. NEWTON'S FACTORY
◇ COLLEGE BUILDINGS
  PARKS

Scale of Half a Mile

Author's Note

The City of Cambridge is one of the principal characters in *The Mathematical Bridge*. Like all fictional characters it is a combination of fiction and reality, both in terms of its geography and history. I hope that, whatever the mixture of fact and imagination, the city's spirit of place survives.

1

New Year, 1940
Cambridge

Detective Inspector Eden Brooke trudged into Market Hill, the city's great square, as snowflakes fell, thick and slow, each one a mathematical gem, seesawing down through the dead of night. Every sound was muffled, a clock striking the hour out of time, the rhythmic bark of a riverside dog, the distant rumble of a munitions train to the east, heading for the coastal ports. The blackout was complete, but the snow held its own light, an interior luminescence, revealing the low clouds above. Brooke stopped in his tracks, his last crisp footstep echoless, and wondered if he could hear the snow falling; an icy whisper, in time with the sparkling of the crystals as they settled on the cobbles, composing themselves into a seamless white sheet.

In the sky to the south a pair of searchlights fidgeted, searching for the German bombers yet to come. Brooke thought of his son, Luke, with the British Expeditionary Force, camped out along the Belgian border, asleep now under the same weeping sky, waiting for spring, the thaw, and the first volley of shells from the east. The war was nearly five months old, and the clash of the Great Powers edged nearer every day, the so-called phoney war stretching out towards the inevitable breaking point.

Brooke walked on through a world he knew well: the city at night, a maze of stone and hidden places, a personal kingdom. He passed the bone-white marble columns of the Senate House and saw King's Parade ahead, a great open thoroughfare, bordered on one side by a chaotic jumble of shops and inns, looking out across a wide snowfield to the stone traceries of the college buildings, and the soaring silhouette of King's College Chapel. The scene was utterly quiet, frozen in the moment. He looked up, snowflakes falling wetly in his eyes, and saw the four great pinnacles of the chapel disappearing into the clouds, as if the building had been let down from the heavens on four stone hooks.

Brooke lit a cigarette, one of his precious Black Russians, and took in the arctic air laced with that strangely metallic edge, redolent of granite islands, and icebergs, and vast grey oceans. The snow, which had fallen now for three consecutive days since New Year's Eve, covered everything in a single folded counterpane, partly obscuring a parked car, all the pavements, a few shop doorways, even the makeshift sandbag walls which had been set up to restrict bomb blast, should the long-awaited air raids finally materialise. Ice clung to the wooden boards which had replaced the stained-glass windows of the great chapel, whisked away to the safety of a city cellar.

Even in this soft light Brooke needed his tinted glasses to protect his damaged eyes: the ochre lenses tonight, providing a subtle filter which produced, for him alone, a gilded world. In his pocket, ready for use, were the green-tinted, the blue and the black. But the city at night had always been shadowy, even before the blackout, gas shortages enforcing 'lights-out' at ten o'clock for most of the years after the Great War. And, in truth, he didn't need his eyes to find his way; he read these streets as if they were set out in Braille.

The silence was broken by the bell of Great St Mary's marking the hour.

Brooke stopped at his usual spot, opposite the gatehouse of King's College. He could just see a splash of yellow light on the stonework where the door of the porters' lodge had swung open. A dark figure appeared with a shielded lantern and trudged off into the Front Court beyond to begin the ritual round of checking doors and windows, and looking out for chinks of telltale light from the rooms of scholars burning midnight oil. A cat, in pursuit, jumped from footprint to footprint, until they were both gone.

Brooke savoured the cigarette, admiring, as he always did, the way the gold filter paper caught the light. Drawing in the nicotine, he took a step forward, turned on his heel and examined the wall above his head, knowing what he'd find: a stone oval plaque which had hung there since he'd first spotted it as a lonely child wandering the city. The frost had clung to the letters, and the roughly hewn decorative symbols of a wine pitcher and a bunch of grapes.

Edward FitzGerald, poet, lived here: 1880-1891

He'd read FitzGerald's masterpiece when he'd been a soldier in the desert during the Great War. The *Rubáiyát of Omar Khayyám*, a translation of the Persian original, had replaced *The Iliad* in his kitbag. Each night, on the long march from Cairo across the northern Sinai with the Egyptian Expeditionary Force, he'd kept up his spirits with the poet's gentle invitation to enjoy the day.

Be happy for this moment. This moment
is your life.

Brooke bent down, made a snowball and launched it at the plaque. Given the horrors of that war, which he'd been lucky to survive, it was a philosophy that celebrated the life he lived.

The white silence stretched on. Perhaps it was the echo of the *Rubáiyát*, but the softly blanketed street reminded him of the desert, the blinding sands between Gaza and the sea which crept over villages and roads, encampments and trees, leaving them just like this: softened and wrapped, parcelled in curves.

It was the desert that had left Brooke a nighthawk, haunted by insomnia, the result of his capture and torture by the Ottoman Turks. Despite the pain — the light of interrogation in his eyes at night, the blinding sun in the day — he'd kept the secrets he had to keep. The king had given him a medal, but he'd never seen himself as a hero. By the fifth day he'd been unable to tell truth from lies. It all seemed like a long time ago.

4

He filled his lungs, held his breath, and felt certain something was about to begin. The unexpected bonus of his condition was this insomniac buzz: a hyperacuity, his senses operating at a preternatural level.

A moment before the sound itself, he heard its forward echo: the pip of a police whistle. Then three blasts, a pause, three more — the agreed signal.

Brooke ran to the corner of Kings Lane, the metal Blakeys on his shoes penetrating the snow to clash with the pavement beneath. He stopped, breathing hard, and heard the whistle again, but louder, and now the *dot-dot-dot* rhythm had gone. Narrow, cobbled under the snow, the dark passage led to the doors of Queens' College below its three octagonal turrets.

PC Collins stood in the street, his black cape swinging as he turned left and right blowing his whistle.

Brooke slowed to a walking pace. The Borough police force was one of the smallest in the country. With only eighteen constables in uniform, he knew them all: Collins, just eighteen, was excitable and what Claire would have called 'skittery'. Brooke detected a note of panic now in the manic whistling. What had unsettled the young constable? A fleeing figure — a student climbing back into his rooms after a secret assignation?

'Collins,' he said. 'Calm down, lad. What's happened here?'

Collins dropped his whistle on its cord.

Brooke slipped off his hat, folding it back into shape, replacing it with a downward tug of the forward edge. The great facade of the college looked supremely unruffled. His father had once brought him here to point out Erasmus's rooms in the third high turret. A symbol of calm, reasonable logic.

Collins stood awkwardly at attention, breathing heavily.

'Sorry, sir,' he said, tongue-tied.

Brooke's reputation went before him: brisk, unpredictable, unable to suffer fools. Getting in the detective inspector's bad books was considered a fatal career move on the Borough. Collins, like the rest of the young constables, would be in the army by the spring if the war didn't end. Like the rest he'd no doubt hoped for a quiet life until then.

'What's happened, Collins?'

'Sir. I was knocking off, on my way home, when I saw the porter out in the street shouting. There's a body in the river, sir, floating downstream. He's ringing the Spinning House now, sir. I've asked for assistance.'

The Spinning House was the Borough's headquarters, a medieval gaol less than half a mile away.

'There's two others out on night beat: that's Jenkins and Talbot. I thought they'd hear the whistle.'

'Good,' said Brooke. 'This body. Did he actually see it? Any signs of life?'

A blank stare told Brooke all he needed to know: Collins hadn't asked.

'When reinforcements arrive, send them down the river, to the Great Bridge, then Jesus Lock. If the body's floating, that's where it will go. The stream's in flood. I'll deal with the porter. Keep up the whistling. Just three blasts then silence. Got it?'

Collins nodded.

'When the others are downriver you go up, check out the bridges. Start with Silver Street. See if anyone's about.'

Collins looked like he was trying to memorise his orders.

Brooke stepped over the high sill through the miniature door set in the great wooden gates of the college and found the porter in his lodge.

'I got through. They're sending help,' he said, standing, dropping the phone, his face utterly devoid of colour.

'You alright?' asked Brooke.

'Follow me,' he said, grabbing a storm lantern and a torch.

Front Court was a well of shadow, but Cloister Court emerged from the night because of its Tudor range of black timber on white plaster. Ahead, Brooke could just see the porter's boots illuminated by the lantern, his footprints inky black.

Under an archway with a single retching gargoyle's head, they emerged over the river on the graceful arc of the Mathematical Bridge, built of straight wooden beams set at a tangent to create a curved span, and — according to disputed legend — built without a nail.

The porter, breathless, stood at the centre, holding the lantern out over the water. The Cam was wild, a chocolate-coloured spate swirling

7

beneath their feet, the surface pockmarked with miniature spiral whirlpools. Occasional shards of ice swept by.

'Right here,' he said. 'There was a sack, like for potatoes? It was gone in a second. I think he was struggling to get out. I heard a voice, sir. Clear as my own.'

'What did it say, this voice?'

'Help me. *Help me*. Just that. And the terrible thing is it was the voice of a child. A boy — I'd swear to it. Who could do that, sir — drown a child like a dog?'

2

Brooke ran back, crossing King's Parade, where he heard more police whistles and saw a radio car in the distance, its feeble, swaddled headlamps myopic in the still-falling snow, disappearing towards the Great Bridge. Opposite Trinity's gatehouse he turned sharply into the old Jewish ghetto, a maze-like neighbourhood of blind alleys, which he'd memorised as a child. Left, right, right brought him into a small yard where the snow had etched the outline of a series of noble heads in stone, supporting iron gutters.

The yard widened to reveal a college facade and a single great door. He executed the long-perfected late-night knock — two taps, a pause, one tap — using his signet ring against the iron hinge. Waiting, imagining the night porter's stately steps, he looked up into the blizzard, each flake in shadow against the luminous sky above. He thought of the snow settling on the swirling river, the child struggling, the double suffocation of the sacking and the water, but most of all the bitter cold.

Doric, the night porter of Michaelhouse, stood in the open door, the great ring of college keys in his hand, turning away already to the interior of the lodge with its panelled walls and the orange glow of a coke fire. Here, on most nights, Brooke took refuge for warmth and the promise of a few leftovers from the kitchens or took a seat by the fire and read the college's newspapers. Doric was one of Brooke's faithful fellow nighthawks, condemned to live life out of the light, at home in the shadowy world of the college after dark, of which he was the undisputed master.

Doric picked up a kettle and set it on the stove.

'Not tonight, Doric,' said Brooke, still on the doorstep. Hat off, he ran a hand back through thick black hair which flopped forward over his forehead. 'There's no time. I need the keys to the college punt. A child's in the water. We may have time, if we're quick.'

Doric grabbed a single iron key from a hook.

'What about Jesus Lock?' he said, turning to a map on the wall which showed the tortured passage of the Cam through the city. 'The river's in flood; it may be open.'

If the lock was open the child might be swept out into the wider river and on towards the sea.

'Ring the lock-keeper, Doric,' said Brooke, resetting his hat. 'If you can find a number. If not, ring the Spinning House, they'll have it. There's a cottage by the gates. Get them to close the sluice too. I'll be there soon.'

'Take this,' added Doric, producing one of the college torches from beneath the counter and handing it over with the key.

Brooke ran back to the river, retracing his steps, almost lost in the falling snow. His blood raced, his heartbeat strained, and it made him consider again the child: *its* heart might be slowing, the blood too, collecting in the ice-cold limbs. Each minute that passed, he knew, took them further away from life. The river could not be more than a degree or two above freezing. The shock alone could be fatal.

Michaelhouse did not back onto the river like most of the other medieval colleges. However, there were plenty of keen college punters and rowers who liked to take to the water, and so a wharf was needed, beyond a locked door, where in the summer Brooke indulged his private passion for swimming in the river. Each night he'd slip into the green water, and slide unseen through the heart of the old city.

Tonight, the Michaelhouse punts lay in a frozen flotilla, chained and covered in a single blanket of snow.

Brooke tackled the icy padlock and set a punt free. As a student he'd been adept with the pole, guiding the flat-bottomed boat out past sun-splashed meadows into the countryside, where the shallow river ran in a shingle bed. Nevertheless, the frost made him clumsy, and he struggled to use the pole as a rudder, swinging out into the mainstream.

Doric's torch picked out the stone canyon which here served as the river's banks, the walls of colleges pressing in on both sides of this stretch of what everyone called the Backs. The beam of light caught flecks of falling snow; student rooms, shuttered and dark; a single owl in an empty carved niche, eyes wide. The current at the centre of the channel was rapid, but in the backwaters created by water gates and docks, steps and bridges, eddies swirled in confused circles. If the child was still afloat, the sack could have snagged anywhere, but there was no sign of life.

Blocks of ice bobbed in the muddy water. The cold river, caught between the damp college walls, had chilled the air. Brooke's breath billowed out as he used the pole to steer under the string of stone bridges which served the colleges, until a sharp turn brought him to the Great Bridge itself, the old Roman crossing which had joined the lower town to the upper, clustered around the castle. From here it was a straight run to Jesus Lock.

On the bridge above, a constable stood, swinging a lantern.

'No sign of the child,' a voice called. 'They're shutting the lock, and Baits Bite too.' Then Brooke was gone, swirling past under the echoing stone arch.

In summer the journey would have required him to use his weight on the pole, like a lever grounded in the gravel bed, to propel himself forward, but tonight the Cam was a torrent and so the river took him on at speed, and ahead he saw quite distinctly the white water of the approaching weir, to one side of the sluices and the lock.

His torchlight swept the flood, left to right, left to right. The river was black but threaded with whirling circles of silver bubbles. On the distant lock bridge, the keeper worked at an iron wheel, inching the sluice gates shut. A police constable, on the far bank, trained a torch on the water as it gushed through the narrowing gap, watching for the child.

The snowfall faltered; the moon appeared through a break in unseen clouds, shining over the wide, bubbling stream. The punt raced onwards, so that Brooke had to cling to the sides. His eyes scanned the water and, for a second, he almost missed it, something not moving with the flood: a glimpse of hessian; a hand, seeming to reach up, breaking the surface twenty yards ahead. In three tumbling seconds he was almost upon it, reaching out, knowing even in the moment that he was a yard short. In an effort to lock fingers to fingers he nearly tumbled out of the boat. Then he looked back, levelling the torch beam, but the hand was gone.

The punt dipped, swung and plummeted though the narrowing gates of the sluice. To the right he glimpsed the lock-keeper's face, shiny with sweat, a hand raised, the eyes wide. Below the lock the cascading flood created a whirlpool, which spun the punt, with Brooke at its centre. Only now, slipping away from the lock, did he notice the thunder of the water as it diminished, leaving a strange, trickling calm. The lock was shut behind him. Had the child slipped through, or was he trapped in the river above?

'Any sign?' shouted the lock-keeper, a silhouette against the searchlight.

Brooke strained to catch the echo of a child's voice, but all he heard was the strange *Brrrr! Brrrr!* of a distant nighthawk in the reeds. He swung the torch across the water's surface.

'Nothing,' he said, in a whisper to himself.

3

Brooke deployed the meagre resources of the Borough to their limit. One radio car was sent to Baits Bite, the next lock downstream, to make sure its sluices were shut too and that they stayed shut, while preparations were made to dredge the whole river at dawn, down from the Mathematical Bridge. Where to concentrate the search? It was probable the child had been swept through the sluice into the lower river with Brooke and the punt, although the locks had been closing, and he might have been caught in the spiralling currents and swept into a side water, a backwater or a ditch.

The Borough's night watch of six constables were set, three on either bank, to walk the mile from the Great Bridge to Baits Bite. The army's motorised river patrol boat was allocated the upper river. A mobile searchlight from an ack-ack gun emplacement at Marshall's airfield was trundled into place on the bank. After the white water fall between the sluice gates, the surface here was alive with bubbles, whirlpools and flotsam — twigs and branches, moss and reeds. Lights blazed in the riverside narrowboats and houseboats, their owners on deck, keeping watch. The WRVS, alerted to the emergency, had arrived with a mobile tea van at the lock gates.

With each quarter-hour chime of the city clocks, hope faded.

Brooke set up a command post of sorts in the lock-keeper's cottage. While its exterior might be charming, its interior was utilitarian, the decoration strictly limited to the green and white livery of the Cam Conservators, the ancient custodians of the river, according to a brass plaque over the door. The front rooms were used to store spare ironwork for the locks, dredging hooks and large drums of lubricant oil for the sluices and gates. The lock-keeper, a widower, seemed to inhabit only a small rear kitchen with a cot bed and a pot-belly stove. But he did have a phone, a wall-mounted Bakelite model with a printed card fixed to one side listing numbers for the locks up and down the river.

Brooke set in motion plans for the day shift to continue the search. The unsaid question was implicit: the search for what? Not a child any more, but a body. There was little doubt the boy — the voice had been high, but definitely a boy, according to the porter — now lay on the riverbed, his lungs flooded with river water. It wasn't just a search for a corpse — the victim's identity would be a clue of itself. There might be more: wounds inflicted, clothes, the drawstring, the sack.

Brooke studied the lock-keeper's chart under a bare light bulb. He'd swapped the ochre-tinted glasses for the green to reduce the painful brightness of the electric light.

The chart showed the Cam, rising in the southern hills, curling around the city, before heading north to the Fens. The child had been thrown in the river — where? The answer had to

15

be upriver of the Mathematical Bridge. Small tributaries — the upper Cam, the Granta, the Rhee — formed a network of streams and pools. How long could the child have stayed afloat before passing beneath the Mathematical Bridge? A few hundred yards, half a mile? By daylight the Borough's radio cars would be assigned to bridges and villages upstream, just beyond the leafy suburbs of interwar semis, where house-to-house enquiries could begin. Had anyone heard a child's cries? Had anyone lost a child?

The map's filigree channels of river and stream, dyke and drain, began to swim before Brooke's damaged eyes. Exhausted, he needed to find a place to rest. The best cure now for the pain was a walk beneath the cold stars, the darkness a salve. And he didn't have to keep his own company, for the city was full of nighthawks, ready with a fireside, or tea, or whisky, and often advice, when a case proved intractable. Or even a couch, or an armchair, if sleep did fall as it often did, without warning, like a hammer blow.

So he abandoned the lock-keeper's cottage and set off back into town. Parker's Piece — the city's great open park — was a ghostly encampment of white bell tents, an army camp since the first week of the war. A few fires burned in the gaps between the tents. With a jolt the scene reminded him of a night in 1934, when he'd been a detective sergeant, shadowing the hunger marchers from Jarrow. The ragged, jobless men had reached the city bounds at dusk. They'd been met with tea and buns at Girton College but with the stern indifference of the Borough when they got to

Parker's Piece. The sense in which his duty, and his sympathy, had pulled in opposite directions had left him wary of demonstrations ever since.

But here, in a military camp, he felt at ease. Claire always said he cut a determined figure: hat; broad shoulders, narrowing down to the feet, which seemed to coalesce at a single point, like a nail driven into the ground. A corporal in fatigues appeared with a torch and checked his warrant card, waving him on with a warning to tread carefully.

In five minutes, he reached the distant iron gates of Fenner's cricket ground. The university's pitch was untroubled by a single human footprint, although the spectral wings of birds, caught at the moment of take-off, dotted the outfield. A short street of large suburban houses led away into a cul-de-sac. The green door of the last house was always on the latch, so he opened it carefully and climbed two sets of stairs to a bedroom.

Detective Chief Inspector Frank Edwardes lay in his deathbed, propped up on a series of pillows, his grey marble skin catching the light of a candle set by a pile of books. The window, ajar to the frosty night air, gave a view of the ghostly cricket field. The moon, now that the clouds were clearing, cast a cold light, creating shadows of the leafless elms which circled the ground.

'Eden,' said Edwardes, suddenly opening his eyes.

They heard footsteps on the floor below. 'That'll be Kat making you tea.'

'I've woken her,' said Brooke.

17

'I doubt that.'

Kat, Edwardes' wife, was a nurse who'd worked with Claire and now cared for her husband.

'Any news from the river?' asked Edwardes.

Beside the bed, against one entire wall of the large bedroom, was a bank of radios. In peacetime, Edwardes had been a 'ham' — an amateur radio enthusiast — one of thousands across the country building simple transmitters, running networks, tracking exotic messages from Europe and beyond. War had brought a prohibition on all radios, which had to be handed in to what they were all learning to refer to as 'the authorities'. There was one broad exception: any ham who agreed to monitor the airwaves for useful data, and send it promptly to the intelligence services, could keep their kit.

Edwardes tracked the Borough's radio car transmissions along with the rest of the nightly 'traffic'.

'No news,' said Brooke. 'There's no sign. I saw his hand, Frank. Nearly got him, but the current's too strong, and the lock gates were open.'

'Well done,' said Edwardes.

'For what?'

'For not jumping in, Eden. No one likes a reckless hero. We all know you swim in the river. But not in the dark, not in freezing water, not in a flood — you had no chance.'

Brooke nodded in agreement. 'You're right. Too cold, Frank. Even for me. And the boy was gone in a moment. There's ice now, great plates of it. Any colder, any longer, and the students will be out on skates.'

Edwardes lit a cigarette and threw his head back. 'I'd like to see that again. That's how I met Kat. Last winter before the Great War, out at Coe Fen. I fell over, she picked me up.' His eyes fixed on the middle distance.

Returning from the sanatorium in 1919, Brooke had abandoned his studies at Michael-house to join the Borough, the damage to his eyes making extensive reading and laboratory research impossible. His father, a distant figure, had won a Nobel Prize for developing a serum for diphtheria, a breakthrough which had saved thousands of lives, possibly millions. Brooke, a hero of the war, still felt the need to carve out a sense of purpose from the peace. The police force had offered a chance to solve logical problems and serve the city he'd adopted as a lonely child.

Edwardes had been his mentor. They'd worked together for nearly twenty years, from war to war, policing the city in the age of the dole queue. Nine months ago, an unspecified canker had struck the old man down. Brooke now had his superior's office, and would have had the rank, but he'd been in no hurry to step into a dying man's shoes. The fiction that Edwardes would return, cured and in fine health, had been carefully maintained. His life would end in this room, and possibly before the first ball was bowled on Fenner's in the spring.

A burst of Morse code filled the room and Edwardes took up a pad, effortlessly jotting down lines of apparently random letters in groups of five.

When silence fell, he studied the note, then laughed. 'Not even in code,' he said. 'One of ours. It's always one of ours. A ham out at Royston. He says he's just picked up a message from Felixstowe that the sirens have sounded. Perhaps this is it at last, Eden. The real war.'

Brooke took the armchair as Edwardes began to describe the latest news from the BBC: fears over a German invasion of Norway, troop movements near the French border. His voice seemed to fade away, and when Brooke closed his eyes he tumbled backwards into a sudden sleep.

When he woke, twenty minutes later, Edwardes was reading. A cup of cold tea stood on the table beside Brooke.

Edwardes closed his book. 'Tell me more about the child in the river.'

'Porter at Queens' heard a voice cry out 'Help me!' Just that. Swept past under the Mathematical Bridge in a sack. I'd guess he'd be four or five years old. A boy. There's no hope, but it would be nice if there was justice. The problem is I can't visualise the killer. Who could do such a thing?'

'You're right. It's beyond understanding. That's your problem — he's the bogeyman, this killer of yours. He comes with a sack to take away naughty children, Santa Claus in reverse. A sack of toys for the good children, just a sack for the bad. If you think it through it says a lot. I'd focus on *why*, not who. The modus operandi is stark. You don't just have a sack to hand. So, premeditation. And it's ruthless, and pitiless, so

I'd say it was professional. It's not a domestic, is it? Where did he chuck him in?'

Brooke started to visualise the bridges upstream of the Mathematical Bridge: Silver Street, the Little Bridges, Fen Causeway . . .

The old man set down his pad with its scrawl of dots and dashes. 'You're not wandering round Cambridge with a child wriggling in a sack — are you?' said Edwardes. 'It'll be a car, or a truck, with the kid in the back, probably unconscious. So he stops, slings the sack over the parapet and drives off. The icy water brings the boy round.'

'God. What a thought.'

Edwardes sat up. 'I'll tell you this, Eden. Odds on he's killed before. And you'll know what that means. It's a cliché, but it's a brutal truth: if he has to, he'll kill again.'

4

At the Spinning House, Brooke slept for an hour in cell six, a stub of candle on a wooden ledge, the darkness like velvet lying on his eyes. Waking, he felt hungry. Claire worked the night shift at the city hospital and when they could they met for breakfast. Brooke shrugged himself back into his Great War trench coat, grabbed his hat and climbed the spiral metal staircase up to the Spinning House's duty desk, where the sergeant reported no news from the river, except that the dredging was about to begin and that the banks had been thoroughly searched.

Brooke stepped out into Regent Street, the old Roman road which ran like an arrow into the city from the low chalk hills of Gog and Magog. The scene was utterly still. Dawn was in the eastern sky. He felt the familiar childhood thrill of having the city to himself, a plaything, a puzzle, a labyrinth. Opposite the police station stood the frontage of the *Cambridge Daily News*, where a single light shone at an upstairs office, and Brooke heard a telephone ringing unanswered. Next to the *News* stood the New Theatre, a dramatic confection of balconies and ironwork. Theatres had been reopened, along with cinemas, and he and Claire had got the last seats in the house the week before to see *Gaslight*. Brooke thought that was a luxury: a nice, neat murder, all tied up in one small house.

He set out for Addenbrooke's Hospital, a half-mile, weaving through the university's science district, a grid of cool, antiseptic brick blocks. He came out opposite the pillared splendour of the Fitzwilliam Museum, with its four sitting lions, which he'd climbed aboard as a child, until an irate curator had dragged him off. Opposite, he turned into the iron gates of the hospital, and looking up saw slivers of light where the blackout blinds had failed. Dawn was rising, casting gold on the steam and smoke billowing from chimneys and pipes.

Once inside, the corridors, glassy and lit, led Brooke to Admissions, his metal Blakeys sounding like gunfire on the polished lino. As he was in the building he felt standard procedure could not be ignored, so he tracked down the sister and told her about events on the river. Had anyone suspicious been seen overnight? They'd treated three cases after nine o'clock: two men who'd fought in the street outside The Eagle and inflicted identical cuts on each other with identical bottles, and an emergency appendectomy. Brooke asked if the Spinning House could be alerted to any admissions of children or victims of domestic violence. Was that the root of the crime, a family at war?

Brooke ran up the stairs to Sunshine Ward. The children were being woken up for breakfast. They lay in thirty iron bedsteads down each side of the long ward, a few feet apart. There was a drifting aroma of stewed tea and burnt toast, and somewhere a radio played the Home Service, a piece of dance band music. The sun, on cue, was

23

beginning to stream in through the windows down one side.

'You're not supposed to be in here,' said his wife, smiling, standing in front of him, holding a bedpan in the crook of her arm. Claire was the sister on the ward, having transferred from Geriatrics. Children were going to be part of their lives again in more ways than one; their daughter, Joy, a nurse herself, was pregnant and now at home after six months administering last-minute health checks on soldiers bound for France from the dockside at Portsmouth. The year promised a grandchild.

At the sanatorium outside Scarborough, where Brooke had been sent after his ordeal in the desert, Claire had often touched him, pulling his hands away from his wounded eyes, or rubbing liniment into his shattered knee, where his captors had put a bullet in the hope he'd have to die, slowly, in the sun, when they'd abandoned him south of Gaza.

He wanted to touch her now, but the bedpan was between them.

'It's an official call. I'm a detective inspector, Sister Brooke.'

He took off his hat, running a hand through the thick black hair, pushing it back off his forehead.

'That means you get a free cup of tea.'

The sister's desk was at the far end, with a view back down the serried ranks. This was Claire's kingdom. She'd grown up the eldest child, with five younger brothers, and so her life often seemed like an endless, efficient attempt to

24

bring order to chaos.

While she issued orders to a staff of three nurses, Brooke noted the disturbing anomaly that was silent children. A few ate their toast and drank tea, others lay still, a drip above one, another being spoon-fed. The soft, church-like hush was unnerving.

Brooke perched his hat on his knee; the injured knee, in fact, which had been rehabilitated through a rigorous programme of swimming initially administered by Claire in a pool at the sanatorium, the germ of his night-time summer passion.

He lit a cigarette. 'Last night someone threw a child into the river in a sack. A boy, alive. The porter at Queens' heard a cry as the body went past. We did our best, although I'm pretty certain it wasn't good enough. I've had the sluices closed and we're dredging the lower river. I've mentioned it downstairs, and apparently there was nothing suspicious overnight. Nothing here? Any recent admissions? Domestic bust-ups?'

Claire sat back, her blonde bobbed hair falling neatly into place. She had a round face crowded with large features, wide brown eyes and a generous mouth. Brooke doubted that any of the nurses had ever seen her discomposed.

'One child brought in from a domestic in Romsey Town, that was the night before last. He'd been hit pretty hard, bruising and cracked bone here' — she placed a finger on the bone ridge above the left eye. 'He's not going home until a constable calls at the house. We've seen the kid before. A regular customer, in fact.'

Brooke copied out an address and name.

'Any more ideas?' he asked, massaging his eyes. 'I need to find a name.'

'I'd try the obvious, Eden: orphanages, the council foster homes, the churches. Other than that, I think I'd just wait. Someone somewhere must be waking up to find a child gone. Just imagine if it was Joy.'

For a moment he saw his daughter as she'd once been: a child asleep in a cot, before he made the effort to push the image aside.

Claire's eyes moved up and down the ward. 'It's the usual dramas here.' She pointed at the first bed on the right and onwards. 'Meningitis, influenza, influenza . . . We've got nearly ten thousand evacuees in town, Eden. The vaccies are part of life. You know we're on half-staff thanks to the war. It's such a mess: when you break up families, everything's up in the air. What do we do with a five-year-old who's crying for his mum when she's eighty miles away in the East End?'

Cambridge had become a city of children. Judged a safe distance from London, and largely bereft of heavy war industries, it was seen as an ideal sanctuary within a few hours' journey of the capital. Crocodiles of youngsters, each child adorned with an evacuee's label, were a common sight, weaving their way into town from the railway station.

'Who'd do it, Claire — murder a child like that? What man would do that?'

'Why's it a man, Eden?' she asked. 'The world's in chaos. The men are leaving for France, for basic training, for the navy, the air force. Families left in pieces. There's plenty of women left who can't cope. They don't all have to suffer in silence.' She wagged a finger. 'Lesson number one, Inspector. Don't make presumptions.'

5

Detective Sergeant Ralph Edison appeared at Brooke's office door at just after eight-thirty, armed, as always, with a mug of tea and a plate from the Spinning House canteen. The waft of fried bacon, several slices of which were compressed in a bap, had preceded him. The smell was poignant, as the imposition of pork rationing was days away and the hypnotic aroma might soon prove a thing of the past. Edison took a seat, the trouser legs of his old suit riding up to reveal clocks on his socks.

The outbreak of war had seen retired officers reassigned to active duty to fill the gaping holes left by conscripts and volunteers. Edison had been in the uniformed branch for thirty years, but Brooke needed a sergeant, and so the sixty-six-year-old had been forced to dust down that second-hand suit. Despite the plain clothes, Edison's natural confident authority allowed him to project a sense of the old uniform, a kind of aura of constabulary power, even as it hung neatly in the wardrobe at home, shrouded in a paper cover.

'Still no news from the river,' said Edison, his voice unhurried, almost stately. 'The only news will be bad news, of course.'

'Yes. Indeed, Sergeant. But we need that body. We've nothing else. No name, no motive, no murder weapon — even the sack might give us a lead. The problem is: where is the body? Nooks and crannies, Edison. We need to look everywhere. It'll turn up eventually. They always do. For now, we need to get on the killer's trail. Today.'

Edison sipped his tea. Brooke often imagined that he could hear the mechanical workings of his sergeant's steady mind, slow but sure. Retirement had promised him time for the allotment. Even now, in the dead of winter, he popped by on the way to the station. Judging by the earth on his hands he'd been wielding a spade, clearing snow perhaps from between the frozen beds of overwintered veg.

'Domestics?' asked Edison, finally.

Brooke pushed a piece of paper across the desk. 'One. That's a note of the name and address. The child's in Addenbrooke's with a cracked cheekbone. Claire says the father's done it before. A constable's down to visit — can you make sure it's been done?'

Edison nodded.

'I saw the child's hand, Edison, as clear as you are.'

Edison nodded as if Brooke needed the affirmation.

'So we're saying a sack with a child — what, three, four years old?' Edison held out his arm straight and curled his fist as if grasping the top of a sack. 'He's only stayed afloat because of the air in his lungs. He's struggling, but he's breathing, coming up for air — he managed to shout out. And there's the cold water. He couldn't have been in the river long, sir. My

29

money'd be on Silver Street Bridge. That's what, fifty yards upstream? Or the Little Bridges on Coe Fen — there's three. Lonely, away from the main road.'

'Check them out,' said Brooke. 'I sent young Collins to take a look at Silver Street last night. See if he saw anything. He's on the second shift so he'll be back in after lunch. The snow was thick, untouched. If that's where the sack was hauled over there'll have been tracks, prints.'

'If he found anything, he'd have reported back,' said Edison.

'Maybe. Double-check. Meanwhile, let's do the obvious, Sergeant. Schools, orphanages, council — anyone who deals with children. The boy's missing. Let's find his name.' Brooke looked at his watch, standing. 'Meanwhile, I'm for the top office.'

Within the Spinning House the euphemism 'top office' was universally recognised. Detective Chief Inspector Carnegie-Brown ruled the Borough with a blunt Glaswegian authority. Her eyrie, a large attic room, had housed, in the days of the workhouse, thirty fallen women in iron beds. She had brought to it an added spartan crispness.

'Good luck, sir,' said Edison, slipping away.

6

Chief Inspector Carnegie-Brown's door was always open.

Brooke hovered, executing a nicely judged cough, noting that his superior was examining a file, glasses held at the bridge of a sharp nose. She sat behind a vast desk, complete with Highland hunting scenes carved in relief, which she'd had shipped down from her last post in Glasgow. Single, tweedy, aloof, she'd nevertheless gained some grudging respect for her straight dealing. Brooke had glimpsed her occasionally on his summer swims, camped out on a day off at Fen Ditton, fly fishing from the bank. She always conjured up a whiff of the Scottish great outdoors.

'Brooke. Good — take a seat. The child — anything?'

Brooke filled her in, but he could tell she wasn't listening, merely composing whatever it was she was going to say to him. They swapped some perfunctory remarks about calling on the county police force for reinforcements in the search. Then she pushed a file towards Brooke across the pristine surface of her desk.

'You can read that at your leisure but let me offer a precis. Prince Henry, Duke of Gloucester, the king's brother, who enjoyed a brief and unremarkable academic career at Trinity College, is to visit our fair city.'

Brooke was no cheering fan of the royal family. He'd been perfectly happy to fight for king and country, but he found the peripheral members of the dynasty he'd met on his duties remarkably unremarkable. In his head, he tried to reconstruct the current family tree. The old king had left five sons. The eldest — the disgraced Edward VIII — had abdicated to become the Duke of Windsor. That left George VI on the throne. Henry was the next oldest. Even then there were more: a younger Prince Richard, certainly; and one who'd died after the Great War, a sickly child, whose name escaped Brooke.

'I know we don't mention Windsor any more,' said Carnegie-Brown. 'With good reason. We don't mention Henry either, for more benign reasons. A man of so little note his nickname is — apparently — the Unknown Soldier.'

Brooke nodded. He dimly remembered seeing a royal prince running in a steeplechase across Coe Fen, cheered on by a loyal crowd, on his return after the war. The city had been dour, grey and exhausted, like the rest of the country. So any occasion for celebration was seized on with a manic intensity. The spectators had hurrahed and waved flags; children perched on shoulders to get a princely view. He recalled a large, fleshy young man, tall but broad, with a round head, shyly raising a hand in response.

'Prince Henry is suddenly much more important than we thought,' added Carnegie-Brown icily. 'The king has two daughters, both yet to reach an age at which they could succeed their father fully, if there was an illness, an accident — or enemy action, God forbid. The family continues to stay in London, and the king wishes, on occasion, to visit the front line. If anything happened we'd need a regent. Henry has been chosen to fill this role. If anything happens he will, effectively, be king until the Princess Elizabeth comes of age. Then he'd go back to being a slightly less unknown soldier. Clearly this scenario is hypothetical. It is not theoretical. Measures have been taken. His personal security is of the utmost importance. If the king leaves the country — as he will do next week to visit France — then Henry is forbidden to do the same, despite his current military role as a liaison officer between our army on the Belgian border and Paris. Either King George or Prince Henry must be safely in the realm.'

There was something in Carnegie-Brown's voice which intimated a less than unbridled affection for the institution it was her duty to defend. Brooke suspected a brooding Scottish grudge.

'All of which amounts to a simple problem: we need to make sure his stay in the city is remembered for nothing more than its bland predictability. County is, in theory, coordinating the security, but in practice the burden of responsibility is ours. He's on our ground.'

Outside of the old city centre, policing fell to the Cambridgeshire force. Its headquarters was less than half a mile away, on Castle Hill. Relations between the two forces were hostile, although no one Brooke had ever quizzed seemed able to trace this bristling antagonism back to any specific event. The prospect of liaison of any kind was not alluring.

She tossed a note across the desk. 'We can call on County for manpower, logistics. There's a number there to call. Ring it, Brooke. Get all the help you can. Let's get this over with and move on. The visit's posted for Saturday 11th January. All leave is cancelled, here and at County.'

Dismissed, Brooke retreated to his office and read the file. The schedule for the royal visit was suitably mundane. Prince Henry planned to arrive by car, take up a suite of rooms at Trinity, then drive to a football match on Parker's Piece between an army side and one raised by the university. He would then go back to Trinity, on foot, to take tea. In the evening he was to be the guest of Queens' College. He would be invited to open the new Fisher Building, an extension on the west bank. There would be a celebratory formal dinner in the Great Hall. He would then return to Trinity to sleep, leaving by car after breakfast for St James's Palace.

Brooke summoned his reserves of patience and stretched out his hand to pick up the phone and get a line to County, but the phone rang as he touched it. It was the duty sergeant from the front desk. A Father John Ward, of St Alban's Church, Upper Town, had rung to say they had been sent thirty-two evacuees from London the day before. They had all been fed and slept in the church overnight. Roll call this morning revealed one was missing.

'A five-year-old,' said the duty sergeant, but

Brooke was already on his feet, reaching for his hat, spurred on by the image of a pale hand breaking the surface of the silver and black river.

7

The Upper Town, and the Catholic church of St Alban's, lay on the far side of the city's Great Bridge, where the Romans had built their outpost on rising ground, which reached a low man-made peak at the crest of Castle Hill. Looking east as a child Brooke had found it easy to believe his father's studied observation that the next encounter with land at that height would be the Urals, beyond Moscow, which helped explain the bitter wind. The whole district had a forlorn air and had been rotting quietly in poverty and squalor since the advent of the Black Death, forgotten for five centuries, except for the wharves on the riverside. Small, mean terraced houses huddled in a warren of streets on the steep bank above the Cam.

Immigrants had come and gone — the Dutch, the Huguenots, the Letts — until the Irish arrived, helping to dig the ditches of the Fens and then lay the arrow-straight railway lines. The Lower Town, spread out in medieval honeyed stone, had made its charitable donations to alleviate the blatant poverty of its poor cousin on the hill: a Free School, a Methodist Mission, a set of almshouses. Unemployment in the thirties had left it squalid and tatty; and even now, especially in the blackout, the Upper Town was a place to shun after sunset. It had a brooding reputation in the town for radical politics, earning it the nickname Red Hill.

Brooke, walking west in the snowy streets, could see the Upper Town's grey silhouette against the sharp, icy-blue sky, comprising a gentle hill, the castle ruins, the county gaol and the high ridge roof of St Alban's. Approaching through the area marked on one of his beloved old maps as Bridgetown, he crossed over the water into transpontine Cambridge. On one side of the street the high walls of Magdalene College — the only medieval institution west of the river — blocked the low sunlight; on the other, a line of ancient houses and shops, in jutting medieval tiers, reached out over the pavement and the narrow road.

As a child Brooke had furtively examined these buildings on his zigzag wanderings between school and home. Each storey was supported by what one of his schoolmasters had called 'lewd' images, ironwork brackets depicting debauchery: a naked couple entwined, a phallus between bunches of grapes, a woman's jutting breasts — all designed, in medieval doublespeak, to ward off the devil. Given his absent father, and his mother's death when he was six, and the lack of siblings, these images had been left to provide a raucous version of the tale of the birds and the bees.

At the foot of Castle Hill, the slums began. A winding street led his eye away, empty washing lines criss-crossing, a small child playing with a wheeled cart in the gutter. A pack of mismatched dogs fought over a clump of chip papers. Unseen, a few streets away, was the 'rookery'

— a tumbledown range of tenements on the sweetly named Honey Hill, an address seen daily on the list of defendants at the magistrates' court. On the right, on rising ground, stood St Alban's, in brutal Victorian grey stone, the lines rigid and machine-cut, without any friendly hints of a mason's chisel. An overgrown graveyard led to a vast porch in which were piled sandbags and wood. As a uniformed constable in the years just after the war he'd often found rough sleepers here, but they were tolerated by the church, and he'd always let them be.

Inside, under a double line of hanging globe lights, children were having breakfast at trestle tables set out down the central aisle of the nave. The pews were littered with bedding, suitcases packed away beneath, evacuee labels still attached. The noise was joyful, a cacophony of chatter, which might have reflected the heady temperature. Warm air was rising from iron grilles set in the stone floors. A priest in a simple black cassock had seen Brooke and was waving him over to where he was dispensing milk into mugs.

He was smiling before Brooke shook his hand. 'Father Ward?'

'Inspector Brooke. Breakfast? I can offer toast and tea. You'd have to be quick, they're like gannets.' That was the sound exactly: a colony of seabirds, safely in possession of a towering cliff. Ward was in his late thirties perhaps, with a finely drawn face, but his thick hair was as white as the snow outside. There was no trace of a regional accent, just the clipped, precise tones of an English university graduate.

38

In profile, Brooke was struck by a Hollywood likeness to a glamorous priest. Claire had taken him to the Regent to see *Boys Town*, in which Spencer Tracy tried to save the soul of would-be gangster Mickey Rooney. There was something of the star's muscular good looks in Ward, overshadowing something more sensitive.

'Can we talk somewhere?' asked Brooke.

Ward handed a crate of milk bottles to a middle-aged woman in an apron, who was vigorously buttering toast. She took it without a word, hauling it up onto the tabletop. Her hair, bright red, was piled up on her head and reminded Brooke of a Georgian print of a society lady with a birdcage in her curls. The sleeves of her blouse were rolled up, one arm festooned with coloured metal bangles from her wrist to her elbow. She was a glamorous sight, despite the sheen of perspiration on her face.

Ward led Brooke to the altar, where a monstrance stood catching the light, its centre circle empty of the host. Here, close to the gilded tabernacle, the smell of incense was almost a physical blow. A side door led into a small office blessed with a single window in the shape of a crucifix into which had been set lurid red and blue glass.

The priest didn't sit. 'I'm sorry to raise the alarm. It's just the responsibility is onerous: these are God's children, and for one night I was their father. So I rang.'

Again, the clear English diction was remarkable. Brooke imagined this voice reading the news on the BBC.

'The child's still missing?' asked Brooke.

Ward seemed to crumple slightly before answering, bowing his head. 'Yes. Sean Flynn, aged five. He arrived with the rest yesterday by train. A total of thirty-two children: twenty girls, twelve boys. They walked here from the station, and we gave them a hot meal. Just soup and bread — but there was enough for seconds, thirds. Mr Lloyd, the grocer from the top of the hill, provided apples too. They were tired, overexcited, so I organised a sing-song. There's a piano, and Mrs Aitken — you saw her outside helping — she can play. It was rather wonderful, all by candlelight. There were tears of course, especially at bedtime. Prayers helped. I locked up at nine, and we did a roll call. We've asked them to keep their labels, otherwise it would be chaos on earth. Thirty-two counted at lights-out and checked against the register. I did a roll call an hour ago when we got them up to wash: there's just one lav, so you can imagine . . . I hadn't unlocked the doors, they'd been shut all night, but Flynn was missing. So I phoned.' He touched the black Bakelite receiver. 'Of course, a lot of them are homesick and so it's no great surprise. We found the small window in the toilet off the latch. It's the only way he could have got out.'

'We're sure he did get out? You've searched the church?'

'Yes. Twice. It's not difficult, Inspector. It's a poor parish and it's a poor church. Marie — Mrs Aitken — supervised the children while I checked everything, the confessional boxes, the

40

sacristy — although that was locked too — the cupboards, the vestment box, everything.'

'Attic, crypt?'

'We've neither.'

'Where do you live?'

'The presbytery next door, to the north. St Alban's — the school, that is — is on the other side of the church, to the south. Three buildings, all clustered round the yard, and all the same depressing architect, I'm afraid. There're no connecting doors. Each one stands alone, although our lives are of one thread — if I can be poetic.'

'Can you show me?' asked Brooke.

There was a side door that led out into the yard, which was clearly used as a playground. Hopscotch squares had been drawn in chalk, and a single set of goalposts drawn on a stretch of blank wall. The church took up one side, the school another, the house the third, all in the same institutional livery: green-painted window frames and doors, red brick, with a few Victorian flourishes.

'That's your house?' asked Brooke.

Ward looked startled, as if he'd not noticed it before.

'Yes. Built for three priests, but with the passage of time . . . I am alone.'

'Where did *you* sleep last night?' Brooke failed to keep the emphasis off the critical word. It wasn't an accusation, but he saw a shadow cross Ward's open face, a look of fleeting disappointment.

'I slept in my office where we've just talked,

41

but I left the door open. Mrs Aitken slept out with the children, in the front pew. She's a saint.'

'I see. And where does she normally sleep?'

'There's a housekeeper's flat, in the presbytery, de rigueur for the time. Catholic priests are not renowned for their domestic skills, Inspector, or compliant, useful wives.'

So, not entirely alone, thought Brooke as he struggled to put aside the idea that he was being fobbed off. The priest's tone had become breezy.

They went back to the office. Ward put a finger on a file lying on the desk.

'I thought you'd want this: young Flynn's details. Have a seat. I'll get you that cup of tea.'

Brooke nodded. An offer of a cup of tea had become the common currency of the Home Front. Sometimes it seemed unpatriotic to even think of saying no.

He read the forms by the red and blue light streaming in through the window. The parents were listed as Gerald and Mary Flynn, the address Askew Road, Shepherd's Bush, London. Flynn had been a pupil at the Sacred Heart, a diocesan primary school run by the Catholic Church. The father's trade was listed as railway clerk. Flynn's scholastic record was compressed into two words: 'easily led'. He could read with difficulty, his mathematics was poor, but he was good at sport, especially football. His height was given at three feet three inches. A brief medical note listed no causes for concern. The boy had been handed over to diocesan officials at King's Cross the day before, his form signed and dated.

The sound of a good-natured riot swelled in

the church, and Ward reappeared with the cup of tea.

'I've just told them Sean's missing and that he's probably hiding in the church. They've to find him. It's a very exciting game and I've set aside a prize of one orange.'

'No one had noticed a missing friend?'

'No — no surprise there. Most children evacuated after the outbreak of war moved en masse, as it were. Whole schools, certainly whole classes. Some parents hung on; perhaps the children were too young, or shy. The government keeps telling us the raids will come. Minds have changed. So the diocese decided to collect up all the stay-at-homes and create a single consignment — if I can put it that way. There are a few friends, classmates, but a lot are on their own, including Sean, I think.'

Ward glanced at a clock on the wall. 'The children are late,' he said. 'I've to walk them next door to the school. There's a welcome assembly, then they'll meet the people who've agreed to take them in. Or who've been told to take them in. Or been paid to take them in. The children are excited. Apprehensive, too, it's only natural. What should I do, Inspector?'

'Let the children finish their search,' said Brooke. 'Then you must get on, take them to school, and I'll see if we can find Sean. But there's something you should know, Father . . . '

Dredging the river was not a private operation. It required boats, and nets, and plenty of constables along the banks. News would get back to St Alban's soon enough. Brooke had no

43

choice but to be honest.

'Father, you need to be ready for the worst. A child drowned in the river last night. We're dredging now. It was a young boy. I'm sorry . . . '

'Oh God, no.' He shook his head, one hand searching for the edge of his desk for support, the other covering his eyes. He fell back into his seat, diminished, momentarily reduced to everyday human scale. For the first time Brooke saw the cruelty in the honorific title bestowed by the church: Father.

8

Brooke unlocked his front door and shouted, 'Home!'

Claire crossed the hallway carrying a casserole dish and paused to kiss him, the heat of the bowl between them. Now that their daughter was back under the same roof, the evening greeting had become more discreet. They used to hold on to each other, to mark the daily reunion.

The old house was draughty, but the light of an open fire flickered from within the dining room, and the few flakes of snow which had entered on Brooke's coat-tails melted quickly on the old rug as he stamped his shoes, which were caked with mud and slush from the riverbank.

'You're on time. Well done. A first.'

'We can't find the boy. It's dark. There's nothing else to do. I'm stumped. Least we know who he was. A vaccie — from St Alban's in the Upper Town.'

Claire bustled ahead to the table, which had been set neatly with what was left of the crystal glasses, his mother's cutlery, even a candlestick.

'What's the celebration?' he asked, swinging off his coat and lobbing his hat onto the stand.

Joy appeared on the steps, taking each one carefully, still in her nurse's uniform from the day shift at the hospital. His daughter was three months pregnant and radiated good health. She looked like her mother, neat and feline, but had his colouring: dark, almost black hair and blue eyes. Claire's natural buoyant energy found its echo in Joy, and the two together seemed to conjure up a little cyclone of activity. Joy had her mother's common sense, but there was no trace of the need to organise, the obsessive drive to check that all was well.

'There's a letter from Luke,' said Joy, answering his question. 'He's well, so we thought we'd be grateful for good news.'

Brooke found a bottle of wine on the hearth, one of his father's red clarets from the dusty cellar, which he poured, sniffing the earthy bouquet.

'How's Doric?' asked Joy. As a child he'd taken her on clandestine nightly visits to the porter's lodge, and she'd been taught to toast bread over the coke fire.

'Thriving. He's been made an ARP warden, which gives him bragging rights over the head porter, so he's quietly triumphant.'

She nodded. 'Mum says you've started sleeping at night. Is it true?'

'No, it isn't. I come home, I eat, I go to bed. I have a regime — at least I'm told that's what I need. The sleeping part of the equation is still elusive, especially when your mother is on shifts.'

'Don't blame it on me,' said Claire, closing the door, boxing in the heat. 'Is it snowing still?'

'A few flakes, nothing more.'

Brooke's insomnia, which had begun in the sanatorium after the war and deepened with the passing years, had become part of his life. But Claire had noticed a gradual decline in his natural energy and spirit, as if the endless days, merging into endless nights, were running him down.

Charged with trying to find the secret of sleep, Brooke had turned to an old friend, a scientist called Peter Aldiss, a nighthawk like himself, engaged on a twenty-four-hour, seemingly endless series of research experiments designed to probe the mechanisms of the circadian rhythm, the inbuilt clocks of nature. Aldiss had been his roommate before the Great War. He'd taken a brotherly interest in Brooke's sleepless nightmare.

Aldiss's regime was founded on the concept of 'establishment': a routine had to be created, and then rigidly followed. When Brooke opened his eyes, he had to go out in the daylight. If it was not too painful he was to stick to the ochre-tinted glasses in order to maximise the brightness perceived. During the day regular walks were prescribed, especially if the sun was out. Meals were to be treated almost as religious ceremonies: three, to mark the phases of the clock, from breakfast, through lunch, to the evening meal. Nothing was to be eaten during the phase designated as 'sleep'. After dinner there was to be a period of relaxation, the long, warm bath in the peaty brown water. (Hot in Brooke's case, as he abhorred the concept of lukewarm.) Then bed, in a dark room even if the blackout rules did not apply, with the window open, the sound of the river percolating across the water meadow. So far, the routine had failed to engender sleep. The nightwalker had abandoned his bed. But each night he tried.

After dinner it fell to Brooke to read Luke's

letter, as both Claire and Joy insisted he had the voice just right. While their son had been with the main expeditionary force sent across the Channel in readiness for war, his unit had been moved south, to reinforce parts of the French army camped along the long-disputed border-lands of the Saar.

Luke's news was domestic, principally encom-passing diet. One passage Brooke liked:

Roper, who was in the last bash, says that they'll have us digging trenches once the frost goes, and then we'll be back where it started in 1914. I don't fancy sharing a billet with rats. The smart money's on an attack in the north, just like the last time. In which case we're in a backwater, which is fine by me. The food here is excellent. We've been stealing eggs and shooting anything that moves. And the Saar's full of fat fish, although their precise identity is a mystery.

Quickly folding the letter, Brooke asked the question that seemed to overshadow the house like the trees on the riverbank.

'And Ben? Anything?'

Joy's husband, Ben, was a submariner. The last they'd heard he was at Rosyth in Scotland, awaiting orders. At Christmas, when they'd met him for the first time, he'd sat quite calmly before the fire and described what it was like to wait, and listen, immobile in the 'fish' — as he called it — on the seabed. If their child was a boy, Brooke thought, Jonah was destined to be the name. Ben, it seemed, liked to sleep when the submarine was lying in the depths, revealing an almost superhuman degree of nerveless composure.

Joy shook her head. 'Nothing. No news . . . What's in the paper?'

'Not much,' said Brooke, unfolding the *Telegraph*, scanning the headlines. 'The Finns are putting up a fight against the Russians, the Chinese are retreating in the face of the Japanese.' He glossed over a report that the government was under pressure to take control of the Norwegian ports before the Germans beat them to it, securing their supplies of iron ore shipped out of Narvik and Tromsø. Action on that coast would bring Ben's submarine into the real war.

'And there's this,' announced Brooke, as Claire appeared in her uniform ready for the night shift, then perched on a chair, removing a set of glass earrings. 'Tonight's offering,' he said. Each evening he chose something to read out loud, usually in an attempt to avoid introspection, and lift the mood. Often the selection was informed by Doric's careful reading of the daily papers at the porter's lodge.

MAN WITH THREE WIVES CAUGHT TRYING TO MARRY THE FOURTH

John Edward Shrike, a corporal in the Royal Lancashire Regiment, was convicted on two separate charges of bigamy at Preston Assizes.

The court heard that Shrike, aged 38, married in 1935, left his first wife due to 'irreconcilable difficulties' and that the parting had been 'amicable'.

After the breakdown of this first marriage he'd moved out of the family home in Croydon, south London, to Ilford, Essex, maintaining his job as an Underground train driver.

He met his second wife in 1936 and they were married at Basildon register office. Shrike lied about his marital status and gave a false place of birth.

Shrike's second wife left him for another man, and he continued to live in their home in Ilford until the outbreak of war, when he volunteered.

His third wife lived in Northallerton, north Yorkshire. He had met her while on leave from training at Catterick Camp. They were married at York register office.

Shrike completed his training and was stationed in Surrey as a gunner, at barracks on the edge of Croydon. His wife and child stayed in Northallerton.

At a dance he met a local woman and proposed at their second meeting. She demanded that they marry in her local church, and the banns were posted.

Shrike visited his first wife, who lived nearby and with whom he had remained on good terms, to ask her to turn a blind eye to the marriage.

He explained to her that he 'couldn't stand the strain of thinking we might all bump into each other'.

She went to the police.

Defence counsel said Shrike was 'hand-some, charming, and told women he was due to inherit a large sum of money'. He found it difficult living alone and missed regular meals when away from home.

The judge, Mr Justice Acre, said, 'Bigamy is in danger of becoming a national industry. There are signs it may prove as prevalent in this war as it did in the last. Women, sepa-rated from family and friends, must beware of predatory men who see themselves as free of the constraints of a binding union.'

Brooke set the paper down.

'The world has lost its mind,' said Joy.

Later, lying in the bath in the attic, Brooke tried to relax. This had been his mother's refuge, three floors above his father's laboratory. She'd installed the bath, and a chaise longue, and a reading lamp. Brooke had lain on the carpet to hear a bedtime story. In those days sleep had been full of adventures, and castles, and quests.

Brooke had issued an order before leaving the Spinning House that the search of the river would resume for one more day. The moment was approaching when he'd be required to call the missing boy's parents.

Missing: it was a concept which haunted Brooke. He'd been missing in the desert. It was what he feared most might befall Luke, which was why the letters were so wonderful.

The bath had grown tepid, so he pulled the plug, watching the water circle. A familiar sense of despair circled too. He wondered how it had

51

come to this, just twenty-one years after the guns had fallen silent on the Western Front. A new war was about to begin. In retrospect it was inevitable.

As a detective sergeant he'd once been called out to a disturbance outside the Tivoli cinema. It would have been 1936 or 1937 — he couldn't be sure, but he did recall the name of the film: *Our Fighting Navy*. A band of anti-war protestors, all students, had gathered outside. A counter-march, a thousand strong, had set out in the spirit of a student 'rag', organised by the Fascist League. Brooke had been forced to order the constables to draw truncheons, as a melee broke out in the foyer. He remembered chants of 'Down with Hitler!' and 'Heil Hitler!' Then someone had let off a stink bomb. It had all seemed very English.

And now, on the other side of the channel, Luke was waiting for the thaw so he could dig his trench.

9

The arrival of sleep was precipitous: he felt his feet falling into an unseen pit, and his consciousness followed, tumbling. The sound of the river beyond the water meadows faded away. So many of his dreams were not dreams at all, but versions of some fleeting, half-remembered moment of his former life. This time he was back in the Great War, on the Sinai coast road, pushing the Turks back, mile by mile, in a cheerless campaign of attrition aimed at the eventual capture of Jerusalem; a crusade, of sorts. The last crusade.

They'd reached a bridge over a river which cut under the road to reach the sea. A river only by name; this was an arroyo, a dry riverbed, the mere fingerprint of the torrent which had run in the few hours after a desert downpour. A line of men lingered on the bridge, looking down. He should have passed by, but curiosity prompted him to order the driver of his armoured car to pull over, allowing a line of horses to take the lead. The sullen crowd of men parted to let him reach the concrete balustrade.

Below him, the arroyo's striations were certainly beautiful, the dry sand threaded in a mazy pattern of lost streams and currents. The image in his dream was black and white only. The usual flotsam had been left high and dry; uprooted trees and thorn bushes, a broken canteen bottle, a line of heavier granite pebbles bowled along by the force of the flood. The dream took on its own reality here, for the images below were preternaturally precise, every grain of sand encompassed in a vision.

Just upstream were the discarded remains of a caravan of fleeing nomads. As the army had marched east, they'd seen deserted villages and camps, women and children trying to escape, the men already gone. It looked as if one of these wandering bands had been caught by the flood. A dead horse lay entombed in the sand, just the rotting head revealed. A few skeins of fabric were half-buried, and some gourds, and possibly a woven saddlecloth. A single cartwheel lay amongst pots and pans.

And a child. A boy lay alone in the dry riverbed, like a swollen starfish, the limbs slightly blue, the face grotesque. The flies were invisible in the buckling desert heat, but the noise, a basal gravid hum, was distinct, and the image shifted like a mirage. A child drowned in a river that did not exist. Brooke looked too long, finally ordering a sergeant to search the body and bring him any forms of identification from the clothes.

There had been nothing in his pockets but a single British penny, Queen Victoria on one side, the date 1899 on the reverse. In reality he'd moved on, only realising later that he should have had the boy buried. In the dream he tried to ask his sergeant to go back and put this right. Every time he made the effort to enunciate the words his tongue felt like dead meat, paralysed at its root. He tried to shout, tried harder, and woke with the final release of a scream.

10

Waking in a sweat, Brooke fled the house and set off for the cottage at Jesus Lock. He'd asked for a constable to remain at the sluices, manning the landline. The night shift had been reorganised to patrol the banks in case the child's body resurfaced. Boat-to-boat enquiries had continued after dark downriver towards Baits Bite. But morale had collapsed; there was now no hope. River wardens, water bailiffs and college porters had all been asked to keep vigilant: the body would appear, eventually. Denied sleep, Brooke felt the need to check dispositions.

At the door of the lock-keeper's cottage he met PC Cable, heading out, readjusting his chinstrap. Cable was a bright, dependable officer, nonetheless destined for call-up to military service before the spring. At this rate the Borough would be reduced to the halt and the lame.

'Sir. The desk just rang. PC Harris, on the far bank, says a woman on the towpath reckons someone's breaking into Newton's factory. Says she saw three men at the security wire. Looks like burglars in the blackout. She's there now showing Harris the spot.'

They turned downriver, past Midsummer Common, the college boathouses on the far bank, and then over Newton Bridge, a nickname now widely adopted, conferred by the hundreds of men and women who worked in the electronics factory on the far side. The building itself was low, with a modernist wave-like roof. By moonlight they could see the brutal simplicity of its construction: three floors, rows of large Crittall iron-framed windows. The whole complex was set back on the water meadows, beyond a frozen football pitch. As Brooke crossed the snowfield, he recalled that the factory made radios and newfangled televisions, and possibly electronic equipment for laboratories. There were several similar factory sites up and down the river, spawned by enterprising university academics who'd taken the city's love affair with mathematics and turned it into a passion for technology.

Ahead they could see torchlight at a wire fence and a group of people in animated conversation: two police constables, what looked like a nightwatchman with a storm lamp, and a woman in a black overcoat with a fur collar and a fur hat.

PC Harris, consulting his notebook, introduced the witness as Dr Augustine Bodart, a fellow of Davison College. She'd been walking home when she'd seen something suspicious up at the wire, which she'd reported to the constable as he patrolled the towpath.

'The constable says a child is lost?' she asked Brooke, a hand to her mouth. She was perhaps forty years old, heavily built, with remarkably agile and expressive features, which gave the impression that she was talking to a not very bright child.

Brooke told her they were still hopeful, that a search was underway. Then he asked her to tell them what she'd seen.

'Three men just here,' she said, and Brooke noted the distinct guttural accent: German possibly, but maybe Hungarian or eastern European. 'Hurrying away towards town. I have no doubt they pass through the fence. I saw their faces, certainly. The labouring classes, perhaps?'

'Did you call out?' asked the nightwatchman. Brooke could see now he was an elderly man, with a grey moustache and a railwayman's cap, who looked extraordinarily worried.

Bodart thought the question a stupid one, because she laughed as she shook her head. 'Certainly not. They are felons. And I was there, on the towpath, not so far away.'

'You raised the alarm?' asked Brooke.

'I told the constable when I saw him on the path a moment later — a minute, perhaps two.'

'No sign of 'em by then, sir,' said Harris.

Brooke took off his hat and ran a hand back through the black hair. 'And you are a national of which country, Dr Bodart?'

The war had made such questions a necessity.

She stiffened slightly, pulling the fur collar closer. 'I am Austrian, Inspector. *Austrian*. The Nazis have invaded my country, as no doubt they would wish to invade yours. I call at your Spinning House once a week to register. I can assure you I pose no danger to the realm.'

She smiled, looking at each of them in turn, apparently pleased with this explanation.

Brooke recalled a newsreel of Hitler's triumphant entry into Vienna. He felt that the concept of 'invasion' had been stretched to

57

breaking point. And, besides, the Anschluss — the annexation of Austria — had effectively made Dr Bodart a citizen of the Reich whether she liked it or not. At the outbreak of war, government tribunals had reviewed the status of thousands of Germans and Austrians living in England. A few hundred had been jailed, ten times that released, but with restrictions on their movements. Regular attendance at a local police station was one such restriction.

Brooke left her to arrange with one of the constables to make a statement at the station, giving as full a description as possible of the three men, while he stepped through the hole in the perimeter fence, aided by the nightwatchman, whose name was Ridley.

'I think we should see what they were up to, don't you?' said Brooke.

Ridley lived in a cottage on the site and dogged Brooke's steps. 'I was just about to set out on me rounds,' he said. 'I did 'em earlier too. This isn't my fault. This place is top security now. They'll not have got in the labs. It's all locked up.' Ridley rattled a bunch of keys at his belt.

Brooke examined the facade, noting that it was top security *now*.

They began to circle the building: the works entrance was at the north end, and a bicycle shed and what looked like a generator at the other. On the far side the factory faced the street and the church of St Andrew's, almost lost in a soaring copse of pines and a great cedar. The south end had no doors, but there was a set of

58

communications aerials rising from a compound. In the corner of the site stood the great mast — a landmark in a flat city.

Ridley followed Brooke's upward gaze. 'Two hundred feet high,' he said. 'The light's to warn aircraft. We had a day out at Ely in the summer and you could see it from there,' he added, with a note of professional pride.

They returned to the main doors which were, indeed, securely locked. They'd checked each ground-floor window on the circuit, and none were broken or forced. Cellar doors, for deliveries, were chained. It looked as if the burglars had fled empty-handed.

'What do you think they were after?' asked Brooke, as he made a note by torchlight.

The nightwatchman shrugged.

'What does Newton make?'

Ridley shook his head. 'Same as always. Radios. TVs — that's what that's for,' he added, nodding to the mast. 'Boosts the signal from Ally Pally, so they can work on getting the picture right. After the war, you see, they'll be making thousands of sets. One for every house, that's what they say.'

Ally Pally — Alexandra Palace, on the northern outskirts of London — had been co-opted by the BBC to test television broadcasts.

Ridley's futuristic vision prompted a moment of silence.

Which is when Brooke detected the infinitely small crimp of a change in air pressure. A lemon-yellow flame suddenly flared at the foot of the TV mast, sending a pain through Brooke's eyes, into his brain, where it seemed to burn its way into his spinal cord. The shock wave put him on his knees; the sound a dull thud, a body-blow, followed by an acid fizzle, producing a cloud of choking fumes.

Struggling to his feet, fumbling for the black-lensed glasses in his pocket, he forced himself to open his eyes. The TV mast was alight, its metal crossbeams blazing in a geometric pattern set against the low snow clouds. Ridley was still standing, but there was blood pouring from a wound above his hairline, and he was shaking violently.

The blast had left Brooke deaf. PC Harris appeared, Dr Bodart in his wake, and was clearly shouting although not a word was audible. House lights were appearing in the streets nearby as doors and windows were thrown open. Down on the riverbank one of the ack-ack searchlights had begun sweeping the scene.

The flames ran up the mast, then flickered and died, leaving a small fire at the foot. For a moment there was an illusion that the tower would crumple and fall, but it held fast on its concrete, box-like base. It was by the guttering flame that Brooke saw a sign painted in whitewash on the concrete, the letters a foot tall.

He made Ridley sit on a low wall while he walked forward towards the mast, the flames dying away quickly now, collapsing into a bundle of odd blue fire.

At twenty feet, Brooke could read the words.

He knew two things: he hadn't heard the bomb fall from the sky, and there'd been no plane overhead. So the explosives had been planted at the foot of the mast, almost certainly by the fleeing 'burglars'. And, although he was no linguist, he knew for certain the message in whitewash wasn't English.

11

In the porters' lodge at Michaelhouse, in the panelled room beyond the counter, a blackboard had been mounted by the lettered pigeonholes. Upon this the head porter scrawled instructions and reminders for the night staff, Doric and his three subordinates. The night porter whistled as he rubbed out a list of proposed duties, which stretched from sweeping the chapel floor to replacing candles in the Great Hall.

Across the now pristine black canvas, Brooke carefully inscribed the words he'd copied from the concrete base of the stricken TV mast. He'd left PC Harris at the scene, and a radio car was making regular hourly visits through the night. A company engineer, dragged from his bed, had examined the mast and pronounced it stable. The bomb, it seemed, was a trifling concoction of a few pounds of low-octane explosives — selected, he felt, for an entirely symbolic attack.

Ridley, the wounded caretaker, had been taken by ambulance to Addenbrooke's. Brooke's ears had recovered, his clothes were merely smudged with ash, and the pain in his eyes had faded to a dull ache. The next logical step was to decipher the message. He had his suspicions as to the language, but not the meaning.

The exotic accents were particularly difficult to transcribe, and he made a mental note to ask County to send down their own photographer to record the exact inscription in situ before repairs began.

Tiocfaidh ár lá.

Brooke, pressed to try a glass of the college claret (collected from unfinished glasses by the head waiter) and the leftovers of that evening's formal hall feast, had time to ponder the strange words.

He attempted to voice the letters in a sound, which produced in turn a strange noise from Doric, a species of guffaw mixed with puzzlement. The porter stood in front of Brooke's cryptic slogan. He was not capable of stillness, and so as he considered the letters his lips contrived a tuneless whistle.

'When does Dr Phipps rise?' asked Brooke. Even in his student days, before the Great War, Phipps was an ornament to Michaelhouse's reputation for arcane passions. Phipps was a linguist, with a special interest in the patchwork of dialects which covered the Indian subcontinent.

'I can get him now, if it's important,' offered Doric.

'It's five o'clock in the morning, Doric.'

'Dr Phipps sleeps after lunch. Often after a *good* lunch, if you understand me, Mr Brooke. A certain decline has set in this last decade. Nighttime he thinks and writes. Before the blackout started I'd clock his window on my rounds. There'd always be a light. Some nights I can see a sliver still.'

Doric's position as night porter had been secured for what they were already calling the Duration, thanks to his simultaneous appointment as both fire-watcher and ARP warden, in command of monitoring the blackout within the college bounds.

Dr Phipps was duly produced, in a dressing gown and boots, and apparently unperturbed by the lateness of the call. Neat, tall, 'a dry stick' would have been the verdict of anyone meeting him for the first time. Brooke had always detected a sprightlier, joyful note.

He studied the blackboard with keen interest for less than ten seconds.

'Yes. Irish — they get annoyed if you call it Gaelic. And famous of course: *Our time will come*. A rallying call for the rebels.'

They'd given him a glass of wine, and he seemed to want to stay, so Brooke asked if the script had any hidden clues.

Phipps studied the letters. 'And this is a faithful reproduction?'

'I tried.'

'Yes. The inflections and accents are precise. It's a rallying cry, as I say. A child would know it, but perhaps omit the smaller diacritics.'

'And so?'

Phipps shrugged. 'An educated hand?'

Brooke left Phipps drinking more wine and set out for the Spinning House. There had been no significant new snowfall, but the frost was bitter. Market Hill was deserted, the all-night tea hut still abandoned, the central fountain a bowl of ice.

Which made him think of the child again, and the cold, deathly touch of the river.

After checking with the duty sergeant at the Spinning House he went to his office and fetched from the cabinet a file of correspondence with Scotland Yard. He had a daybed, which he'd bought on the quayside at Alexandria in the war. Some carefully painted scenes adorned the woodwork: the blue Nile, green rushes, a red sun. It was a bed in which he never slept, reserving the cells below for snatched moments of the abrupt bouts of sleep which punctuated his days. The daybed was for reading.

Quickly he found the relevant set of three memoranda, all addressed to his superiors:

URGENT. A GENERAL ALERT.
ALL CHIEF CONSTABLES

He noted Carnegie-Brown's neat scrawl in the margins, signing off in lieu of the chief constable, who saw his role as purely ceremonial. A lieutenant-general from the Great War, he was rarely seen in the Spinning House, except to welcome dignitaries on the doorstep. All operational files went direct to Carnegie-Brown. She'd passed them on to Brooke, with the languid comment, 'Watching brief, Brooke. Cambridge is hardly a Fenian stronghold.'

The first letter detailed the declaration of war against the United Kingdom issued in Dublin by the Irish Republican Army almost precisely a year earlier, several months before Germany's invasion of Poland had precipitated a wider

65

conflict. The IRA planned a campaign, code-named the S-Plan — S for sabotage. Their aim was to win back Ulster, or — possibly — to impress their German allies, with whom they imagined they might one day join forces. The Irish government, fiercely protective of neutrality, had locked up rebel leaders. The bombing on the 'mainland' carried on, hundreds of low-key attacks aimed at small-scale infrastructure: local power stations, railway lines, post offices, letter boxes, telephone exchanges. Smoke bombs were set off in crowded cinemas. Damage was limited. The stated aim had been to kill no one, but mistakes were made, and there were lethal casualties. The campaign had appeared to dwindle.

Why had it reignited here, in sleepy Cambridge? And why target a TV mast? Brooke knew no one with a set. He'd seen one working in a shop window on Petty Cury, showing a shadowy two-minute Mickey Mouse cartoon. Removing the mast hardly amounted to a vital blow against the body politic, let alone the body economic.

He lit a Black Russian and watched the smoke rise to the nicotine-coloured ceiling.

He felt his nerves, down legs and arms and at his temples, suddenly freeze. It was a moment he recognised: the moment of disturbing revelation. He'd missed the obvious, because it had been in plain sight. Sean Flynn, an Irish Catholic boy, had been kidnapped and murdered, drowned in the river, twenty-four hours before a unit of the IRA had carried out an attack at an electronics factory on the bank of the same river. Brooke sat up. He saw again the pale hand of the drowning child, and then — his imagination instantly in top gear — the red heraldic hand of Ulster, dripping blood.

12

The dawn was lost in fresh flurries of snow, the light of the day diffused in mid-air, creating a grey, teeming world. Flakes stuck to Brooke's eyelashes as he set out towards the hospital, so he kept his head down, and was only able to catch sight of the great stone paws of the lions which guarded the entrance to the Fitzwilliam Museum, before turning sharply to cross the street. Here he had to use all his childhood knowledge of the city to prevent a tumble into the open runnels which at this point replaced the ordinary gutters. The snow had filled them entirely, but they were two feet deep and treacherous. Built to carry water in a 'new river' from the hills, they'd brought a stream into the heart of the town for centuries. As a child he'd fashioned paper boats at school, and then let them sail down the street, watched by puzzled pedestrians. One of these featherweight ships had survived its journey all the way to Fitzbillies bun shop, and now stood on the mantelpiece at home.

He leapt the first runnel, packed with snow, then crossed the road and leapt the second.

By the time he reached the stone portico of the hospital, the front of his coat was white, and he had to stand, stamping, to shift the flakes and ice. It was only when he'd finished that he realised Claire was there too, in her nurse's coat, cradling a steaming mug.

'Bunking off?' he said. He put his arms around her and they stood in close contact for a ticking minute, enjoying the intimate heat.

She offered him a sip of the scalding tea.

'I heard about the explosion,' she said. 'Priestly, the porter in the laundry, said he was outside clearing snow and thought it was a bomb. He was in the last lot.'

'That's why I'm here. Caretaker took a bit of shrapnel.' He decided to leave aside the fact that he'd been standing beside the caretaker at the time.

'We had a soldier in earlier, broke his ankle playing football in his barrack hut — idiot. Anyway, he said the inside story was the bombers were these Irishmen — the rebels?'

Brooke shrugged. 'Looks like it. It's a bit amateurish. Not much more than a firecracker.'

'So what's worrying you? I can tell that look.'

'The child in the river. Could be — almost certainly is — an evacuee from London. Irish Catholic. Which is one of those worrying coincidences that you know can't be a coincidence. I'd put money on a link, wouldn't you?'

She watched the snow falling. 'I came down for a chat with Joy. It's our secret rendezvous.'

'How was she?'

'Alright. Worried, sick with it I suspect, but you'd never know. She's got your ability to screen her emotions from the outside world. Or is it a disability?'

Brooke examined her face. 'Lipstick?' he asked. 'Is that allowed?'

'The ward's freezing, they had to shut the boilers this afternoon and the heat's not cranked up yet. My lips were blue and unsightly and hardly an advertisement for good health. Besides, I make the rules. It's started a trend on Sunshine Ward — we look like the Tiller Girls!' She laughed and slipped the hood off her head. 'Come on, I'll show you . . . '

Inside the main doors she turned left and down concrete stairs to the basement. This was their secret place. When the shifts allowed they'd meet in the warmth of the boiler room, to which Claire had secured a key. Brooke said that if they were ever caught it would be a scandal and the *News of the World* would label it a love nest.

Brooke's hopes were dashed when Claire switched on the lights. The boiler room had been transformed into a new ward: brass bedsteads stood in military lines, a few inches between each.

'They shut the boiler down to move some pipes to get them all in,' she said. 'Sixty beds. It's for air raids, so we don't get overwhelmed. We can't have beds out in corridors, or worse, in the street. And they've taken the locks off the doors,' she said sadly.

Brooke let her go back to the children's ward while he headed along the main ground-floor corridor to Admissions.

Ridley, the Newton factory caretaker, was in a bed, under a bright light.

'I'll live,' he said cheerfully, shaking Brooke's hand, although he looked frail.

His chest was bandaged as well as his head.

'I can go home when the doctor's had a look. That's after breakfast. I can't sleep.'

'How are you getting home?'

'Company's sending a car. A week off too. Managing director's been in already. That's Mr Tyndale. First time I've ever spoken to him. I told him straight that nobody got into the factory. Kept asking, mind you.'

Ridley's hand strayed to the bedside table and a pair of glasses.

'He said I wasn't to talk to the press, and if you asked questions I was to tell you to ring his secretary.'

Brooke took off his hat. 'Unfortunately, Mr Tyndale is not the chief constable, Mr Ridley. If I ask any questions, and you don't answer, I will have to ask them again at the Spinning House.'

Ridley swallowed hard. 'Yes. Of course. I was just saying . . . '

He bent his arm stiffly and managed to extract a business card which he handed to Brooke.

'Embossed,' he said approvingly.

Mr Tyndale was listed as managing director and founder.

Ridley nodded, filling his lungs. 'He said to say if you came round that the factory manager — Mr Forbes — would answer any questions that he could on-site. He'll be there now.'

Brooke wondered what they were making in their factory which could account for the institutional secrecy. Television might be the sensation of the century, but on the brink of a world war a few missing sets were unlikely to register in terms of the fate of the nation. Or did the production line at Newton's turn out something more precious?

13

Edison was at his desk in the sergeants' room when Brooke came down from his office, spreading out on a large table an assortment of vegetables: carrots and beetroot, turnips and Roman cabbages. Edison's expertise with vegetables was widely admired. His generosity was also welcomed, but — as he explained — largely the result of his four children growing up and 'flying the coop'. Brooke worried fleetingly that the advent of spring might present his detective sergeant with an unbearable dilemma: to report for duty, or to drill his onions.

Seeing Brooke, he stood, then threw a stiff arm out to indicate the largesse. 'Can't keep 'em, Mr Brooke. The shed's freezing. And there's only so much room in her larder. So I've been sent out to distribute the crop. Help yourself — the rest'll be in soon and they won't stand on ceremony. Hungry beggars.'

Brooke went to the window and looked down on the station yard. Edison's retirement plans were not entirely confined to the allotment. He owned a Wolseley Wasp, a fine motor car which he polished to a sheen, and whose engine was tuned to continual perfection.

'Too icy for the car?' asked Brooke.

'No. She's fine. I walked in to pick up this lot. Once the salt's on the roads she can hold her own,' said Edison, a note of hope in his voice that he might be sent out on constabulary business, which would entitle him to a vital supply of petrol coupons. 'The desk filled me in on the factory raid,' he said. 'Sounds a bit slapdash to me.'

Brooke took a seat. The sergeants' room held lockers and tables, usually adorned with packs of cards. A sink and kettle completed the suite. Edison lowered himself into a chair.

'Indeed. Nevertheless, the Home Office will want chapter and verse. I'm seeing the factory manager at Newton's now. Then I'm back to the river to see how the dredging is going. We can't ignore the possibility of a link, Edison. The murder is a precursor for the bomb, I'm sure of it.'

'You think the kiddie got in the way?'

'Maybe. I'll need to tell the parents soon that their son is missing.'

That corrosive word again: 'missing'. Was it better to wait and see if he could furnish news, good or bad?

'In the meantime, I'd like you to concentrate on our Fenian bombers.'

Brooke brought him up to speed on the inquiry so far. The 'bomb' at the Newton factory, or at least its remains, had been packed away and sent south by train for analysis. Brooke had spent an hour on the phone with Scotland Yard. Their advice, when he finally tracked down a diffident inspector in Special Branch, was to focus on the explosives, not the bombers.

Previous IRA devices had proved to be a concoction known as Paxo, after the popular stuffing brand for chickens, a bland mixture of sage, onion and breadcrumbs. The IRA recipe employed large quantities of potassium chloride, sulphuric acid and iron oxide. And they'd needed a 'factory' to mix the explosives in, somewhere out of the way, where they could gather all the ingredients together.

The Special Branch inspector had been blunt. 'You'll know your own patch, Brooke. Finding the bombers is futile. The Irish stick together, whether they believe in the campaign or not. Christ, half the men are in *our* army, and they're all volunteers. But you won't get a cigarette paper between 'em. No. Look for the chemicals, look for the factory.'

Brooke met Edison's watery eyes. 'Let's get our men, and uniformed, on the job. See if we can check the local chemists, builders, anywhere they could have got the mixture for the bomb. And then there's this mysterious 'factory' — again, brief uniformed branch, let's see if anyone has clocked anything suspicious. A warehouse, a garage, a lock-up, let's get eyes on the street. And don't forget Boudicca,' added Brooke. The Spinning House dog unit consisted of one bloodhound. 'If we need help, County have their own dogs. Delegate all that, Edison. Your duties are out of town.'

Scotland Yard was coordinating the hunt for the IRA bombers in England, through the direction of Special Branch. But the most active, and successful, inquiry had been in Coventry, following a bombing in the city the previous summer. A bicycle had been left outside a shop in the city centre with explosives in the pannier, attached to a timer. The explosion had killed five and injured seventy. One of the dead had been a young woman out shopping a few days before her wedding day. One of the city's main shopping streets had been reduced to broken glass and rubble. Two men had been arrested, charged with murder. They'd told the court the real target had been the telephone exchange, but a disastrous mistake had been made. It had cut no ice with the judge. They were in prison in Birmingham awaiting execution, while the Irish government pleaded for mercy.

'I want you to go to Coventry nick, they're the experts apparently. Read the files, Edison. We need suspects — names, a link to Cambridge. Anything that catches the eye. You have family there?'

Edison stiffened slightly in his chair, setting down his cup.

Brooke had met Mrs Edison once, at her husband's official retirement presentation in the Spinning House's great hall, the chamber in which women of ill repute had once been set to work at their spinning wheels when the building was a prison-cum-workhouse. Mrs Edison had looked ill at ease, overawed by the formality, including the chief constable's stiff speech of commendation.

'That's not a problem?'

'No, sir.'

'Remind me. Mrs Edison was born in . . . ?'

'Milltown Malbay, County Clare. Now the family's in Coventry — that's her sisters, and a brother. They're all close.'

'Good. You can take the Wasp. I've authorised the petrol. DI Harvey is your man in the city. He's got the files. They've made progress: the people who did it are for the drop, but they know who helped, and who kept silent when they should have rung the police. Their conclusion is that while each IRA cell is separate, there is a coordinator — and probably a supplier. The bomb is easy to assemble, but the fuses are trickier. They need to be brought in, maybe even across the water from Dublin, and then fitted by an expert. So we need to find a link to our bomb. Anything you can find. The only way to find these people is through *intelligence*. You're to be our expert, Edison. If you need to stay in Coventry, stay. A hotel's fine if it's difficult staying with the family.'

'Sir. No — Marianne, the wife's sister, she's got the room now. A widow, and the children all gone. I went to her wedding.' Edison shook his head. 'That's half a century ago. That was in Milltown. What a place, sir. There's a beach there that you can't see the end of, and a great hillside, dotted with cottages. We did think, when I retired, that we might go there, buy a house, see out our days. The light's quite different too — it sort of glows. And Mrs Edison likes a good sunset. And you can grow anything if you've a cow to provide the manure.' Edison considered the array of vegetables. 'There's been trouble, sir, in the city, since the outrage.'

Anti-Irish feelings had been running high since the bombing, with demonstrations, and strikes in factories with large numbers of immigrant workers. Irish labourers had been forced to quit lodging houses by irate landlords. Incidents had been recorded beyond Coventry: in London, Birmingham, Portsmouth.

'I know, Sergeant. You may not have heard the latest.' Brooke produced a folded newspaper from his coat. 'The chief constable of Coventry, a Captain Hector, has told the *Daily Telegraph* — no less — that he is not of Irish descent but a 'perfectly good Somerset man'. Whatever that means.'

'The people I know, sir, they're no friends of these bombers,' said Edison. 'They're patriots. Not like these men, they're out for more. They've no friends in Coventry or anywhere else.'

Brooke grabbed his coat and hat. 'Just tread carefully. One of the victims was a young woman out shopping for her wedding dress. They identified her by her engagement ring, nothing else, Edison. It's an overused word — carnage. Anyone else dies in this campaign and we might have a full-blown riot on our hands.'

14

The Newton factory confounded expectations once Brooke was through the doors: hushed parquet corridors led past two large production halls, but there was no thunder of machinery, or hissing steam, just a hum of small drills, the whirr of extractors, a gentle precision tapping overlaid with band music on the radio. Hundreds worked on the factory floor, women with their hair in turbans and pristine white overalls, in long production lines, soldering irons in their hands. The men sat at individual desks, surrounded by drifts of electrical components, banks of radios and eviscerated TVs. Some peered into the innards of gadgets with the aid of large anglepoise magnifying glasses. It was the smell that Brooke would recall: the distinct metallic tang of electricity, the whiff of a thousand blown fuses.

The offices, on a floor above, preserved the slightly brittle hush of a public library. A bank of secretaries typed with lightning dexterity, opposite a matching array of women operating comptometers, adding, subtracting, computing at a dizzy speed. Brooke sat at a coffee table, spinning his hat slowly in his hand, his eye sliding over copies of the *Radio Times* and brochures for the latest batch of TV sets. The prices were a cause of scandal in the Brooke household, and had been used to deter his son and daughter from the idea that they might have one installed. A *Newton Newsletter*, lying amongst the magazines, boasted: *Official statistics show TV ownership close to 20,000.*

Ralph Milton-Forbes, factory manager, ushered him into a large office, set at the corner of the factory block, with a wide view of the river, and the city to the south. Downstream, Brooke could see the police launch directing the dredging, a flotilla of small boats in its wake. The fruitless search was due to end, finally, at dusk.

'I'm Rafe Forbes,' he said, delivering a firm handshake. Brooke noted the contradiction, the dropping of the double-barrelled surname but the insertion of the upper-class diminutive for Ralph. Silver hair was slicked back off a wide, open face, which made him look like he'd been running at speed. A Great Dane lay under his desk, its long legs stretched out as if to dry.

'We'll have it fixed in a week, of course,' he said, standing at the window, looking out at the blackened TV tower. Men were at work building a scaffold, repainting scorched metal.

'Ministry's slapped a D-notice on it as well — so our bog-trotting friends won't even get any publicity.' Control of the press, via the 'advisory' system of defence notices, had invited a level of self-censorship unthinkable before the war.

Forbes looked at Brooke, noting the thick black hair flopping forward slightly, the ochre-tinted glasses. 'I'm told by Special Branch I should be as open as possible. Answer questions, that sort of thing. In the last lot I was at the Ministry of Supply, flying a desk. Maths, statistics, that's my bag. Apparently, the king gave you a medal for bravery in the desert. They said you'd served with Lawrence of Arabia.'

Brooke took a seat. 'I saw him twice, Mr Forbes. Once across an open fire at an oasis, once from half a mile, in the white robes on a horse. If that constitutes 'serving with' then they're right.'

Brooke broke out a fresh cigarette. 'Why do you need Special Branch's permission to talk to me? I thought you made TVs and radios. The IRA are targeting communications. Ridley — the caretaker — said the mast was to pick up the BBC from London. So that explains that. Hardly top-secret stuff.'

'Ridley should keep his mouth shut. We all should. Cambridge is full of all sorts these days. Jews for one, Irish, Germans, Austrians — it'll be the Eyeties next. Mussolini's that far from coming in on Hitler's side.' He held up his hand, thumb and forefinger almost touching. 'Bloody city's full of 'em.' Forbes straightened his tie.

'We checked the building last night,' said Brooke. 'It seemed secure.'

'Yes, yes. They didn't get in. Good job. The mast's bad enough. It is a TV receiver, Ridley's right there, for our research bods. Audience for commercial service is tiny — but one day, Brooke. One in every home. No. It's what they may have been after that's the problem. What they got close to.'

He grabbed a countryman's heavy tweed coat from a stand and clicked his fingers, bringing the dog laboriously to its feet.

'I'll show you outside.'

The dog led the way down a concrete staircase to an outside door. Forbes produced a bunch of keys attached to his belt. 'Three sets,' he offered, before Brooke could ask. 'Me, Ridley and the managing director — he lives twenty miles away, but they're there if we need them. None of the keys from any of the three sets are missing. None of the doors were forced. So, ipso facto, no one got in.'

'A copy is easy enough to make,' offered Brooke.

'Not if you keep them close,' said Forbes, throwing open the door to reveal a snowy scene running down to the river.

'And Ridley?' asked Brooke.

'You can trust Ridley. Not the brightest of men, but loyal. Worked on the shop floor, copped a bullet at Passchendaele, came back a hero. So he got the job, and a tied house. He's sound. Why? Think he's a covert Fenian, do we? He's an Englishman, Brooke.'

The dog ran manic circles in the snow. Two sets of goalposts were the only indication that a football field lay beneath. A dismal concrete changing block stood behind one of the goals, disfigured by damp, with unpainted shutters. Beyond was the perimeter fence.

'How do you get through the fence at the main gates?' asked Brooke.

'After dark there's an electric lock. You need the six-figure code. Again — just the three of us.'

Forbes began hurling a small ball for the dog, which tore off, returning at speed, leaving a chaotic set of paw prints.

'Right, Inspector. You didn't hear this.' Forbes surveyed the scene. There was nobody within sight, either on the riverbank or in the fields. 'Imagine I'm a radio transmitter and I send out a pulse of signal like this.' He had the ball in his hand, and threw it into open space, waiting for the dog to bring it back. 'Until now I've been throwing the ball and getting nothing back, unless Gawain here intervenes. Same happens with radio signals, send them out into the ether, never hear of them again. Unless this happens.' He threw the ball at the wall of the changing block and collected the return before the dog could run it to ground. 'It's that simple. I'm a transmitter. When I collect the ball I'm a receiver. If I was one of a line of transmitters strung out here across the field, we could all chuck balls at the sports pavilion. Then we could analyse the way the balls came back, and we could work out the shape of the pavilion, and its distance, because we know how fast we threw the ball. Radio waves, you'll know, travel at precisely the speed of light. It is a highly effective system.'

'You're making these transmitters and receivers here?'

'Yes. Well, a key component. The Germans are into this too — and the Yanks, and the French. Everyone knows it will work. We've known for decades. We just need the technology. We need a production line. We used to call it the telemobiloscope. Now we call it RADAR because that's what the Yanks want to call it. Get it right, you can spot aircraft, ships, storms at

83

sea, airships — you name it.

'There's a line of receivers down the East Coast from the Tyne to Kent. It's called Chain Home. If the German bombers come, and they will, that line could save London, Brooke, and thousands of lives, hundreds of thousands of lives. What we don't want is for someone to see the kit and work out how to block it.

'The IRA are a bunch of peasants with pitchforks, that's not the problem. But we know they'd like to impress the Germans. Our enemy is their friend.' He pointed at the blackened TV mast. 'Want my opinion, there's nothing to worry about. It's a bloody great mast, they failed to blow it up, end of story. However, London's jumping. We're reviewing security.'

The police launch went by on the river, a net being stowed on deck.

'Any news on the lost child?' Forbes had produced a cigar, a narrow cheroot, which he lit with a silver lighter.

'There's no hope, now. An Irish Catholic child, so we can't rule out a connection with events here. Perhaps the child got in the way somehow, or saw something they shouldn't have, or someone they shouldn't have.'

Forbes produced a plume of smoke. 'Sounds a bit far-fetched. More likely to be a nasty little family drama, don't you think? You know what the problem is? Mongrels. Won't be an Englishman, Brooke, I'll wager you that. Gawain here — '

He patted the dog, and as he fussed with the noble head, Brooke noted an enamel badge on

Forbes's lapel of a full moon, etched with the letter *G* in blue.

'She's pedigree,' he said, straightening up. 'I breed 'em, so I know. Know the parents, know the child. That's what it's all about, this war, Brooke. True blood.'

15

Brooke entered St Alban's through the oak-studded door, which closed silently behind him, restrained by a damper. A large straw mat had been set on the parquet floor to soak up the snow and slush, and so his first footsteps were silent too. He stood for a moment, brushing flakes from his coat. At the far end of the nave, Father Ward sat in a pew, side-on to another man, whose head was bowed, so that they appeared to be whispering together. Brooke coughed, and they both seemed startled, Father Ward rising awkwardly to his feet.

'Inspector, news?' asked the priest. Brooke was struck again by the man's energy, as he advanced to shake hands. So many priests and vicars simply faded into the fabric of their own churches. Ward, by contrast, seemed too big a character for the modest nave, the threadbare furnishings of a poor parish.

Brooke briefed him on the operation along the river and the pressing necessity to contact Sean Flynn's parents to warn them that their son was missing. As Brooke talked he examined the other man: round-shouldered, slightly shambling, with thinning red hair and a clean but worn suit. He was studiously avoiding Brooke's eyes, revealed now, as he'd taken off his glasses.

'You know our head teacher?' asked Ward. 'No? Liam Walsh.'

Walsh's hand was oddly lifeless, pale and cold. Brooke guessed he was perhaps forty years of age, but he looked beaten down, as if the responsibilities of his position were a literal burden. He mumbled a few words, the Irish accent replete with a Dublin edge, in marked contrast to Ward's newsreader English.

'There is a development, Father,' said Brooke. 'Can we sit?'

Walsh made to leave, almost tripping in his haste to quit the church.

'It concerns the whole community,' said Brooke, raising his voice. 'So perhaps the head teacher could stay?'

Walsh nodded several times, as if trying to convince himself of the wisdom of the inspector's suggestion, then subsided, sliding back into the pew.

Brooke outlined the series of events which had begun with the explosion at the Newton factory — the message left behind, the three men spotted leaving the scene — before moving on to briefly summarise the IRA's S-Plan and reminding them of the attacks which had occurred in the last year, including the fatal, reckless outrage in Coventry.

When he'd finished there was a bemused silence.

'There's no evidence of a link with St Alban's?' asked Walsh, summoning mild indignation. 'You can't think — '

'The congregation is mostly Irish,' stated Brooke. 'A child is missing, possibly murdered. It would be remiss to discard the possibility of a link.' He quickly outlined the logic behind looking for suspects here in the Upper Town. The missing boy was an Irish Catholic. He had been abducted twenty-four hours before the IRA attack. Did he pose a threat to the bombers and their fellow travellers?

Ward patiently listened. 'Yes, I see. We have to face these issues, I suppose. Although we don't know yet, do we, that the boy is dead. He could be trying to get home or hiding. And if he is the victim, and there's a link to the Republicans, then it's more likely to lie in *his* past, not ours.'

Brooke thought this was an intelligent observation. 'Indeed. I accept that. We will look at the family when we can. In the meantime, Father, we are here.'

Brooke spread out his arms to embrace the church, the school, the community.

Ward nodded, glancing at the head teacher as if to summon his support, but he said nothing.

'The congregation is Irish, yes,' said Ward. 'Predominantly. And poor. Certainly more Irish than the Big Church.' The Big Church was a Cambridge landmark, the Church of Our Lady and the English Martyrs, a cathedral-sized Victorian statement on the corner of Parker's Piece. 'We're not just Irish. There's Spanish refugees from the war. Basque Catholics too. And Poles. Again, often poor, often in need of practical help. Catholic scholars, theologians, go to St Edmund's House, the university chaplaincy. We live very much in our own small world here, Inspector. It's marked by poverty, not hot-headed revolutionaries.'

'And the school?' asked Brooke, turning to Walsh.

Walsh considered the question carefully, his hands pressed together as if in prayer. 'The majority of the older children were born in Ireland, certainly. And several of the teaching staff, myself included. Many of the children were born here. But their parents — yes, one or both may well be Irish citizens. The children have a right to be here, Inspector. Many of their fathers are soldiers of the king.'

'The local community is patriotic?' asked Brooke.

Ward raised an eye. 'There's a Gaelic Society, a hurling club, song nights in the pubs. Liam here offers them classes in the language of their fathers, and of course they are instructed in their religion. The rites of passage are observed: first communion, confirmation, and the Mass and benediction. These are simple people, Inspector. They live quite literally from hand to mouth. If you're looking for Fenians, orators, whipping up the poor, I think St Edmund's might be a better place to start. We don't get many intellectuals in the pews of St Alban's.'

'But they'd have sympathy for the cause?' Brooke persisted.

'There are many causes, Brooke. Ireland's free already — although not free enough for some, it's true. And there's Ulster. And then there's the war itself. They are guests in a foreign country, at least some of them are. The rest are here by right. I'm an Englishman, a public schoolboy from Ampleforth and Oxford. *They* don't seem

89

to have a problem with that.'

Brooke wondered how well the priest really knew his flock.

'And yourself, Mr Walsh? An Irish citizen you say. So you'll be registered at the Spinning House?'

'Yes. And my wife. It's the law. We reported as instructed. I have no objection to that.'

The far door of the church, which led to the playground beyond, opened to reveal the children in frantic motion on the snow-covered yard.

A young woman hesitated on the doorstep, as if she'd been rendered in stone.

'Father, forgive me. Liam, will you be free for science or . . . '

Walsh leapt to his feet. 'No, no. I'm coming.'

He inclined his head as if seeking permission, but Brooke waited instead for an introduction.

'My wife, Inspector,' said Walsh, and the gleam of proprietorial joy was unmistakable. 'Kathleen.'

She took a few steps forward. Her principal feature was her youth in present company. Twenty-five, possibly thirty, with fine skin and the kind of jet-black hair which shimmers and reflects, like a liquid mirror. Short, lithe, with a neat bust, she could have been a schoolgirl herself. She was a decade younger than her husband, at least. And her voice was a marked contrast to all the men, exhibiting a musical lilt, suggesting the ability to hit a note at will. It was difficult, even in church, to avoid the adjective 'radiant'.

'The inspector thinks young Sean's death is

linked to the Republican bombers,' said Walsh, a note of laughter in his voice. 'We're all under suspicion,' he said, trying to catch the priest's eye.

Ward acted as peacemaker. 'He's doing his job, Liam. Until we know the truth, what other motive can we find?'

Mrs Walsh had, in a heartbeat, taken on a flushed, angry complexion. 'They might sing patriotic songs on payday, Inspector. They might even give a few pennies for the rebels. But violence? To kill a child?' She summoned up a note of defiance, her soft accent thickening. 'You'll find no sympathy for that in the Upper Town.'

16

Back in his office Brooke raised the blind and watched night rise beyond the brick cenotaph that was the tower of the university library. Venus glittered alone in an icy-blue sky. The dredging of the river was over. He could hardly justify the cost of the operation on the first day, let alone into a third. The lack of a body condemned the case to shaky foundations. All murder inquiries proceeded from the corpse: it offered a necessary starting point scientifically, but more importantly as a physical expression of a moral imperative. Its presence in the morgue demanded retribution and justice. Its absence merely prompted questions. And duties. He'd have to ring Sean Flynn's parents in the morning.

For an hour Brooke sat at his desk. There was no news from Edison, so he presumed his sergeant would be gone until the next day at least. He rang the presbytery of the Church of Our Lady and the English Martyrs, the city's Catholic mother church, and was referred to the diocesan office in Norwich. He rang and was surprised to be answered by a young priest, who asked him to hold.

Waiting on the line he recalled the cathedral itself, a cube-like Victorian edifice which stood on the city's skyline, looking down on the soaring spire of its medieval predecessor. When the phone was picked up it was the dean, who took a note of Brooke's request to see the files on Father John Ward and Liam Walsh, head teacher of the diocesan junior school of St Alban's.

'Routine enquiries,' said Brooke, arranging for a messenger from the local police station to pick up the documents in the morning.

'There's no news?' said the dean. 'Father John spoke to the bishop. If you speak to him tell him we're praying for the child.'

Brooke rested the phone on its cradle. He should go home and eat, although the house would be empty. The thought of the hot bath was enticing, but leftover stew not so.

Grabbing his greatcoat, he set out into the snowy streets.

A glittering tram rumbled past on Regent Street, and the pavements were crowded with workers intent on getting home before the blackout began or the siren sounded.

Brooke cut down All Saints Passage into the old Jewish ghetto. The porters' lodge at Michaelhouse offered a coke fire. Brooke, discarding Aldiss's specific advice to preserve a fast until late evening, devoured a bowl of leftover roast potatoes and a single leg of a spatchcocked guinea fowl, leaving the pathetic slim bones on the plate.

Something about the discarded skeleton, feather-light, made him say out loud what was on his mind.

'We've not found the child.'

Doric knew him well enough not to speak. The porter poured a cup of tea and, standing by the fire, rocked back and forth on his flat feet, a hand fluttering at a loose thread on his tunic.

'They've dredged the river and found nothing except dead dogs and bicycles,' said Brooke. 'I know I saw his hand. The body must be there, but if his lungs were flooded he'll have sunk to the bottom. We may never find him. It'll be one of those forgotten wartime mysteries, Doric. Once the real war starts nobody will be bothered about the life of a small child.'

'The parents?' said Doric.

'I've to ring in the morning. I'm not looking forward to it.'

Doric had moved to his small desk, where he had been clearly engaged in polishing silver. The night shift was his realm, of which he was monarch. The under-porters reported to him. The lofty authority of the head porter was a mere rumour. The quiet order of the panelled room, the rhythmic cleaning of a silver plate, seemed to inspire the porter, who stood and went out into the store, returning with a rolled paper tube, which he set out on the counter.

It was a navigator's map of the river, showing locks, pools, cuts and ditches.

'You could ask them to drain the river, Mr Brooke,' he said, his swollen fingers worrying at the edge of the map.

Doric had worked at Trinity before the Great War. He explained that it had been relatively common practice in the last century to ask the Conservators, the ancient guardians of the river, to open the sluices downstream and allow the river to flow out and away, exposing the foundations of the colleges along the Backs, so that repairs could be made to brickwork and

94

bridges, docks and drains, and regular maintenance carried out on lock doors and sluices. These operations had often been planned for dry summers, but a big freeze — such as the one forecast — was also ideal, in that the narrow headwaters would be iced up and unable to refill the stone channel of the Cam.

'The trick is you can't do it in the wet, you see, because the headwaters will flood and keep the water level up. Open the sluices now and you'll see the river bed in hours. Open the sluices and you'll see if your boy is there.'

Brooke studied the map. 'What if there's a thaw?'

'There won't be. Johnston, the night porter at Benet's, says the meteorologists are all betting on a big freeze. Hard as iron, by the weekend. And of course, once the river's frozen your body's locked away for days, maybe weeks. So now's your chance, Mr Brooke.'

Brooke took his chance. Out on the riverbank it was clear the meteorologists were right. A haw frost was settling on the water meadows, creating an exquisite landscape of ice: bone-white trees, the grass and reeds like sugared candy, the river itself almost choked with miniature ice sheets jostling under the bridges.

The lock-keeper at Jesus took his request for the river to be drained with equanimity.

'Can be done, of course,' he said, tipping a cap back off a wide forehead. 'I'll need to talk to Clayhythe,' he added, walking to his cluttered office and picking up the phone.

Clayhythe was headquarters: a stylish, even

eccentric, house on the banks of the lower river beside a dock, a mile from the village of Waterbeach. The pinnacled, geometric house was rumoured to contain on its top floor a single room, the Conservators' sumptuous dining hall. Here the masters of the river, empowered to charge tolls at the locks, met to consider their duties — the care of the Cam from its headwaters at Byron's Pool to the last lock at Bottisham. Their coffers were raided to pay for dredging, a lock gate, a stone wharf or a new towpath. Or a sumptuous feast.

A brief conversation, which included a verification of Brooke's rank and position, established the schedule. A signed note from the chief constable's office would be required, retrospectively, as a formality. The sluice gates at Jesus Lock would be opened immediately, and those at Baits Bite below. A freezing cold snap was forecast to deepen within forty-eight hours, so time was short. It would take less than twelve hours for the river to bleed away into the Fens. By dusk the next day the riverbed would be exposed. Brooke would have a full six hours to search its course from Mill Street to Baits Bite. Then the sluices could be closed, to allow water to collect, in time to meet requests from several colleges and the fen skating clubs for rinks to be prepared on the water meadows. Speed skating was planned for the river itself, the course marked out by barrels set on the ice.

'No time like the present,' said the lock-keeper, leading Brooke out to an iron wheel which he began to turn to open the sluice gates.

The river, stirring, began to pour through the gap in a muscular green wave. Finished, the old man swept sweat from his brow. 'It's a few years now since we've drained the river,' he said. 'Who knows what you'll find.'

17

The city streets were deserted now, the surface of the snow on the pavements a crisp carapace through which Brooke's shoes crunched as he walked back towards the Spinning House. A constable on his beat, passing the Round Church, saluted. The prospect of the cold house at Newnham Croft was even less enticing than it had been at dusk, so he ducked off Sidney Sussex Street into a long alleyway, already home to half a dozen roadsters, vagrants who fed off the bins and sought shelter at night. It amazed Brooke that the city had any rough sleepers at all, given its almost preternatural ability to attract a cold wind. The Fens, to the north, seemed to harbour the arctic airs, then release them, at full force, into the streets.

A metal fire escape led up to a flat roof, across which Brooke walked, lifting each foot out of the thick snow. On the far side a ladder rose twenty feet to a second flat roof and the last fire escape, which did a smart double switch-back before decanting him onto a platform, a wooden ledge, designed to claim the highest point at this corner of the city, with a panoramic view of the river, the Upper Town, the medieval colleges clustered below. At nearly ninety feet, the lookout — an official Observer Corps post — provided a bird's-eye view, a living map.

The post was circled with sandbags to a height

of several feet, and in the rear corner, against a wide chimney breast, a conical steel hut had been set, out of which emerged Josephine Ashmore, rearranging her immaculately tailored uniform and touching her short brown hair, which — expensively cut — dropped precisely to her collar. A gas mask in a leather case bobbed at her hip, transformed from a vital lifesaver into a fashion item.

Her face brightened. 'An honour indeed. A visit from the Borough. How thrilling.'

They stood companionably at the sandbag parapet. In the city below a few cars crept along in the brick and stone canyons, peering forward with the help of swaddled headlamps. The snow's interior light revealed heavy clouds above, which had rolled south since sunset.

'Tea?' asked Ashmore.

Brooke took up a pair of field glasses and completed a *tour d'horizon* as the kettle boiled. The Observer Corps had six lookout posts in the city, providing 360 degrees of cover. The East Coast radar stations were on standby to issue alerts, which would reach the conical hut by landline. Ashmore's job was to report any useful military intel back to the airfield at Duxford, to the south of the city. Using a fixed metal plotting table, she had been trained to track the course of incoming EA — enemy aircraft — by sight and sound. After a raid, she was to plot fires.

'Tonight's orders?' he asked, accepting a steaming mug.

'We're on standard alert for a German bombing raid, which never comes,' she said. 'The gossip is that they'll attack in France later this month, once the snow's gone. Berlin won't want us providing air cover for our boys, so maybe we'll see them then, trying to destroy the runways, catch the kites on the ground. Then we'll go all misty-eyed about those boring nights when nothing ever happened.'

Jo Ashmore's life, before the war, had contained very few boring nights. The Ashmores had lived in the villa next to the Brookes at Newnham Croft, beside the river. The children had been friends, the two families entwined in that peculiar way which means nobody can recall how they got to know each other so well. As a child she'd played hide-and-seek in the house with Brooke's daughter, Joy. While Joy had gone into nursing, Jo's life had drifted. There'd been a racy lifestyle, London parties, a scandal with a married man. Her father, a professor of history, had demanded a low profile. Irony had placed her on this giddy rooftop.

'Any instructions on the IRA bombers?' he asked.

'Pages of it, Brooke. Piles of bumf. We're to keep our eyes open for anything suspicious close to the usual targets. Postboxes, pylons, telegraph poles, gas mains, power stations, masts — just like Newton's. That was a sight, I can tell you. I thought the whole thing was coming down. And they cut through the wire?'

Brooke nodded, resettling his hat on his head, the rim lower over his eyes.

'It's all still small beer,' she said. 'Put the bomb on a bike, wheel it up to the target, then bugger off. They're not exactly courageous warriors are they, Brooke? But there's word . . . '

She sipped her drink, smiling, teasing. Even as a child she'd been drawn to the pale, heroic figure of the man next door, shrouded in the legend of Lawrence of Arabia, a wounded warrior, but always silent when it came to stories of war and victory. The children would watch him coming home along the river, hands in overcoat pockets, the hat, the legs tapering to neat brogues, the crack of the metal Blakeys on the path. There was always a note of menace in the figure, which meant they invariably broke cover and ran ahead screaming, desperate to hide in the house.

'Go on,' said Brooke. 'What's the word?'

She fetched a batch of typed order papers from the hut, held together with a military bulldog clip.

'The theory is that the bombers are out to impress the Germans. They're not doing very well, are they? So far they've killed a dozen civilians by accident, and burnt a few postboxes, and interrupted a couple of nights out at the flicks. They want Berlin to think they're an army behind the lines. So the thinking is that they're moving on and up. First off, we're to keep an eye on major infrastructure — petrol stores, swing bridges, bridges generally, airfields. And locks, and sluices. Runways too. And on the Fens, pumping stations. Flood banks. There's a whole platoon camped out at Denver Sluice to make sure we can all sleep safe in our beds, protected from the possibility that a single bomb could let

101

the tide flood in. Imagine that, Brooke. Even Berlin would notice the sudden appearance of an inland sea.' She took a gulp of tepid tea. 'Every Observational Post, or OP, has a list of targets to monitor. That's my priority.'

She pointed down below, where the street led into the distance, and over the Great Bridge. 'Blow that up and there'd be pandemonium, Brooke. Major north — south route. Principal river crossing. The army predicts chaos, and they should know, they're brilliant at creating it. Anything suspicious, especially after dark, we're to ring the military at Madingley Hall. Personally I don't think they'd bother. Too obvious. If I was them, and I wanted to prompt an international shindig, I'd go for a munitions train. We get two, three a night now. A mile long, Brooke. Takes twenty minutes to rattle past. Derail it, you've got a nightmare. Derail it and set fire to it, they'd hear the bang in Berlin.'

In the silence, on cue, they could hear the distant rattle of a train.

Brooke considered her profile, the lips slightly parted, the eyes bright. His daughter had whispered that Jo had a new paramour, a pilot, and that this one was different, not just a moustache in an open-top car, trailing a silk scarf. Something had certainly lifted the mood on the draughty rooftop OP. Did the new man visit her on the rooftops? Change was certainly in the air. Brooke had noted subtle alterations: a small mirror had always hung in the hut at just the right height for Jo to apply lipstick. That was gone. And she no longer lit her cigarettes with an extravagant striking of a match, but discreetly, a lighter cupped in her hand, her head turned away. And there was something less fragile about the smile.

'There's wilder rumours,' said Ashmore, hiding her face behind the field glasses. 'One of the OP men said he'd been told by a mate, who'd overheard a conversation on the train, that when they caught one of the bombers after Coventry he had plans in his pocket: Buck House, apparently. They're all still in London — the King, the Queen. And they tried to kill Chamberlain's son — you heard that?'

Brooke nodded. 'Not exactly earth-shattering, was it? The bomb was in a tobacco tin, Jo. And he was *in* Ireland.'

'Maybe. But we're on alert. We've got this Prince Henry visit on the cards. You can just imagine the fuss that'll cause. And there's more and more bumf from London on the IRA. These two bombers are waiting to hang at Birmingham. If they swing, the IRA will strike back, they have to.'

She laughed then, her beautiful face lit up by the prospect of judicial execution and mayhem.

18

Brooke, respecting the letter of his new regime, set out for home, a bath, a meal and a moonless bedroom. Walking home along the river path he welcomed a growing sense of fatigue, even exhaustion. At Newnham Croft, where the river arrived from the chalky hills in a series of pools and cuts, streams and ditches, the landscape was oddly silent; ice, like a spell, had stopped the flowing water in its tracks. Lifting the snicket on the gate he observed the house, one of a pair of Edwardian villas, with fancy decoration reminiscent of a railway station or a vicarage. It had been his home all his life, and in the last twenty years a family home. In the desert, in his cell, he'd dreamt of walking up the path, and so this simple action always lifted his spirits.

Opening the door, he resisted the urge to shout 'Home!', knowing that Claire was still on the night shift, and that Joy might be home but would be resting. The staircase led past her room. He noted the light under the door and wondered — but really knew — if she was lying awake thinking of Ben, even now, perhaps, suspended in the brown, cold, murky depths of the North Sea. In the attic room he ran a bath, hot and steamy, but felt too tired to get under the water. The late-night meal of reheated stew he couldn't face either, so he lit a fire in the bedroom, set his glasses on the bedside table and struggled under the heavy covers.

Sleep comprised approximately twenty minutes of a tumbling dream. He was on the bridge again, the one on the desert road across the Sinai, looking down with all his comrades. This time it wasn't a dry arroyo, but a tumbling flood. Then he was wading out into the water, trying to pluck a child from the stream, but each time he reached out the boy's hand eluded his. They were trapped in a whirlpool, so that this opportunity to fail was repeated and repeated. The child had no name, but he was still compelled to shout it out, the syllables mangled because his tongue felt mired in glue, its root sluggish and unresponsive, so that all he could do in the end was emit a strange animal wail from within his throat.

When he woke, Joy was at the end of the bed with a cup of tea.

'I heard the shouts,' she said. 'Well, they're not shouts, are they? There's something insistent, frustrated. I'm worried, Mum's worried. I don't think it's getting any better, do you?'

The fire was still burning, so Brooke could see her face, and he thought for the first time that he caught the ghost of *his* father in her features, something about the steady, detached observation.

She sat while he sipped the tea and lit a cigarette.

'Why do you smoke those things?' she asked, nodding at the Black Russian.

'Your grandfather smoked them. He had a silver box in his laboratory downstairs. I think that was his father's. It was etched with his name: Dr E. E. Brooke. I used to steal them. It was my one and only rebellion. A dull child.'

She laughed, one hand on her belly. 'There was a call, from Ben's mother. She got a telegram from Rosyth. The boat sails at dawn for a patrol in the Northern Approaches; she's very good on the jargon already. I think that means the Arctic, Norway and beyond. So I can't sleep either, but I'm going to try.'

'I'll read,' he said, and she wished him goodnight.

An hour later he slipped downstairs, noted that Joy's light was out and struggled into his greatcoat on the mat, winding a scarf round his neck before plucking his hat from the newel post at the foot of the stairs.

Outside the frost was astonishing, so cold he felt it icing his hair, stinging his eyes. His nose and throat began to ache slightly, as if succumbing to a subtle anaesthetic.

Aldiss's laboratory was in the science quarter beyond the redbrick facade of the Sedgwick Museum. They'd been students together in those halcyon months before the Great War, sharing a set of rooms in Michaelhouse. Aldiss was brilliant, but in a singularly unimpressive style. On meeting him for the first time most people would have guessed he was a not very bright provincial solicitor, perhaps, or a bank clerk. He left verbal pyrotechnics and high-flown creative hypothesis to others, specialising instead in a trademark remorseless logic. It enabled him to construct faultless, exhaustive experiments.

The laboratory, on the fifth floor of a faceless interwar block, was a hothouse. Along one wall, in a series of pens, were up to a hundred guinea pigs, emitting that strange collection of noises which don't quite amount to a sound at all, the movement of the softest fur, the tiny jaws working at seeds and grain, the skitter of the weightless feet.

'I'm taking advantage of the cold snap,' said Aldiss, producing a bottle of malt whisky from a fume cupboard and pouring two large shots into a pair of beakers. Aldiss was one of Brooke's more welcoming nighthawks. The research was, by necessity, ceaseless, and so visitors served to enliven the tedium. It was always a malt whisky, usually from Skye, and of a decent age.

Aldiss was an expert in circadian rhythms, those innate cycles which give animals and plants the ability to be ready, in a hormonal sense, for the inevitable challenges of life. For some months he'd concentrated on the effects of light. Beyond the laboratory's three steel doors he kept cockroaches, fireflies and hamsters, exposing them to carefully regulated patterns of artificial solar radiation. Brooke, on his nightly visits, often stood amongst the glowing fireflies as Aldiss checked the cameras which recorded their movements and their luminescence. One visit to the 'roach room' had been enough. The scuttling of the insects' carapaces on the concrete floor had unsettled him.

Now Aldiss had moved on to the effects of heat.

'Enjoy it while you can,' he said, touching the

radiator momentarily. 'On the hour I'm opening the windows. As I said, it's a chance I can't miss. I can vary the heat, ratchet it up, let it cool down, but even I can't deliver a blast of boreal air. So this is a golden opportunity. I'll have to stop talking to you when the time comes. I need to observe, Brooke. And that's a serious business.'

'I can't sleep,' said Brooke.

'I'd worked that out,' said Aldiss, running a hand through what was left of his hair. He had a lumpen head, a kind of boulder of pale skin, which now seemed slightly too heavy for his neck. He was constantly lifting it up to meet Brooke's eyes.

'I've kept to the regime, your regime, without results.'

'Yet,' said Aldiss, checking the clock on the wall. 'As a scientist you were never scrupulous, were you? When you say you're following the regime, why do I doubt you? The bath, for example?'

Brooke shrugged. 'It was late. I lit a fire in the bedroom. It was warm.'

Aldiss shook his head. 'Yes. *It* was. But the idea is that *you* are. A bath alters your body temperature and — it is thought — that triggers the release of certain hormones, and precipitates a descent, as it were, into a sleep-like state. Patience, Brooke.' Another look at the time. 'I must get ready.'

Brooke went to a bench where Aldiss displayed the latest issues of scientific magazines for his students. Brooke may have abandoned his formal studies but he liked to keep up with the latest developments in the natural sciences. Above the bench was a noticeboard and his eye went immediately to one headlined:

VISIT OF PROF. JOHN ARKWRIGHT,
KING'S COLLEGE LONDON

THE INTERIOR OF NYASALAND

It was not the subject of the debate that seemed to leap off the poster but the symbol at the top of the page: a capital letter G set on an image of the moon, identical to the badge he'd glimpsed on the lapel of the factory manager at Newton's, Rafe Forbes.

'What does this mean?' he asked, pointing at the symbol, as Aldiss put on a coat.

'The Galton Society,' Aldiss said. 'Been going for years. Back before our time, Brooke. Francis Galton — the statistician, geographer, polymath. Moribund now, I suspect. Galton's reputation isn't what was.'

'Could you ask around, see what they're up to?'

'I could. I will. It sounds like they're up to listening to thrilling tales of Empire. It'll be a bunch of old buffers. I'll report back,' he said, executing a lazy salute. 'Now, ready?'

He moved along the north-facing wall of the laboratory, throwing open the windows. The mechanical action of the hinges created a small wind which blew bone-dry snowflakes into the room. The somnambulant hamsters began to stir under their solar lights.

'Genetics too, of course,' he added, apparently prepared to chat while making initial notes. Brooke saw that each hamster was marked with a small label attached to a foot, like a consignment of evacuees from the East End. 'Remember Bateson at Trinity?'

Brooke could hardly forget. William Bateson had been one of the grand old men of science in their student days.

'He coined the word 'genetics', Brooke. He relied on Galton to some extent. And there's a thought. Perhaps your mistimed circadian clock is nothing to do with your time in the desert. Maybe you inherited the disability, if disability it is. And now, I must work, and shut up.'

He sat on a high stool, his breath clear in the air, annotating a graph paper chart with an arcane code, recording the increasingly rapid movements of the once sleepy guinea pigs.

Brooke stood, stunned by the idea. His father, a professor of medicine, had certainly been a nighthawk himself. After the death of Brooke's mother, the old man had been a fleeting and distant figure, leaving his son to his schoolwork and to wander the city, under the loose administrations of a series of nannies. When his father did come home he'd retreated to his personal laboratory in the basement of the house. Tired, but often elated, he'd appear at breakfast to drink tea.

The idea that his insomnia was somehow a family gift made Brooke feel strangely elated too.

19

Brooke retrieved the latest edition of the London telephone directory from switchboard, collected a cup of tea from the canteen and took the steps to his office as a man walks to the gallows. The call had to be made. Sean Flynn had been missing for two full days. The search for his body on the river had been abandoned. The dry riverbed would be revealed tonight. His parents had a right to know the likely outcome of such an operation, and the likely outcome was that they'd find the five-year-old's body in its sack. Father Ward, at St Alban's, had rung the Spinning House an hour earlier to confirm that the missing child had not reappeared. When the boy's mother visited the city, as she was scheduled to do on the coming Saturday, along with other parents anxious to see their children, it was likely she might have to formally identify the body laid out in the morgue.

Brooke looked out over grey, snowy rooftops. The day itself was stillborn, the light in the sky filtered through a haze of falling ice, flecks of snow. Brooke switched on his desk lamp, adjusted the blue-tinted glasses and searched for Sean's father's name — Gerald J. Flynn — and the address listed in his file west of Shepherd's Bush. The Flynns took up several pages, with many of the addresses clustered in west London and north London, both thriving Irish migrant communities. There was one G. F. Flynn, in Wood Green, north London, and then a long line of G. M. Flynns. Brooke felt his heart skip at the relief, and he tossed the book aside.

Switchboard put him through to Shepherd's Bush police station. A note was taken of the Borough's request for a constable to visit the house. At this stage Sean Flynn was simply missing, but the parents should be told that they should brace themselves for bad news. Brooke suggested to the duty sergeant at Shepherd's Bush that Mary Flynn kept to her planned visit to Cambridge for that coming Saturday. Her husband should accompany her. If this was not possible, then a friend or close relative should be with her. The Borough would relay any news to Shepherd's Bush in the interim.

Finished, Brooke stood and, looking down from his window on the yard, spied the Wasp below, the windscreen flecked with snow, the bonnet steaming. Ice encrusted the headlamps and handles. Five minutes later Edison appeared, with tea and biscuits, the snow melting on his great overcoat, which he laboured to shift off his broad shoulders.

'Progress, sir. And a name — well, almost a name. Certainly, an address.'

'From the start, Edison,' said Brooke, lighting a cigarette.

As his sergeant fished out his notebook, Brooke noted that the pensioner was looking considerably younger than he had on his first day back on duty. Detection, rather than the carrying out of uniformed duties, was clearly his metier.

Or was it the speeding thrill of the Wolseley Wasp?

'After the Coventry bomb they picked up two of the men pretty sharpish,' said Edison. 'The rest of the organisation went to ground. Killing five people wasn't in the plan. Nor was having two of their men on death row. The bomber they didn't catch, the one who brought in the orders and the fuses, was long gone. He's the one they needed, of course, because he's the link with Dublin.

'Then they had a stroke of luck. The two bombers wouldn't talk, but the Irish community — the clubs, the pubs, the churches — they were shocked, outraged. CID was able to put together a description of the outsider — tall, slim, handsome, with a widow's peak — and they came up with at least two names he'd used while he was in the city. Second stroke of luck, he used one of them — John Fitzpatrick — to book a room in the Caledonian Hotel, near King's Cross, a week ago.

'Special Branch came in the front door, chummy was at the bar, although they didn't know that. He did a runner, in his shirtsleeves, despite the snow. If he's got decent paperwork and the necessary Irish ID card he'll be back in Dublin by now, in a new suit. Upstairs at the Caledonian, in his room, they found his coat on the hook; no wallet, but a diary, with names. Well, eight sets of initials at least, and eight partial addresses. So, *T. H., 18 Station Road*, that kind of thing. He'd have memorised the towns I suspect, and his compatriots' full names.

I had a look at the list and spotted *Honey Hill*. They were ringing round, but no one had thought of Cambridge, and I'm pretty sure it's unique.'

Honey Hill was at the heart of the Upper Town rookery, the dilapidated ghetto of rooms and attics in which the poorest lived. The area was overcrowded, insanitary and, after dark, off limits to polite society.

Edison produced a notebook. '*P. O., 14B Honey Hill*. It was top of the list, which could mean nothing, or it could mean Cambridge was next to cop it.'

'The Newton factory bomb,' said Brooke.

Edison held up a finger. 'Maybe. That's certainly them, but there's a pattern, with this S-Plan. So far each cell has been responsible for *two* bombs. They get two ready, blow one, pretty quickly blow number two, then close down the cell and bugger off. So I reckon there's one to come, sir. Unless the death of the kiddie has spooked them.'

Brooke sat back in his chair and considered the large map of the city which hung on the far wall. Cambridge was not an industrial city, but there was no doubt it comprised some high-profile targets, as Jo Ashmore had gone to some lengths to list.

'I need to tell Madingley,' said Brooke. 'The top brass can drum up the manpower. If we're going to put a guard on all the targets, we'll need a battalion.' He stood. 'You need a rest, Sergeant. A few hours at least — that's an order. But first set a watch on Honey Hill. Let's keep

114

out of the way if we can. Use the local constable on the street. Nothing heavy-handed. Let's get a spyhole: a house opposite, a corner shop, whatever it takes. Let's clap eyes on the mysterious P.O.

'A description would be a good start. Then we can match it to the eyewitness account from the night of the explosion. We've got a rough idea. I'll check now and see if the witness can't do better. Her first effort was an Irish caricature. I'll see if she can add detail. Meanwhile, we keep watch on Honey Hill. But anything suspicious, Edison, anything we can't deal with, we get this P.O. character off the streets and in a cell downstairs. We take no risks. At all costs we must stop a second bomb.'

20

Brooke, using the map he'd drawn in his mind as a child, set off for Davison College, via a series of alleyways which led down to the water meadows. A small herd of cattle stood steaming on the far side of the river, as he traced a route over a series of small wooden bridges, known as the Little Bridges, to Newnham village. The mainstream itself had been reduced to a trickle, banks of gravel revealed, peppered with snow. By nightfall the upper river would be dry and the final search for the lost boy could begin.

Once across the fen the Victorian colleges began: estates of brick, with brutal ark-like chapels and sturdy turrets. Bicycles were chained to every available yard of wrought-iron railings.

Dr Augustine Bodart's brief statement, made at the station the day after the explosion at Newton's, said that between the hours of nine and six she was to be found in her laboratory at the college, a foundation for women, set at the far reach of the city, with fields beyond, dotted with rugby posts. The college's facade presented a particularly depressing vision, with prison-like ramparts, designed to repel the vices of the city, or — more succinctly — men.

The porter said that the inspector would, indeed, find Dr Bodart in the laboratories. A junior porter would accompany the visitor on his forward journey, as all outsiders required a chaperone. The route led through a small door, reminiscent of Alice's gateway to Wonderland. And what lay beyond was indeed a world of its own: a great garden, hidden from the city, protected by the encircling wall of college buildings.

Here, secretly, the grim neo-Gothic of the new colleges had been abandoned for something much more joyful: white wood replaced stone, windows reached down to the ground, a sense of playful decoration gave the buildings a seaside air. The garden itself, despite a central parterre and monument, was otherwise informal, dominated by exotic trees and sweeping, snowy lawns.

The junior porter, a youth whose last growth spurt had left his trousers two inches short of his shoes, had clearly judged Brooke's moral fibre as adequate, as he was promptly abandoned at the first of a series of arrowed signs marked LABORA-TORY. The path led through a small wood to a cluster of prefabs, the roofs studded with skylights from which an extraordinary golden light radiated, gilding the tree boughs above. Brooke swapped the green-tinted lenses for the blue and stepped inside.

Bodart stood alone in a white lab coat, tending a long line of small plants laid out in pots beneath three great lights, each set within silvered dishes. The intensity of the golden beams was excruciating for Brooke, so he turned his back and swapped the blue lenses for the black. The heat was subtropical and humid, and somewhere a boiler throbbed, possibly beneath their feet. It reminded him fleetingly of St Alban's — an image that, looking back, he should have noted and considered.

Bodart gestured to the roof, the makeshift prefab walls. 'Science for women!' she said. 'We are permitted to use the laboratories in town. Permitted by men. I prefer to be a master in my own hall. You say this?' The animated eyes caught the light and Brooke found himself smiling in response.

Bodart, who wore glasses on a silver chain around her neck, asked if she could complete her current set of observations before giving full attention to the detective inspector. Five minutes, no more.

Brooke dabbed at his forehead with a handkerchief. He tried to concentrate on Bodart's work. He thought the plants were sweet peas. Those induced by the lights to bloom were arranged in lines by colour: white, blue and red. Others, about to bloom, waited in wooden trays. The work, whatever its purpose, seemed to involve meticulous observation. Notes were transferred from clipboards to ledgers. Numbers were written up in chalk on a large blackboard, broken into grids. Each plant was examined by eye, at close quarters, as if every leaf and stem held within it the secret of life.

Finished, Bodart ran a tap to fill a glass of water and pulled up a chair. A sturdy woman, she'd tied back her grey hair in a tight bun. The mobile face refused to succumb to inaction. Her eyes flitted over Brooke's face, as if collecting data from a particularly fascinating pot plant.

Brooke established the basics quickly enough. She lived in a houseboat on the riverbank, preferring what she termed 'the world outside' to a college room. Her work, on plant hereditary sequences, kept her at college late. She reprised her statement given verbally on the night of the explosion. Walking home she'd seen the three men climbing out of the gap in the security wire at the factory. Wanting to raise the alarm, but afraid of alerting the men to her presence, she'd backtracked along the towpath towards town and met the constable walking towards her. He'd told her to wait on a bench, while he ran to the scene.

'So you saw the men, and then the constable, almost immediately?'

'Yes. A few seconds, half a minute perhaps. Good fortune, certainly.'

'And how far away were you, when you first saw these men?'

She looked into the mid-distance, as if trying to see them again. 'Thirty yards?'

'Did they see you?'

'Perhaps. They were fleeing, yes? So they have no time for anything but to run. The criminal is a degenerate. They do not pause to reflect. The pattern of behaviour is animalistic.'

'I see. But you saw them. You *reflected*. This wasn't just a fleeting image. The light was good?'

She waved a hand. 'The moonlight, the snow, so yes. I can see them clearly. These are for here . . . ' She held her glasses up to her eyes, her free hand a foot away. 'For reading and observing.'

'It is possible we have found one of these men, Doctor. I need to compile a full description of them all.'

Brooke took out his notebook and they began

carefully to build a picture of the three men. Bodart, a trained observer, was an expert on detail. One was 'hulking', a 'typical labourer', with heavy bones, and a black jacket stretched across a broad back. She thought his trousers were tucked into socks, revealing what she called worker's boots. She thought he wore a heavy jumper, running to a thick neck — almost 'no neck at all'; in fact, merely a continuation of the shoulders. The face was heavy, with dark eyebrows, 'gone to fat' and rounded. Clean-shaven, with a heavy 'lantern' jaw.

His accomplices were less conspicuous; lightly built, one with light fair hair and tall, the other dark, but partly obscured by a hat — a 'cap' — pulled down tight. He had been the smallest of all, perhaps five feet six, with very slim limbs. Night-vision had wiped any colour from the scene.

'Did they speak?' asked Brooke, although he was trying to recall her initial description given at the scene on the night of the blast. Had she not described them all as of the 'labouring' classes?

For a moment she hesitated. 'I think the big one, who held open the gap in the fence, said 'Move!' — but no more.'

'And they ran south, towards the city?'

'I did not see this. I quickly turned away. Clearly they run, because your constable finds them gone.'

Brooke asked if — when — they had a suspect in custody would Bodart be available to identify the man.

Bodart seemed taken aback. For ten long seconds she was quite motionless.

'Yes. Certainly — forgive me. I am nervous of the authorities. But this is my duty. I am a guest in your country.'

Brooke stood, picking up his coat.

'What's life like on the river?' asked Brooke. He found Dr Bodart an enigmatic figure, her life lonely and self-contained. 'Quiet?'

Her face brightened, fluid again, manufacturing a smile. 'Not at all. Private, yes. But I have neighbours, friends. The houseboats are a village, yes? The English do this well — they combine the respect of the person with the collective good. I approve,' she added, nodding. 'It is idyllic,' she said, pleased she'd found the right word. Then her face darkened. 'But this child . . . '

'We've been dredging the river. There's no hope now. The boy was murdered. Tonight the river will be drained. We may find the body.'

'So it is true?' She shook her head. 'In war countries clash. Empires. Soldiers. This is sometimes necessary. Darwin sees this.' She covered her eyes for a moment. 'But this, an innocent, this is unforgiveable. A crime against nature.'

Turning to go, Brooke thought he saw something in her eyes: sadness certainly, even a weariness with the world, but also a trace of fear. Looking back from the door he saw that she had put on her glasses and picked up a pot plant, examining its leaves.

Walking back through the now falling snow of dusk he was struck at the vividness of Bodart's

121

descriptions of the three bombers: the hulking, the fair, the dark. It was as if the clinical certainty of her experiments had given her a clarity and simplicity of vision in the real world, outside the cloistered laboratory.

Crossing back over one of the Little Bridges on Coe Fen, in sight of the Spinning House, he wondered if the forcing of the plants under light meant they grew so quickly their progress was actually visible — a tiny green, soft bud, opening to reveal the simple secret of its colour, red, blue or white. Not for the first time he felt that his damaged eyes had saved him from such a life, observing minutiae, recording results, building a career out of patience.

In the end he might have found the experience deadening. For the second time in as many days he was forced to consider the possibility that his disability had been a gift.

21

As dusk fell, the snow, which still lay on the rooftops and in the parks, seemed to connect to an inner source of illumination, brightening as the sky darkened. A brief thaw in the hours after noon had been ruthlessly reversed, leaving a lethal patina of ice on the pavements and saw-tooth icicles hanging from eaves. Brooke collected a torch from the Spinning House and, swaddled in his Great War overcoat, set out briskly for the river: not the central stretch held between the stone college walls, but the upper reach at Mill Pond, where the chalky streams flowed down from the southern hills, wandering into the city through the water meadows.

The mill pond itself had formed a deep pit over the centuries as it swirled before slipping under Silver Street Bridge. Even now, with the river almost drained away to a trickle, its gloomy green depths were untouched, hidden beneath a cataract of ice. The languid stream that crossed Coe Fen to feed it, which he'd crossed earlier, was now a dry bed, with nothing more than a streamlet glistening as it threaded its way through the gravel and sand.

Cold air slumps into dips and shallows, and so, as Brooke descended the steps to the punt dock, he felt the temperature drop. A boatman was checking the chains on the craft — twenty or more, set in parallel lines, lying now on the riverbed below. Here a police constable stood by a brazier set on the gravel, in which a flame flickered.

'All in order?' asked Brooke.

'Sir. I'm to guard these steps, and the dock. Downstream all the other steps are watched too, until you get to the Great Bridge.'

The PC nodded over Brooke's shoulder. 'Here're the troops.'

The town's Civil Defence depot had agreed to lend the Borough twenty men for the night. Mostly too old for military service, or too young, or conscientious objectors, they formed an unlikely battalion. They came equipped with torches and an assortment of garden tools: rakes, brooms, hoes, and one with a wheelbarrow.

Brooke got them all to climb down the steps to the riverbed while he stood on the dock, a stage above his audience.

'My name's Inspector Eden Brooke,' he said. 'We're grateful for your help tonight. The river's almost dry. A child was thrown in the water two nights ago, in a sack. We need to search the river from this point down to Baits Bite.

'The child was last seen passing beneath the Mathematical Bridge.' Brooke pointed downstream. Beyond the modern span of Silver Street Bridge they could just see the dim outline of the wooden wonder itself, a ghostly curve, magically constructed of straight beams.

'I'm sorry it's such grim work. There's hot soup and tea at the Great Bridge and the far lock. Keep your eyes peeled. Anything suspicious, unusual, anything that catches the eye, tell one of the constables.'

By the flickering orange flames of the brazier, Brooke could see their startled eyes. In the strange light they looked oddly threatening, a lynch mob perhaps, waiting to light torches, setting out for the shantytown across the tracks.

A police van arrived and disgorged half a dozen uniformed officers co-opted from the County force. They brought with them a large steel chest within which were stored dozens of waxy batons.

Brooke brandished one. 'Once upon a time these were useful,' he said, handing them out. 'The bus company gave them out to conductors on foggy nights so that they could walk in front of the bus, clearing the way. A slow journey home, but a safe one.'

He lit the end of the first baton and held it aloft, the flame an intense red-blue, guttering.

'They last an hour. We've replacements at the Great Bridge.'

They set out under Silver Street, a forward line, then a second, double-checking, the lights dappling the curved stonework as they passed beneath the bridge. At Queens' College two students watched from an open window, calmly smoking.

The Backs followed a familiar pattern as they paced downstream. The left bank was largely open water meadow, unseen from the depth of the riverbed. On the right bank ran high college walls crowding in, beetling over the river.

They marched on, keeping to a ragged rhythm, the occasional shout identifying jetsam on the riverbed: a bicycle, a holed punt, a brass key on a wooden tag. The pacing line moved onwards, as the constables to the rear examined the finds. Ahead, Brooke could see King's College Bridge, out of whose shadow they eventually emerged to see the pinnacles of the great chapel, moonlit, against the stars. The marching men generated their own cloud of condensation, a match for the cattle Brooke had spotted earlier on the meadows.

More jetsam, mostly found under each of the following bridges, emerged as they tramped north. Pint glasses, wine glasses, a few bottles, a silver plate with the arms of Clare College embossed, a broken crystal decanter under a set of student windows, a dead cat tied to a brick opposite Wren Library.

At the Bridge of Sighs Brooke paused, lighting a cigarette.

The familiar electric buzz of exhaustion made his heart race. In the summer he loved to swim here, at the point where the college buildings took up both banks of the river. The torchlight played over the covered bridge, which led from St John's medieval courts on the right to the Victorian neo-Gothic on the left. The tunnel of stone which arched between was dank and threatening, in perfect harmony with the reputation of the bridge's Venetian original, which had led prisoners from the Doge's Palace into the republic's great gaol. Brooke could just see the shadowy forms of students crossing within the covered bridge, condemned to obey the dinner gong, which sounded faintly.

They pressed on, coming quickly to the Great Bridge, where a mobile tea kitchen had been set up and hot sausage sandwiches were dispensed, wrapped in greaseproof paper. By now, with rationing finally in full flow, everyone had learnt to eat such offerings quickly, putting aside any serious examination of the nature of the meat within. Sausages were universally known as 'mystery bags'. The work squad tucked in, gathered up on the parapet, glad to be free of the cloying icy air trapped below.

Brooke looked downstream. The pattern switched for the first and only time: Magdalene College lay to the left, the broad wharf to the right, and then open parkland. A few narrowboats here, and then houseboats, all either beached or lying in dark pools, their heating and pumps working to repel the advance of ice.

A twenty-minute break, then back down the steps to the dry river. The town slipped away behind them. Ahead the lock at Jesus stood in silhouette against a brilliantly lit treescape, illuminated by a pair of ack-ack searchlights, ordered up by the military at Madingley Hall.

But first the lock: the two lines of volunteers came together to file through the gap of the open sluice, led by Brooke, then splayed out to try and cover the wide bed as it began its long sweep northwards to the distant sea. On both sides houseboats sat at odd angles, several lit within, people out on deck watching in silence as the search moved relentlessly forward. From one boat, a tumbledown wreck festooned with rigging, jazz music played for a few seconds then fell silent.

The searing lights transformed every pebble, every discarded bottle, making them as vivid as artefacts in a gallery, each with its own black shadow.

Brooke saw the sack first, thirty yards ahead, within a hundred yards of the approaches to the sluice, where he'd seen the pale hand sink below the black water. At first his heart lifted; the sack looked spent, almost empty, flat on the gravel bed. It was a cruel illusion, for as he approached he saw it lay in a large pothole in the shingle, surrounded by thin ice. The body had found its own shallow grave.

Beside the sack he stopped, the torchlight at his feet. The hand of the child still lay outside the hessian bag. The rhythmic pacing of the search line faltered and then stopped behind him, conversation dying away. Everything fell quiet for the length of a prayer. Brooke stepped forward and with a pocket knife cut the drawstring of the bag. The hessian flopped open, to reveal both arms, the top of the head covered in a swirl of black hair, flecked with ice, bloodied where a wound cut deep. He slit the bag lengthwise. The body, frozen and stiff, remained in its foetal ball.

He set the lantern down. Its light revealed the outstretched hand and the bare left arm. On the lower arm were the inky remnants of a child's game. Brooke recognised it as hangman, in which one player choses a secret word, set out in blanks, which their opponent has to guess, letter by letter. Each unsuccessful guess adds a single stroke to a little picture of a man on a gibbet. The word unrevealed stood at *A–CH–A–*. On the scaffold a man dangled, the single stroke across his neck indicating death, and for the boy, a final childish victory.

Brooke stood still, the crowd at his back, but felt himself overwhelmed by a sense of loneliness, a rare emotion, and — selfishly — he wondered if later, after the body had been taken away and he'd done his duty, he'd have time to walk to the hospital to see Claire, to touch her, and feel the warmth beneath her skin.

22

The line of men stood in silence, their blazing torches held above their heads.

'We'll search on, to Baits Bite, once the body is removed,' said Brooke, addressing them again, as he had just an hour before. 'There may be other evidence. But go back to the Great Bridge now, get a hot drink. Things need to be done here. It'll take time.'

Reluctantly the line began to turn away, leaving one old man, his head still down in prayer.

Two constables were set to guard the spot, storm lanterns placed on the glittering shingle beside the body. Bending down to adjust a wick, Brooke caught sight for the first time of the child's face: an eye glazed as if with ice, bloodless lips revealing small milk teeth. And something else glittering on his coat; a small enamel badge depicting a gold cannon on a red background.

The searchlights thudded out of power, leaving the lanterns as an oasis of light in midstream. Across the city the bells began to chime the hour.

Brooke sent one of the constables to the nearby home of the force pathologist, Dr Henry Comfort, a university man who taught at the Galen Anatomy Building, a few hundred yards from the Spinning House. The twin appointment was a tradition stretching back to the turn of the century and recorded in gold lettering on a board in the lobby of the Spinning House. Dr Comfort's standards were rigorous: he would examine the victim in situ before allowing the body to be taken to his morgue. Sean Flynn would have to lie in his shallow grave a little longer.

A constable arrived from upstream, brandishing a fiery baton. They'd found something back by Mill Pond, tangled up in a rusted bicycle. It took them twenty minutes to march up the riverbed, a small crowd gathered now on the Great Bridge, watching but silent. Walking under the elegant curve of the Mathematical Bridge, Brooke saw ahead that the burning torches had been set in a ring, thrust into the shingle, around the carcass of a bike lying under Silver Street Bridge. At this spot a set of steps led down from the parapet to a small wooden dock, where a punt and two dinghies were tied up, lying now at an angle on the stones.

'We missed it first time,' said the constable who'd been left to watch over the Mill Pond steps. 'But I had a second look.'

Beneath one wheel, Brooke could see a hessian sack, a twin to the one in which the child had been bound, but badly stained with what could be blood. An electric torch, held close, revealed the true colour, a deep rust-red. Gently, Brooke took a corner of the material and began to lift it, until a heavy object dropped out. Stepping back, they could see a metal wrench, a foot long, double-headed. The maker's trademark was deeply etched — STANLEY TOOLS — while the

131

surface of the metal was elegantly cross-hatched with lines. Something dark, possibly more blood, was caught between the spaces of the metal nameplate.

Around one end of the wrench was a piece of heavy string attached to a label which was blank. Brooke found his fountain pen and used one end to flip the label over: damp, discoloured, but it still bore the name *Sean Flynn* in a loopy feminine hand, followed by the address of St Alban's Church.

Scrawled in pencil was a note: *See you soon. Mum.*

23

Walking back to the Spinning House, Brooke felt, for the first time, that he could *see* the crime: a car or van parked on Silver Street Bridge, the snow falling heavily, the streets empty, the first sack hauled to the parapet and dropped into the flood, followed by the second. Did the killer think the child was dead? Within a minute the van would be gone, while the child — stunned into consciousness by the icy water — had floated down to the next bridge, where his cry for help was heard beneath the Mathematical Bridge. The second sack, perhaps used to clean the 'murder' scene, had sunk, weighted with the wrench, which looked a likely candidate for the murder weapon.

On that night Brooke had despatched PC Collins to check Silver Street Bridge. What had he found? Why had he not reported back? Had Edison checked?

The snow had been heavy, but tyre tracks must have been visible, and snow may have been brushed from the parapet. The killer, if cool-headed, may even have still been at the bridge. Had he watched in horror as the sack floated away, the child's voice echoing in the stone canyon between the college buildings? Had he heard his final call: *Help me!* Even if he'd fled he'd have left a trail, a trail quite visible for an hour or more, before the snow could have obliterated the tracks.

The duty sergeant on the desk at the Spinning House checked the roster: PC Collins was marked as off sick.

'I know Sergeant Edison left us a note,' offered the duty man, flicking pages. 'Yes, here it is. We had to check out a domestic in Romsey Town — we did that, nothing to report. And send a constable round to Collins' house, but the inspector told us to hang fire. Bit delicate apparently. The file's gone upstairs.'

He raised his eyes. 'Top office. She's in, sir. At her desk.'

Brooke found the door ajar, a desk lamp illuminating a drift of paper.

'Ma'am?'

'Brooke. The search?'

Brooke gave a brief résumé of the night's events.

'A blow to the head?' she asked. 'A fatal blow of itself?'

'Possibly. But the water intervened. That's the reality,' said Brooke. 'Dr Comfort's at the scene now. The discovery of the second sack pinpoints the bridge where the child was thrown into the water. I sent PC Collins to check it out on the night. He's now off sick and there's been no report back. I understand there's an issue?'

Carnegie-Brown took off her glasses and cast them aside, signalling for Brooke to take a seat.

'I see. Then we do indeed have a problem.'

She steepled her hands. 'Collins is missing. In fact, from what you've just told me, I'd say you may have been the last person in authority to have seen him. He was on his way home at the end of his shift when he responded to the incident at Queens'.

'He lives in the family home at Chesterton. An empty house, it appears, as his mother's dead, father's in the Merchant Navy. One older brother, in the army. He got his own call-up papers last week.

'A bit of a loner according to the sergeant, but he did confide to one or two people that he didn't want to join up. He'd considered applying for registration as a conscientious objector. Apparently, the family has a military history — his father was in the Great War. Won a medal at Jutland. So you can see the problem. He talked to one of the uniformed inspectors about trying to stay with us, which was not possible of course, not at his age.

'My judgement was that he'd done a runner, Brooke. In fact, that was our working assumption. I sent a woman police constable round but the house, as I say, was empty. Locked up.'

Brooke saw Collins' face then: the panic, the flushed cheeks. He'd tried to calm him down, then he'd sent him to Silver Street Bridge. What had he found there? Had he encountered the murderer? Had he followed the trail?

'If he discovered the killer still on the bridge he might have come to harm,' said Brooke. 'We'll search the far riverbank, just in case. He wasn't the only constable out that night; we'll ask around, see if anyone saw him about. We shouldn't presume the worst,' he added. 'The prospect of war may have been too much for him. The likelihood is he's simply run away. I'll get someone to check his file, see if we can find other relatives. Maybe he's holed up somewhere hoping it'll all be over soon. Fear is a corrosive emotion. It can eat a man up.'

Carnegie-Brown was nodding. 'We'll find him soon enough, Brooke. He'll be sweating it out somewhere, as you say, regretting he let his nerves get to him.'

Brooke stood, softly punching out his hat into something like its proper shape.

'Progress on the Fenians?' asked Carnegie-Brown.

'Edison has tracked down a link between the Coventry bomb and a suspect here in Cambridge. We're watching his rooms in the Upper Town. When we've got a decent description, we can see if he matches one of the three men our witness saw at Newton's.

'For the record, Coventry's view is that the IRA's modus operandi in this current campaign usually involves *two* bombs per cell, then they close down, go to ground. I'm hoping our suspect will lead us to bomb factory, or his accomplices. We need a break, ma'am. We need one soon.'

24

Rigor, and the icy water, had locked the body of Sean Flynn in its curled self-embrace, but under the lights in Dr Comfort's forensic laboratory the arms had slowly unfurled like pale, fleshy spring leaves. The back of the head, shaved clean, revealed the brutal wound which had broken the skull. Brooke was reminded of an eggshell, cracked open by a single blow of a silver spoon.

Comfort, tetchy and unusually brisk, had come to a forthright judgement. 'Lethal force, Brooke. He'd have died if untreated. Drowning intervened, but only by minutes.'

He wiped blood and hair from his hands. 'The lungs are flooded. There is no doubt as to the actual cause of death, but as I say, that is entirely a timing issue. The blow to the head is what ultimately ended his life. The person who delivered it must bear all the responsibility. The tragedy is, of course, they are unlikely to find that much of a burden.'

Dr Comfort offered one other observation, although it was technically beyond his remit, but perhaps he was keen to move on from the corpse. 'The golden cannon, Brooke,' he said, indicating the badge on the boy's jacket, which had been laid out with the other clothes on a dissecting table. 'An ardent fan, no doubt, of Arsenal Football Club, but that hardly narrows the field. Last year, according to Whyte, they won the First Division title.' Whyte was one of the doctor's autopsy 'servants', poised at the far end of the lab to wield the heavy tools of the trade. 'The team is internationally famous, I'm told. Thousands of children must have been dazzled by the glamour. Perhaps he dreamt of playing himself one day.'

He moved back towards the corpse, using a long metal pointer to indicate the inky tattoo on the lower arm.

'And a game of hangman, of course. I wonder when English children started playing that? A century ago. Two, three, five? No wonder he won. The key word's tricky: *A*, dash, *C*, *H*, dash, *A*, dash. Any ideas?'

Brooke shook his head. He'd played at school with all the rest, but there had always been something malevolent about the imagery. He'd found the tension imposed by the rules — that he had to guess the word by trying out the various letters — strangely unpleasant. He did the obvious, as they all did, and tried the vowels first. Each wrong guess added a pen-stroke to the stickman's image, until at the last the neck was broken with a single dash. It was just a game, a proxy death, but the anxiety always lingered.

'I doubt it's relevant,' he said, finally, looking away.

'As you know, Brooke, I'm no advocate of judicial execution,' said Comfort, cleaning a scalpel under a tap preparatory to starting the dissection of the body. 'But if you find out who did this I'd like a ringside ticket at the gallows.

138

But then that's a swift death. A broken neck . . . '
He clicked his fingers. 'This lad suffered terribly,
and I think someone should pay for that, don't
you?'

At a further click of the fingers Comfort's
servants moved forward with a trolley upon
which were arranged saws, knives, mechanical
dividers.

The moment of existential obliteration was at
hand, and Brooke had no stomach for it tonight.

He brandished a note. 'This was waiting for
me at the lodge below. I must go. We've found
one of the Fenian bombers — or at least a fellow
traveller — up on Honey Hill. Edison's at the
scene. I have been called to inspect the dispositions. For that would be a criminal failure, to let
the man slip away. He could be our murderer.'
He adjusted his hat. 'I'll leave you to it, Doctor.'

Brooke fled before the saws could start their
work.

On the doorstep he stopped and lit a cigarette.
They'd always known the boy would be dead.
But without a body the victim had inhabited a
kind of earthly purgatory. Now, at least, he had
been released from that, although the cruel
ordeal was not over. The autopsy was underway,
the reassemblage of the body would take place
for the purposes of identification, and then
storage would follow, in one of Comfort's steel
drawers. And there it would lie until the coroner
released the body for burial; an order which
relied on Brooke finding the boy's killer.

139

25

As Brooke walked up King's Parade a neat line of choirboys, exiting the great chapel, broke ranks at an unheard word of command and began a frantic battle of snowballs. Otherwise, the city centre was quiet, although the faint sounds of a piano were drifting from the doors of the Mitre, in Bridgeland. As he crossed the river on the Great Bridge a clock struck ten. Climbing Castle Hill, he cut off to the left around the base of the slope, turning up an alleyway by the Old Ferry, an inn infamous for Saturday night brawls.

Edison's note was precise: when free, Brooke was to proceed at the first opportunity to the Castle End Working Men's Institute in the Upper Town. He was *on no account* to enter by the front doors, but to climb Pound Hill from the Old Ferry and slip into the delivery yard at the rear of the club. He should knock there to gain entry. Not for the first time Brooke was impressed by Edison's natural authority and confidence, in that he had clearly taken charge of the operation on the ground.

Brooke followed the path laid down for him by his detective sergeant. His shoes slid badly on the ice and snow of the hill as he climbed away from the river. The Stuke — as the institute was affectionately known — was a red brick and cream confection, a Gothic folly paid for, according to a plaque, with donations from several colleges. The blackout screens over the lancet windows were brutally efficient. The club looked dead, except that a telltale column of white smoke rose from the chimney. Walking to the back, Brooke followed Edison's instructions and executed a sharp knock on the wide doors marked CELLARAGE.

The steward, in a white shirt and tie, let him in without a word. Down a corridor Brooke glimpsed the bar, and beyond that a large room dotted with tables at which men in pairs shuffled dominoes. Cigarette fumes hung in the air, whisked aside by sudden belches of pipe smoke. The radio played something orchestral and improving: Vaughan Williams perhaps, or Britten.

'Old timers tonight,' said the steward. 'I've told 'em we've got family staying. They're not stupid, but they know when to keep mum.'

Up the stairs Edison sat by candlelight at a dormer window, cradling a pint of beer.

'Sir. Anything from the river?'

Brooke briefed him on the latest: 'I left Dr Comfort to complete the autopsy.'

The news clearly gave Edison some food for thought, as he nodded, taking several sips from his beer. Brooke waited for the steward to bring him the whisky he had ordered, and then pulled up a chair beside his detective sergeant.

'Which house?' he asked.

'Well, sir, not so much a house as a warren. Sorry for the summons, but the next move's tricky. I thought you'd want to see for yourself.'

Opposite them a small street ran off Pound Hill, no more than a wide alley, a hundred yards long. This was Honey Hill. On either side,

141

tumbledown buildings, mostly wooden-framed, teetered over the pathway. A patchwork of roofs, dotted with chimneys and windows, completed a picture of a medieval hovel, transported unchanged into the twentieth century.

'A slum, really,' said Edison. 'We didn't want to alert anyone to our interest, so it's not been easy. The buildings form one interconnected block. There are at least six landlords, with flats to rent, rooms to rent, beds to rent. I checked with the council: there's three toilets and a single bath. All of it's facing demolition. Water supply is by a standpipe at the far end.'

Edison shook his head, sipped his pint again, and set it aside.

'And he's in there, is he?'

'Yes, sir. Local constable knew the name. Patrick O'Leary — so, *P. O.* He's a regular in the Spinning House cells of a Saturday night. Drunk and disorderly, a common assault last October. Drinks in the Commercial at Mitcham's Corner. I got a detective constable to follow him home from work. He's a builder's labourer.' Edison checked his watch. 'Got home two hours ago. He went in the third door on the right. As I say, the place is a warren, but there's no way out except down the street, unless he's got a head for heights and he's desperate, in which case the rooftops would work. But if we go in we can watch the streets. He'd have to come down eventually.'

A door opened on Honey Hill and a dog loped out, squatted down in the snow, and trotted back inside, the owner unseen but for a hand.

'One other thing,' said Edison. 'From what I was told in Coventry it's very unlikely the bomb factory's here. Thin walls, loads of people about — it just doesn't work. It'll be a garage, a lock-up, a cellar.'

'If we watch him he could lead us to it?'

'That's it, sir.'

Downstairs they heard the cacophony of dominoes being shuffled on tables and a sudden convivial hum.

The blanket of snow along Honey Hill was unblemished except for the dog's stain.

Brooke lit a cigarette.

'As you say, Edison. A tricky decision. We could have him in the cells tonight. If we lost him there'd be hell to pay. Any telephone lines in the block?'

'Not one, sir. Nearest box is there.'

At an angle they could see down Pound Hill to a telephone box under a fir tree. The snow had made a neat pyramid of its roof.

The dilemma was clear. If the IRA cell had plans for a second bomb and O'Leary spotted he was being watched, he could alert the rest. They'd all go to ground, but they might decide to set off the second bomb first, especially if it was already in place or preparations were complete. Or had the murder of Sean Flynn thrown them into panic? Perhaps the rest of the gang would come here, to Honey Hill. Or O'Leary might lead them to his comrades.

It was a trap, but they needed time for it to be sprung.

'I'd be much happier if that telephone box

143

wasn't there,' said Brooke. 'What if he knows we're watching? What if he raises the alarm?' He weighed the odds and made a decision. 'Let's watch him tonight, tomorrow, see what he does, who he talks too. We might get lucky. I'll get a shift rota set up so you can get a break. Let's keep a watching brief.

'I'm off to London to see the parents of Sean Flynn in the morning, after I've told Father Ward the bad news first thing. I can't just ring the local nick and leave a message for the parents that their boy is dead. I'll tell them face-to-face. And it's a chance to find out more about Sean, and his family. I'll be back by dusk. If nothing changes here we'll pick O'Leary up tomorrow night, at midnight.'

Brooke slipped down the stairs, ordered Edison a fresh pint and went out into the snow. Standing in the silence he fished in his overcoat pocket. The penknife had been his mother's, so it had a pearl handle, although the blade was worn because she'd used it to prune roses. He walked down Pound Hill, slipped into the phone box and cut the wire.

26

On Trinity Street, walking home, Brooke paused
beneath Jo Ashmore's lofty rooftop eyrie. The
compacted snow dulled the usual *rat-a-tat* of his
metal Blakeys on the pavement, and the frost had
frozen the water in the drainpipes, and so the
silence was complete. Which is why he heard the
laughter: Jo's liquid voice certainly, but not alone,
up at her Observation Post. The man's voice was
understated, and soft, but with a teasing edge.
Brooke, in the shadows smoking, examined his
response. He felt displaced, and disappointed to
miss Jo's youthful company and the hot toddy,
and the panoramic view of his city. But there was
also a sense of fatherly comfort, that her long
exile above the roofs, looking down on life, was
drawing to an end. Looking up he thought he
could see cigarette smoke drifting out over the
street. Their words grew softer and Brooke imagined them getting closer, which made him feel
like a voyeur, so he fled.

He set out again for home and a hot bath,
even some food, respecting the letter of Aldiss's
strict regime, but opposite the ghostly white
walls of the Senate House he came to an abrupt
full stop, catching on the still air the savoury
aroma of freshly fried bacon. Following his nose,
he entered Market Hill, the square empty but for
a few stalls swaddled in tarpaulin, and a single
splash of electric light where the regular tea hut

had reopened despite the cold snap.

A platoon of soldiers crowded at the hatch, while a group of tram drivers, still in uniform, clutched steaming mugs, gathered round a small brazier from which smoke dribbled upwards in a vertical column untouched by any breeze. Rose King, proprietor, was Brooke's oldest and most reliable nighthawk. The cafe was usually open twenty-four hours a day. The bitter winter weather had forced a brief shutdown. Now she was back in business. Rose reserved the night shift for herself, leaving the daylight hours to her three daughters.

Brooke's first beat as a uniformed police constable after the Great War, a north — south line through the old city, had taken him across Market Hill four times a night, a journey which never managed to reveal exactly where the 'hill' lay, given the piazza and the streets about were all fen-flat. In an old book on the city's ancient history Claire had bought him one Christmas he'd found an answer to the riddle: there was no hill, for the old Saxon word had at its root the concept of a meeting place. Height was, apparently, a secondary quality.

It was certainly a good place for nighthawks to meet.

The soldiers parted to let Brooke get to the counter.

'Well, well. It's the night detective,' said Rose, sloshing a dark tannic soup into a large mug. She carefully tucked away a lock of grey hair under a colourful headscarf. 'The usual?' she said, placing two rashers on the griddle.

Rose's counter was her stage, and every movement a dramatic gesture. She cut two slices of bread and coated them with margarine, with a single sweep of a broad knife.

Armed with two cups of tea she came round to stand with Brooke, close to the flames which had begun to flicker amid the smoke, her fingertips poking out of woollen mittens.

'Cold night,' said Brooke.

'Getting colder. But people get used to it, so we thought we'd show willing. Open all night for nearly twenty years, Brooke, so England expects. Can't let the customers down. This is the Home Front. And it ain't gonna get any warmer, is it? The ice is here for a week, maybe more. Just listen.'

Rose was a student of folklore, particularly when it pertained to the weather.

Brooke strained his ears yet could hear nothing but the soldiers talking, so he shrugged.

'Exactly,' said Rose, triumphant. 'Most nights this time you can hear the trains in the yards; the wheels, the couplings. Silence means a north wind. Not down here, up there . . . ' She pointed skywards.

'How are the girls?' asked Brooke, keen to keep the conversation rational.

'The big news is that Dawn's pregnant. Her first, and she didn't even know. I told her — it was plain as a pikestaff. Hair shining, eyes bright, cheeks like apples. She glowed. Sure enough she's three months gone.'

A fleeting image came to Brooke, of the radiant Mrs Walsh, the young wife of the head

147

teacher of St Alban's School. Was there joyful news for the head teacher? Did he know?

Brooke told Rose about Joy's baby and the prospect of being a grandfather, and that Claire was already painting the old nursery below the attic. A cot had been purchased, but stored in the garden shed, to avoid bad luck.

Rose beamed, delighted to find any evidence of continuing superstition. 'The other girls have got their hands full. We've taken in three evacuees.'

'Londoners?'

She nodded. 'East Enders. It's a bit of an eye-opener, I can tell you. Bath time's an innovation. And the language . . . Still, the money helps, and if you put the ration books together you can rustle up a decent meal.'

The idea that the government paid for the upkeep of the children had not occurred to Brooke. There were supposed to be ten thousand children in the town billeted with families. The city had become a giant playground.

'Any sign of the parents?'

'They took the kids home for Christmas, but they're back now. The government keeps saying the children need to stay put, out of harm's way, but a lot are going back. Ours will follow, you watch. Unless the bombs start to fall. Then it will be full steam ahead, backwards. Like everything else. The more they go on about not panicking, the more likely everyone will. They'll be stuffing the kids on any old train out of the Smoke just to get them safe, you see.' Rose drank her tea. 'How's your boy?'

148

'Luke? We just watch the post for letters. He's stuck on the Belgian border waiting for it to all start. Joy's man is on submarines. She's trying to keep from thinking about it, but it's not working. You know they have to volunteer for subs? They won't send anyone down who doesn't want to go. I'm amazed they can raise a crew, let alone hundreds of them.'

They fell silent, watching the fire.

'I had the Civil Defence lot here an hour ago, all talking about the kiddie you found in the river.' Rose sneaked a sideways glance at Brooke's face, lit by the flames. 'You'll find the killer. I know you will. But if it don't happen, or if it takes time, don't take it personal. Go home, Eden. Sleep.'

Brooke resettled his hat, executed a mock salute and slipped away.

27

Brooke found the children of St Alban's in the playground, swarming in that peculiar way unique to the under-tens: a version of Brownian motion, the haphazard oscillation of molecules in gas. Brooke always imagined that he could hear the telltale noise of buzzing bees. The speed of circulation had been vastly increased by a fresh overnight snowfall. The cramped yard had a single drain, which had spilt over and frozen, so that through the milling crowd the occasional child shot by at speed. Snowballs flew in all directions. The informal discipline of St Alban's stood in sharp contrast to the cliché of Jesuit cruelty. Mrs Walsh, the head's wife, was in the middle of the melee, cheerfully swinging a very small child around as if about to launch a Highland hammer.

The school building was two storeys, with large metal grilled windows, and a single white statue of St Alban set in a central niche. Christmas decorations still obscured the interior. For the first time the identity of the patron saint of the school and church struck Brooke as significant: St Alban, the first martyr of the English. Had it been chosen to smooth the cultural waters, to dampen Victorian fears of an Irish takeover of the wider church?

As Brooke entered, a bell rang out in the playground. Liam Walsh, the head, met him in the central corridor of the school, the backbone of the rudimentary ground floor. Today he wore a threadbare corduroy suit and ran a hand back through the thinning red hair. Children, oblivious, scuttled round him at speed. At the far end of the corridor a Virgin Mary stood in a grotto, the flesh painted in realistic tones, a light burning in a silver dish, Bernadette kneeling amongst the rock flowers.

Walsh's eyes, examining the parquet floor, rose slowly to meet Brooke's, but he must have read there an intimation of what was to come. 'Bad news, Inspector? We've been praying. The children at least were hopeful.'

Brooke told him the boy had been found. There was no doubt it was Sean Flynn.

'I'm going to London this morning to tell the parents. We'll have to wait for a formal identification of course, possibly at the weekend,' said Brooke. 'But as I say, the child fits the description of the missing boy. We found the body below Jesus Lock, his ID label upstream. He'd been coshed, a blow which would have killed him in its own right. We must find the man who did this, Mr Walsh. I'd like to speak to the children again.'

Walsh was silent, head bowed, and Brooke realised with a shock that he was praying. A brief, fleeting sign of the cross released him, and he led the way towards the Virgin at the end of the corridor. Around them the children streamed back into the classrooms, the building filling with the smell of damp wool and soaked leather.

'We've put the evacuees in the same class for

151

now,' said Walsh, his whisper-like voice even less audible than usual. 'They're all of an age, and we have the room. And they're a disparate crowd, many of them travelled alone, without friends, but they're closer now. All this must be terrifying.'

They entered a classroom. The children sat in pairs at desks, listening to Mrs Walsh call the register. In front of the class she seemed older, but nonetheless still remarkably youthful in comparison to her husband. She managed to radiate good health even here in a damp classroom, in the stark white light flooding in from the playground.

She called out the children's surnames, nodding briefly as each stood, then sat.

'Thank you, Mrs Walsh,' said the head. 'If I may. We must pray for the soul of Sean Flynn, children. It seems that God has decided that he may never come back to us. We must pray for his parents, and his brothers. Sean will be in heaven soon, but we must pray for him nonetheless.'

The children stood uncertainly and joined in an Our Father.

Brooke thought about the missing child. Frank Edwardes was right. The abduction, the murder, were clearly planned. But the child was a visitor who knew no one. How could this small boy have represented a threat to anyone? Did the family have links with the IRA? Had he met his killer at some point between leaving his home and lights-out in the church? Who had he met, and where?

'Children,' said Walsh, motioning for them to

sit. 'This is Detective Inspector Brooke, from the police. He's trying to find who took Sean, who wanted to hurt him. There's nothing to fear. He simply has questions. Speak up if you can help with the answers.'

Brooke noted that despite the head's mild manner and the friendly tone, the children had listened to him in complete silence. One of the girls at the front had produced a handkerchief and held it over her mouth. The boys' good humour had evaporated entirely. As Brooke took up a position in front of the blackboard every child followed the movement, transfixed.

The story of the evacuees' journey to Cambridge and St Alban's was quickly established. They'd parted with their parents at King's Cross and boarded a special train which had separate compartments, with a single corridor. Sean had shared with five other children but had made particular friends with John McQuillan.

McQuillan stood up when asked. As a policeman in uniform, Brooke had noted the effect authority could have on a child. This was of a different order. The boy looked terrified.

'Did Sean say he was happy, or unhappy? How was he, John?'

The boy's shoulders were in constant squirming motion. 'Dunno,' he said.

'John,' warned Mrs Walsh. 'Speak nicely.'

'Don't know, sir.'

'Did he cry when you all left London?'

'Only the girls cried.' The boy fidgeted, pulling up a sleeve on his jumper to reveal an ink-spotted pale arm. Brooke caught a glimpse of a sketch of a football corner flag, carrying the letters *QPR*.

'Did you speak to any adults on the train?'

He shook his head. 'Sean and I talked about football. Then we played I spy. We had to spot church spires and cows. A woman gave us squash, and a bun.'

'Yes. And you played hangman, didn't you?'

McQuillan looked wary. 'Yes, sir.'

'And Sean won?'

McQuillan nodded.

'Then what? What happened when you got to Cambridge?'

The boy was clearly tongue-tied, so Brooke motioned with his hand for him to sit down.

A confident girl called Alice took up the story. 'They gave us squash again outside the station. There was a van, with a counter . . . And there was a sweet shop too, and if anyone had pocket money they could spend it. Then we all had to use the toilet. A woman showed us where, because they said it was a walk to the school. Then Mr Smith arrived and said we'd to follow him. So we did.'

Mr Smith, Mr Walsh explained, was the school caretaker.

'A man gave us flags,' offered McQuillan, eager to reclaim the story. 'Mr Smith didn't see because he was at the front. But we took the flags.'

The other children joined in to describe the man handing out flags. Large, in a donkey jacket, with dirty fingernails. They'd all waved the Union Flags in their double line, holding hands.

'They try to welcome the evacuees,' explained Walsh. 'They give out flags, or balloons, or sweets. Even cakes.'

'I didn't like the man,' said one of the girls confidently. 'He smelt of whisky,' she added, then flushed, perhaps realising she'd given too much away about life at home.

'Where was this?' asked Brooke.

One of the other boys, slightly older than the rest, had a clear memory. 'There was a memorial, to the Great War. A soldier striding along. I liked him.'

Brooke nodded. 'The Homecoming' was a statue at the bottom of Station Road. A bareheaded young soldier marched into town, with a glance towards the station as if expecting his comrades to join him. The figure was joyful, victorious, and the warrior carried a laurel wreath. The soldier was modelled on a friend of Brooke's from his student days, a Trinity man who had indeed marched back victorious, or at least alive.

'Did he say anything?' asked Brooke. 'The man with the flags?'

'He said the flag was for me — Mary,' said one girl. 'We all had our labels, so he could see. He told Patrick that it was a good name to have, didn't he?'

Patrick nodded.

'Did he read all of your labels?'

Several children nodded.

'What did he sound like — did he have an Irish accent?'

None of them spoke, but several nodded.

The rest of their first day had run to a strict

schedule. The children were given a meal in the church, asked to make up their overnight 'beds' on the pews, and then taken to the school playground, where Mr Smith organised games. They were back inside by six, where they had tea, and Father Ward read them stories. They'd had a singalong, with Mrs Aitken at the piano. The doors were locked, a register taken and the lights turned out.

Brooke asked to see the caretaker before he left. Joe Smith, who they found shovelling snow in the playground, turned out to be a surprise: twenties, fresh-faced, he'd taken the job while waiting to be called up. His father was already out with the expeditionary force in France. His accent was pure London East End. Even leaning on his shovel, he projected a sense of potential motion: knees rising perhaps, arms pumping, as he ran into the distance.

Walsh told him that they'd found Sean's body in the river.

They all stood in silence until the head teacher rested a hand on the young man's broad shoulders.

'An athlete, our Joe,' he said. 'He runs like the wind, up at six and off along the river like a whippet. And he's a wonder with a football in the playground.'

This recommendation delivered, Walsh seemed suddenly crestfallen, as if he'd realised that he'd traduced the general air of grief. 'I must go and tell Father Ward the news,' he said. He hurried away, back into the warmth of the school.

Brooke asked the caretaker about the man

who'd given out flags, but the children were right, he'd not seen him, and he'd been astounded at Speaker's Corner, on the edge of Parker's Piece, when he'd turned back to see the children waving their flags.

'Not a sign of 'im. But they all had the flags, and wavin' like mad. It was a sight. It certainly cheered 'em up. A few people clapped an' all. People on the street, a few on park benches. It's good to see. A welcome really.'

'Did you meet Sean later, in the playground?'

'Oh yeah. I've got to know John since — John McQuillan — and they stuck together that first day. They was both football mad. Good too, I got 'em overlapping, tracking back, keepy-uppy. They had skills, no question.'

Brooke stepped closer to Smith. 'I'm sorry to ask this. We're pretty certain it is Sean we've found, but it would help to be sure.'

Smith nodded, rearranging his feet as if called on parade.

'I'm going to see his parents in London now. They have the right to know quickly. We will need a formal identification. That may take a few days to arrange. It would be a great help to me if I could be certain of the child's identity now. Would you — could you — identify the body for us unofficially? It would take a moment.'

The colour drained from Smith's energetic face. 'Yes. Of course. If it helps. I can see his face now. So I could, yes. But there's still hope is there — that there's been a mistake, and it's some other kid?'

Brooke replaced his hat. 'I'll get my sergeant to send a car. Perhaps an hour, no more.'

He touched the hat rim and turned away.

28

Brooke slept fitfully on the train, opening his eyes between troubled bouts of unconsciousness to see the winter landscape rattling past. Descending the shallow funnel of the Lee Valley, shadowing an ice-locked river, they reached the north London suburbs, smoke from factories obscuring dismal streets where, in contrast to the Fens, the snow seemed to be in retreat. Barrage balloons squatted over a colony of gasometers in Hackney, and a tram, running alongside the tracks, shed lurid sparks from the pantograph above, which seemed to glide along the wires. Then they were in Liverpool Street, the concourse packed with soldiers, smoking, camped out on kit bags. The reek of damp clothes was overpowering.

Outside, the air was freighted with coal and petrol. He found a call box and rang the Spinning House. The sergeant had a note to hand: Joe Smith had no doubt, the boy in Dr Comfort's morgue was Sean Flynn. Brooke replaced the receiver, let the change chug from the metal box and stepped out into the bustling city. On the Tube, forced to play sardines, he thought the general mood was sombre, even defeated, which was odd, given the war was yet to start in earnest. Perhaps it was the thought of the dull sacrifices to come: hunger, cold and separation.

In contrast his present task was simple enough. He had to tell Mrs Flynn that the body had been found and that it was her son, although a member of the family would have to complete the official identification. Finding his killer was the Borough's priority. All available officers were currently trying to hunt down the mysterious man who'd handed the children flags while making sure he read the labels attached to their suitcases and cuffs. Was he a local character? Uniform branch would check the shops, the pubs. The donkey-jacketed Irishman was their prime suspect, and a close match, superficially, for both Dr Bodart's lumpen Celt, seen at Newton's factory moments before the bomb blast, and Patrick O'Leary, labourer of Honey Hill. He'd tell Mrs Flynn an arrest was imminent. It might help.

From East Acton Underground station, he set off down Uxbridge Road, then turned into a district of comfortable three-storey villas. Askew Road was very different. Here were smaller cottages, two-up two-down, but of a superior quality, with small neat gardens in front and fresh paintwork in various Victorian colours, a detail which gave the game away. A single colour would have signalled a common landlord, but the variation pointed to ownership.

Number 36 was like the rest save for a poster in the downstairs window: ARP WARDEN.

Brooke knocked, took his hat off and held it at his chest, slipping his glasses into a top pocket.

The woman who answered the door was in a pinafore, slightly flushed with some domestic

160

task. Brooke would have placed her age at between thirty and forty. Squinting into the darkness of the hallway he thought her eyes were green and striking, set wide in a plump face.

'Mrs Mary Flynn?'

'Yes. What's wrong?' At some level she knew already, because she took a quick step backwards and nearly fell, one hand leaving a white floury handprint on the wallpaper.

'Detective Inspector Brooke, Mrs Flynn. From Cambridge. I think Shepherd's Bush sent a constable round about Sean.'

She nodded, dropping her hands to her apron, working out the truth on a more conscious level. If Sean had been found alive they'd have relayed another message through the local constable. This strange, pale man, with amber-tinted glasses, stood before her like an undertaker at the graveside.

She rallied. 'I see. Of course. Come in.'

She told him to take a seat while she fetched her son Bobbie, as her husband was at work. Brooke said he could come back later, but she shook her head. Somewhere in the house he heard a muffled conversation, and then quite distinctly the sound of sobbing.

Brooke waited. The room was tiny but set out in a cameo of middle-class suburban life, with a mantelpiece, three armchairs, a tiled grate and a table inlaid with the image of an elephant carrying a potentate.

When Mrs Flynn returned her eyes were red, her cheeks wet. Bobbie was a teenager, in working boots and a collarless shirt, and he stood behind his mother as she took a seat. The boy stared belligerently at Brooke.

'I'm afraid it is bad news,' said Brooke.

Her head dipped. Bobbie made a move towards his mother but then took a step back.

'We retrieved the body of a boy from the river. The school caretaker has identified him as Sean. Obviously, we must arrange for a formal identification by a member of the family, but I don't think there's much doubt . . . ' Brooke had promised himself that he'd use the word itself — 'dead' — because in the long run it was therapeutic, but his courage had failed him at the last. So much for the hero of the desert.

Mrs Flynn seemed to be studying Brooke's lips.

Bobbie overcame his inertia and gripped his mother's shoulders. 'Sorry, Mum,' he said.

'Gerald, my husband, said we should fear the worst,' she said. 'So we are prepared.' Her eyes had begun to focus on the mid-distance and the blood had drained from her face, leaving thin lips slightly blue.

She patted her son's hand and he fled, presumably to the kitchen, as they listened to the sound of cups and a tap running.

'Bobbie's got shift work on the railway, stoking coal. He's on a double today, again. He's tired, worn out really. We all are. He'll be old enough by the spring, and then he'll be gone too.'

This gave Brooke a glimpse of the nightmare with which she lived.

'The Royal Engineers, like his big brother,' she added.

By the time Bobbie appeared with a tea tray she was crying again, but the breakdown of appearances seemed to help. Without prompting she told Brooke what Sean was like: a bit of a loner, the baby of the family. Bobbie sat with his tea on the floor, his back against the wall, his feet to the unlit fire, nodding agreement. As his mother spoke her accent was more fully revealed, an Irish brogue emerging from behind a brittle English, middle-class screen.

'Can you think of any reason why someone would want to do this to Sean?' asked Brooke. 'We think — in fact, we're convinced — that someone killed your son. It wasn't a random act of violence, it was planned and executed. Do you see?'

There must have been a railway nearby because in the sudden silence they heard the clash of couplings.

'It's not a pervert, is it?' asked Bobbie, his fists balled.

'No. Not that. We have to believe that whoever did this knew his victim — or at least knew of him. Does the family have any enemies, anyone who'd wish to do you harm?'

'We'll talk to Dad,' said Bobbie. 'But we're just a family.' He shrugged. 'We're not important.'

Brooke felt this was a curious statement. Bobbie's place in this family, his emotional position, seemed out of kilter. While his mother grieved, he seemed shocked — even disturbed — but also somehow disengaged, intermittently angry or disinterested.

'He could have gone last year with the rest,'

163

said his mother, already blaming herself. 'I just couldn't bear it. The parting. So we hung on. Most of his class went to Essex in August. The whole school. A few stayed, but it was no fun for Sean. And if it did start, the bombing, it might be too late. Gerald said we should use our heads, not our hearts. St Alban's was the last chance, so we took it.'

She pressed her hand quickly against her lips as if she'd said something terrible. Brooke could tell that the reality of her son's death was coming into focus. What could she see? A grave, perhaps. A coffin.

'You were born in Ireland, Mrs Flynn?' Brooke asked. It was a curious fact that while the house was laden with pictures and ornaments, not a single item echoed a Gaelic influence of any kind.

Her chin came up. 'Yes. Cork.'

'And your husband?'

'Dublin. But he came here as a child. Grandma lives in Kilburn. Grandpa's dead. We're Londoners now.'

'And your family?'

'I've not been back, not for a few years.' She glanced at some Christmas cards still on the mantelpiece. 'I've registered at the police station, so's Gerald. We've done nothing wrong.'

Brooke nodded, running a finger round the rim of his hat, studying the boy, who seemed reluctant to meet his eyes.

'Sean's death — certainly his abduction — coincided to some degree with a bomb attack in the city by the IRA organisation. One of many

164

around the country, of course. Nevertheless, a pointed coincidence.'

Bobbie actually laughed. 'You'll find no sympathy for that cause here, Inspector. This is our country now. Dad's for making our lives here. We work, we don't dream. That's what he says.'

'No friends, workmates, neighbours, with such sympathies? Violence is a last resort, but surely others support the wider aim — a united Ireland.'

'Dad says we have no time for politics.' Bobbie levelled a finger at Brooke. 'The copper who called said Sean just slipped away, that he'd slept in a church but wasn't there in the morning? How does that happen? Whose fault is that?'

His mother looked shocked. 'Bobbie. Don't.'

'It's alright,' said Brooke. He outlined the facts as they had them. Sean's abduction was as yet unexplained. He might have been taken from the church, or slipped away himself and then been abducted later, from the street.

Brooke considered withholding the details of the child's final minutes, but decided they deserved an account, in part — *his* account.

'A college porter saw him in the river. He cried out for help.'

Mrs Flynn rocked back slightly in her chair.

'I'm sorry. The water was icy cold, so he wouldn't have suffered. I got a boat and caught sight of him downriver, but I'm sure it was too late. It was over very quickly.'

Brooke wondered if any lie he'd ever told had brought such comfort.

'We will find who did this, Mrs Flynn. I can promise you that,' he said, standing, pushing his hat into shape. It was a rash promise, and it made him think of Rose's warning: *Don't take it personal.*

Bobbie stood too, studying his mother. 'I can miss a shift, stick around?' he offered.

She shook her head. 'No. Go to work. Can you phone your father from the yard?'

Bobbie nodded.

'I'll go to church now,' she said.

They all left together, walking along the crowded streets to the Church of the Holy Blood on the corner. Bobbie embraced his mother, then disappeared down a flight of concrete steps into the Underground. His mother repeated arrangements for her visit to Cambridge: she'd get the train arriving at just after ten. Brooke said a car would take her to the Spinning House. A formal identification would take place in the Galen Building.

'You'll not be alone?' asked Brooke. 'Mr Flynn, perhaps?'

She didn't answer.

Brooke nodded anyway, adding that she could also visit the school and the church if she wished. He reminded her, finally, that any funeral arrangements would have to await the coroner's decision to close the inquiry, and that that might take some time.

They shook hands, and Brooke said again that he was sorry to have brought such sad news. He watched her climb the steps into the church, past a life-size wooden Christ, bleeding on a crucifix.

Turning away, lighting up a cigarette, he was struck by the degree to which the loss of the boy seemed to be the mother's alone. The absent father, the slightly calculating Bobbie, seemed peripheral to her grief. The age gap between Sean and his older brothers also begged questions. On Saturday he'd undertake more searching enquiries, but for now his duty was done.

29

The sun was setting over Cambridge by the time Brooke unpacked himself from a crowded compartment and set out down Station Road towards 'The Homecoming'; but this evening the striding victorious soldier-scholar seemed to mock Brooke's inability to unravel the death of a five-year-old child. That was one of the certainties of war on the battlefield: you knew your enemy, and you knew when he was beaten. The art of detection was a subtler affair. The family of the dead child might be dysfunctional and oddly distant, but he'd discerned no motive for murder. Which left the IRA bombers. Tonight, time would run out for Patrick O'Leary. The Irishman's Honey Hill rooms would be raided by the Borough. The questions he would face ranged from his role in the S-Plan to the death of an innocent child.

Brooke contemplated the snow which had collected on 'The Homecoming', particularly in the German upturned helmet, which was amongst the victor's spoils. It reminded him that it was at this spot that the children had encountered the mysterious, patriotic Irishman, handing out welcoming flags and reading labels. It had been young John McQuillan, Sean's new-found friend, who'd recalled the encounter. McQuillan seemed a nervous child, alternatively garrulous and tongue-tied. Had he told the whole truth?

Brooke checked his notebook: he'd asked the

efficient Mrs Aitken to phone the Spinning House with the address of the family looking after the boy. The house was in New Town, a cluster of working-class streets which lay beyond the soaring spire of the Church of Our Lady and the English Martyrs; lowly St Alban's mother house. Saxon Street was so close to the church the shadow of the spire cut across it like a knife. Brooke encountered a throng of children and teenagers playing with home-made sledges in the road. The din in the narrow, damp street was hellish. The door of No. 57, ajar, opened into a carpet-less corridor. Three children, two boys holding fast to a toddler, pushed past him on the doorstep, screaming that they were off to join in the fun.

In the back kitchen a woman sat at a table watching a man eat a plate of mince and mashed potatoes.

Mrs Harper shook Brooke's hand and said her husband, Sidney, had just got home from a long shift at the sugar beet factory and so she'd let the children out for fresh air.

'Does 'em good,' she offered, putting on a kettle. Mr Harper worked his way steadily through the mince, helping himself to a bottle of beer which he decanted by the inch into a tin mug.

'How's John?' asked Brooke.

Mrs Harper set him a chair close to the coal fire.

'He's upstairs with my youngest,' she said, with obvious pleasure. 'That kid deserves a good home.'

Mr Harper grunted, pouring more beer. He caught Brooke's eye. 'A drink?' he said.

They got him a glass and a bottle, and he sat, enjoying the heat and listening to the distant hubbub of the children in the street. The light was almost gone, so the relative brightness of the fire grew by the second.

'Hasn't he got a good home back in London?' he asked.

'He's not happy. I think he misses his mate — the boy that's been taken. Cruel that. They met on the train and just clicked. It happens when you're that age. Ron, my youngest, tries his best, but you can see Johnny's lonely.' She thought about that. 'Well. More lost, really.'

She took a breath, as if deciding. 'Back home there's just his mum, by the sound of it. There's something wrong, but we can't get to the heart of it. He keeps asking how long he can stay with us. I've got five nippers. It's like a travelling circus in 'ere. It breaks my heart that he doesn't want to go home.'

Mr Harper nodded.

'I want to know if young Sean said anything to him he hasn't told us yet,' said Brooke. 'We found the body, you see. So it's murder now.'

'Go on up,' said Mr Harper. 'I'm gonna throw a snowball,' he said, lumbering towards the front door.

Mrs Harper shook her head happily. 'Grow up, do, Sidney Harper.'

Then they heard steps on the stairs and two boys fell into the room. The bigger, presumably young Ron, fled after his father. Mrs Harper said

John was to sit, and she gave him a mug of tea, announcing that she'd take her chance and make the beds upstairs, leaving them alone.

'It's pretty cosy up there,' she confided. 'Least they keep each other warm.'

Brooke could see the boy was still terrified. He was sure now that the haunted look betrayed more than an unhappy home life.

'I've just been to London to see Sean's mum,' he said. 'She can't think who would have wanted to hurt him. Did he say anything to you, John? I know I asked. But it's difficult standing up in front of everyone. Mrs Harper says you're unhappy. She thinks you're unhappy about home, but is it really about Sean? Is there something you wanted to say? You can tell me.'

'What's going to happen?' he said.

'Nothing's going to happen to you. Should it?'

He studied his cup of tea. 'We played games on the train. He liked games. I love 'em. We had a ball, so we dribbled up and down the corridor. We got the girls to scream. We broke a window in a door. That's what I didn't say. The guard, when he came round, said we'd cop it, lock us up, throw the key away. When he went, Sean started a fire.'

'A *fire*?' said Brooke.

'Yeah. There was rubbish in a bin and he had a box of matches.'

'Where'd he get those?'

'Kitchen drawer at home.'

'But you didn't burn the train down, did you?'

'It went out.'

'Shame.'

'He stole stuff too.'

There was, for the first time, a sly note in the story.

'Chocolate at the station from a counter. I had to point at something on a shelf — the sherbets — and he took two bars: Fry's. We had 'em on the walk down.'

'Bit of a crime spree. Was it all his idea?'

'Yeah. He said he did it lots. Maybe he took something and that's why the bloke came and took him away? Maybe it was small. D'you look in his case?'

'Just clothes, John. Bits and pieces. A box of Owzthat.'

'We played Owzthat on the train,' said John. 'I was England, Sean the Aussies.'

'The man with the flags, did he speak to you, or Sean?'

The boy looked up for the first time. 'He said we were to wave the flags. He looked at our labels. He said he had family in London, too. A place called County Kilburn, or sumfink.'

Brooke smiled. 'That's right. So many Irish they think it's an Irish county. It's a grown-up's joke.'

The boy looked more relaxed now that he'd confessed to vandalism and petty theft. Had this been the root of his obvious anxiety? Perhaps going home represented the threat of retribution for past crimes. Brooke doubted Sean was really the chief instigator of their spree.

Brooke put his tea mug on the hearth. 'Sean didn't mention the IRA, did he? You know who they are?'

'Sure. I'm not stupid. We talked about football. Talkin' about the IRA isn't polite. My mum says that if you hear anything you best forget it.'

They sat in silence for a moment, then Brooke stood. 'I'm sorry you've lost your friend, John.'

'I don't want to go home,' he said. 'I want to stay 'ere. It's fun.'

'I'd take one day at a time,' said Brooke. 'I'm sure your mum loves you a lot. But she'll want to keep you safe. That's why you're here. If the Germans send planes over London she'll not want you back too quick. Who knows . . . it might be a long war.'

30

The slush had frozen on Honey Hill, creating a series of miniature crevasses and arêtes, so that the short, cobbled street seemed to ooze out into Pound Hill like a miniature glacier tumbling from a microscopic alp. At some point during the day the temperature must have risen above freezing, because a series of small streams had sprung from the crushed snow, but they were solid now, arrested in the act of flowing down the hill to join the river below. Brooke noted this was full again, but strangely sluggish, the gleam of the surface clouded with layers of thin ice. By dawn a perfect frozen surface would run through the city like a silver thread, a paradise for skaters.

The Stuke was quiet, the bar below long shut, the steward in bed, although Brooke doubted he was sleeping, given that his snooker room was currently occupied by half a dozen uniformed police officers and a bloodhound. The radio car had crept up Pound Hill and was now parked in the rear yard. Patrick O'Leary was not a suspect Brooke intended to let slip. The time had come to pop him in the bag. Another detective sergeant, a late addition from the County force, was also present, and armed. His orders were clear: to stay in the rear of the advance party, led by Brooke, but to be available if O'Leary appeared and was armed himself or threatened to use a gun. Constables were to draw their nightsticks.

174

Bells marked midnight as Brooke left the Stuke by its front door. Edison followed in his footsteps, leading the uniformed constables. The presence of armed officers had set Brooke's nerves on edge. He approached the front door of 49 Honey Hill with caution but reminded himself that his suspect was almost certainly sound asleep on the third floor, room five. Many of the residents of Honey Hill had come and gone in the last twenty-four hours, but most certainly not O'Leary — a giant of a man, according to the local constable, at six feet, with a donkey jacket stretched across sideboard shoulders. And the head: everyone mentioned the head, a cannonball, with eyes sunk in pudgy flesh.

Brooke called for light, and the torches swung wildly as nightsticks were transferred from hand to hand. Edison signalled for a constable to step forward with an iron ram and without a word he took the lock out with the first blow, the door with the second, kicking splinters from the threshold. A dog started barking and birds' wings rose from the roofs above, precipitating an avalanche of snow.

Led by Brooke they stormed the stairs; by the second landing, lights had begun to appear below doors, and one was open by an inch, revealing a woman's frightened face. Bare boards led them up the last flight to O'Leary's door, which they took out with the ram, standing back to let Brooke enter first, the armed officer on his shoulder. A blackout board was against the wall, so starlight lit the mean space before someone

175

found the light switch.

'This is the police, Mr O'Leary. We have a warrant and we are armed.'

The sentence was out before Brooke had fully comprehended the scene.

It was impossible to look at anything but O'Leary's body, one leg still up on the bed, his torso on the bare boards, his head thrown back — or rather, the mass of bone and flesh, blood and brains, which had been his head. The first image which came to Brooke, and which would be indelible, was of some animal dead on the road: a fox perhaps, or a badger, reduced to offal. The dead man wore long johns, heavily stained with sprayed blood.

'Christ,' said one of the constables and staggered back out into the corridor to vomit.

Brooke threw the sash window open and looked down, then up.

'Nothing,' he said.

The room had an empty grate and was icy cold, so there was very little smell from the corpse, just the red-meat tang of a butcher's shop. Otherwise the room was unremarkable: a wardrobe, a bed, a table, a sink and a draining board, all quite neat and clean. The walls, once papered, were now a collection of various remnants, and held a single framed picture of a young boy with boxing gloves, both hands held to his chin in a defensive pose. On the bedside table was a battered slim volume of poetry, the back broken so that it lay open.

Brooke felt the dead man's hand. The flesh was still warm.

'Sir.' A constable stood by the bed, his boots carefully placed just beyond the pool of blood which encircled the crushed head. He was pointing up at an open attic hatch above the bed.

They stood for a moment listening, but the noise from below, as the residents gathered on the landings, was raucous. A drunken, slurred voice demanded to see a warrant card, while a dog barked erratically.

They moved the bed, carefully lowering the dead man's leg to the floor, discovering a small suitcase, which held old newspapers, largely the sporting pages, and a complete change of clothing, including a pair of new black brogues. A chair placed on the table allowed Brooke to get head and shoulders into the attic space. A torch revealed a room which stretched the entire length of the short street — about sixty yards from end wall to end wall, running over all the upper floors. With a boot on a constable's shoulder Brooke hauled himself up the last few feet so that he could stand astride the trapdoor, his torch beam almost too weak to penetrate the distant shadows. Various bays beneath the roof beams had been used for storage: rolled carpets, a stack of tiles, cardboard boxes of books, a pyramid of drainpipes laid against the end wall.

In the torchlight something glittered on the floorboards. Kneeling, Brooke examined, but didn't touch, a lump of yellow waxy material, a slightly luminous teardrop, the colour of onyx perhaps, or clarified butter, about two inches long. He unfolded a handkerchief and picked it up, slipping it into his pocket.

Below he could hear the rooming house still in uproar, tenants being dragged out of bed to give statements, a woman screaming in a perfunctory way, as if to ward off a persistent wasp. Boots tramped up and down stairs.

On his knees at the trapdoor he saw Edison below.

'I want silence,' he ordered.

His sergeant disappeared and issued calm but terse orders.

Gradually the official silence spread down through the house, leaving the dog barking, until it too was quiet. In the street a car engine spluttered and died. The house took over the principal soundtrack, the timbers ticking and cracking.

Brooke heard a footstep above his head, almost exactly at the apex of the roof. The second footstep was as distinct, a further stride towards the end wall. Then he ran for it, the footsteps multiplying, swift but sure along the roofline. Brooke tracked him until at the far end he found a single skylight, which was open so that he could stand within it, his head outside. A metal ladder ran from the side of the sill up the incline of the roof, which he scaled on hands and knees.

He reached the apex, where a flat walkway ran the length of the building. Nothing moved. Casting a glance below he saw a yard, the remains of a metal fire escape petering out about ten feet below, to be replaced with a dangling rope. He had no fear of heights, but the scene below seemed to drop away, then come back into focus.

The view across the chimney tops was vividly Dickensian; dark roofs, in confusion, linked by stairways and ladders amid a forest of stacks and pots, out of which smoke drifted. Brooke stood, eyes wide for movement, but the scene remained static save for a cat sauntering across a wooden walkway high above the yard. A constable appeared below, his torch swinging from side to side like a lighthouse beam.

He saw the fleeing figure once, a fleeting second — maybe two — caught in silhouette fifty yards away, moving between two chimney stacks and then dropping from sight. A man, almost certainly, a jacket perhaps, certainly no great winter coat. Brooke was struck by a sense of a body in fluid, rapid movement, an indication of the brutal power, perhaps, which had crushed Patrick O'Leary's prodigious skull.

31

Two murders within three days, and a bomb attack, demanded a rapid public response from the Borough. Despite the distractions of war, the city expected its streets to be safe, even after dark, unless the sirens wailed. O'Leary's brutal killing rang alarm bells. Would the violence spiral out of control? Was the second bomb attack now inevitable? A constable had been despatched to the Spinning House to alert Chief Inspector Carnegie-Brown of developments. She, in her turn, would no doubt call the chief constable. The downward weight of bureaucratic pressure for action would be intolerable by dawn. Not for the first time, Brooke's insomnia was a positive boon.

With Father Ward's permission, he commandeered St Alban's Church in order to set up an incident room close to the scene of the crime, with the added bonus of a fixed telephone, an office and heating, thanks to the caretaker, who had been woken and dragged out of bed to stoke up the boiler. Within minutes hot air was rising from the Victorian gratings, enveloping the nave in a warm fug laced with the lingering aroma of incense.

Constables came and went, reporting to Edison and taking tea from Mrs Aitken. She duly delivered a mug for Brooke to the office, taking the seat on the opposite side of the priest's desk.

He sensed that the lowly designation of 'house-keeper' failed to catch Aitken's status at St Alban's. At times she appeared to outrank Father Ward.

'They say a man's dead, up on Honey Hill. An Irishman? Is this right, Inspector?' she asked, meeting him eye to eye.

She'd brought her own cup with her, which she held, finely balanced on its saucer, in one hand. There was something about the accent, to Brooke's untrained ear, which set it apart; it lacked the musical note and had a sharp urban edge.

'Yes. He went by the name O'Leary, a Patrick, but it'll be an alias. A big man, a navvy, but even by their standards a workhorse.'

'Sounds like a Music Hall Paddy then. Thick in the arm, thick in the head. Is there nothing to set him apart from the crowd? It's a small community. We might know him here, you know.'

She took a hairpin from a pocket and expertly corralled some strands of hair that had fallen from the red crown.

'He liked poetry. There was book beside his bed, in Gaelic I think, but I'm no expert.'

She looked through Brooke for a second, her left hand shuffling the coloured copper bands that crowded her right arm between the wrist and the elbow.

'You'd be surprised how many can still use the old tongue, Inspector. Even here, in the Upper Town.'

Brooke thought of the carefully executed slogan on the base of Newton's mast. What had Dr Phipps said? *An educated hand.*

181

'But can they write it?' asked Brooke.

There was a clatter of cups from the main body of the church and Aitken jumped to her feet. 'That's a very rare skill,' she conceded. 'I'd better go. Father Ward's a menace with the urn.'

Alone, Brooke could feel the presence of the church and the school, pressing down, pressing in. The priest and the housekeeper, the head teacher and his wife, emitted a distinct tension, a brittle wariness. He'd felt it that first morning when he'd answered Ward's call and had set it aside as the understandable reaction to the loss of the child in their care. But there was something else, something watchful. The priest's file, delivered from the diocesan office in Norwich, had been blameless. Brooke had checked with the Spinning House on the Walshes and Aitken — all Irish citizens, and all duly registered with the authorities and issued with appropriate ID cards. What was he missing?

The phone rang. The duty sergeant reported that the house on Honey Hill had been searched from the basement upwards, revealing no more clues to the shadowy identity of the butchered Patrick O'Leary. The pathologist, Dr Comfort, was at the scene. Snow had begun to fall steadily after Brooke's brief glimpse of the fleeing killer — for that had to be their working hypothesis, given Comfort's tentative statement that the time of death was less than an hour before the discovery of the body. Brooke had thrown a cordon around the Upper Town, aided in part by the telltale carpet of snow. The radio cars, placed at strategic points, had reported nothing

— literally nothing, not a single moving human being, let alone a vehicle, but they would keep watch until dawn.

The contents of O'Leary's suitcase were being re-examined by Edison at a trestle table set up in the nave. The dead man's pockets had given up little more: a wallet with a single five-pound note, about ten shillings in loose change, a handkerchief and a very small piece of the mysterious waxy material Brooke had discovered in the attic. The wardrobe door in the room had been blocked by O'Leary's shattered head. Its contents would only be retrieved when the body was moved, a grisly task left to the pathologist and his men, at hand to haul the Irishman away to the morgue. O'Leary's fellow tenants were all being interviewed, but the initial consensus was that he spoke to no one and that nothing had been heard from the attic during the preceding week. What little detail could be gleaned characterised O'Leary as a cliché: the hard-drinking, hard-working navvy, although one woman did say he'd once mentioned a family back in Ireland to whom he sent money.

Brooke, rising stiffly from the desk, went out into the church and found the priest, alone, sitting quietly in a pew.

'Thank you for letting us use the church,' said Brooke. 'I take it no one knows this man by name — Patrick O'Leary?'

Ward shook his head. 'I said a prayer for him, but I'm struggling to find it in my heart to mean a word of it. A bomber, you say, and there's no doubt?'

'Not much. I think one of his comrades feared he was about to fall into our hands. So he silenced him. And I think he took something with him.'

Brooke produced the yellow teardrop of wax.

The priest took it, testing the scent, but shook his head. 'A chemical, for the explosives?'

'Possibly.'

'A wicked man, amongst wicked men. They want to unite Ireland, Inspector, when half its people are paupers.'

Brooke wondered then about Ward's background. He'd mentioned Ampleforth — the stately Catholic public school on the high moors of Yorkshire, and Oxford. The accent certainly dripped class and money, but perhaps he'd seen enough of the world to inspire genuine sympathy for the plight of Ireland.

'I think I'd start with the poor, wouldn't you?' he asked. 'Solve their problems. Then move on to grand designs. It's the worst folly. Although I understand the need they have, even the poor love their country. It's all they've got. You can't take that away.' The priest licked his lips as if he'd said too much. 'Did this man kill Sean?' he asked.

'It's a working hypothesis. No more. We have no evidence the murder and the bomb are connected. However, the *circumstantial* evidence is strong. And the description fits that of the man who handed out flags to the children, who read their labels — *and* the eyewitness account from Newton's factory.'

Aitken joined them and took an empty cup

184

from beside the priest.

'Sean's mother, you've told her the boy's dead?' she asked. 'Joe said you'd asked him to view the body, to identify the child, and that there was no doubt. He cried to tell me.' She shook her head. 'He won't forget that sight, I'm sure.'

'There's no picture of this man from Honey Hill?' asked Ward.

Brooke told Edison to retrieve the framed picture they'd taken from O'Leary's room from the evidence bag. The priest and the house-keeper, touching side by side, studied the young face between the boxing gloves, but shook their heads.

Brooke produced a cigarette, but remembered where he was, slipping it behind his ear. 'Mrs Flynn is coming up at the weekend for the formal identification,' he said. 'She may want to see the church, to meet you all. It's going to be a difficult visit I'm afraid.'

'Poor woman,' said Aitken clutching her elbows. She looked to the priest for comfort and he lay his arm, stiffly, across her shoulders.

Brooke eased his neck back until the bones cracked, studying the plain wooden roof. 'Of a Sunday, Father, what size is the congregation?'

Ward looked at his hands as if he needed the digits to compute the number. 'At Easter, Christmas, St Alban's day itself — three hundred, maybe more. Of a Sunday, perhaps half that. There are familiar faces of course, but transients too, following work, following family.'

'And soldiers,' offered Aitken. 'We see them

once, twice, and then they're gone.'

Brooke nodded. 'This Sunday, the Epiphany, I'd like to take names, see if we can find a link with O'Leary, with his confederates. We'll need to check registrations too — for those who are Irish citizens. We need to find out if this man was known to anyone in the community. Maybe he made friends, or saw people outside the church: the pub, the shop. Please — both of you — keep this to yourself until the day.'

Ward nodded. 'If you really want to catch everyone at one time, in one place, I'd try the school tomorrow evening. There's an Epiphany play. It's the highlight of the season, if I say so myself. It starts at six. There's more tea. Everyone comes. It will finish at seven promptly, so your men can come then.'

Brooke nodded, making a note.

Dr Comfort arrived with two constables weighed down with the contents of O'Leary's wardrobe, which they began to lay out on the tables.

Comfort didn't shed his coat. 'Brooke,' he said, with a curt nod of acknowledgement. 'Autopsy tomorrow I think. I'll advise of the time. For now, what can I say? You saw the man's head. It was beaten to a pulp. There are no other wounds, and no signs of any medical condition except the usual attrition associated with hard labour. The skin — and the surface arteries — and the eyes, suggest heavy drinking.'

Brooke nodded. 'A cigarette outside?'

They stood together in the porch, watching the snow fall, smoking in silent communion for a

186

minute. The pathologist's car, a polished grey Rover, stood in the playground.

'Deliberate, certainly,' said Comfort eventually, as if answering an interior question. 'The face, that is. It's been obliterated, there's no other word for it, Brooke.'

'Yes — a clear intent to obscure identity,' he agreed. 'We have a name, but it won't be his. My guess would be that the killer knew we had his picture somewhere, on file at the Yard, perhaps? On a wanted poster? The rogue's gallery of IRA men is impressive. He'll be on it. This way we're in the dark — at least for a few hours. The confusion buys them time. Let's hope they don't use it to plant another bomb.'

Comfort briskly rearranged a heavy scarf at his neck. 'Frankly, the injuries tell us more about the killer, don't you think? To do that, Brooke — to disassemble a man's head with a weapon — requires strength, and a disregard for humanity on a wider scale. And this is the man, perhaps, who despatches a child in a sack in the river. What a monster, Brooke.'

Back inside they examined the items taken from O'Leary's digs: two more threadbare suits, linen shirts, socks, pants, two pairs of boots and a fine woollen overcoat, almost new. Inside the breast pocket lay a Catholic missal, a book for following the responses and prayers and readings of the Mass.

There was no sign of a wallet. But the missal contained a single bookmark, and as was the custom, it carried the image of a saint: in this case St Alban. The image was brightly coloured, with gilded letters, and showed the wealthy Alban sheltering a priest in his house from pagan Roman soldiers. The back carried the name Father John Ward, and the address of the presbytery and telephone number.

The message read:

Go forth in the name of the Lord

An inscription had been added in a confident hand:

Colm — God will remember your good deeds

It was signed by the priest.

Ward had to retrieve reading glasses from the office to study the inscription.

'Good heavens,' he said. 'It's Colm, Colm Hendrie. This terrible man O'Leary was really gentle Colm?' He looked around the church, saw Aitken and beckoned her over. 'Marie. Look at this.'

Again, shoulder to shoulder, they studied the words and letters as if memorising the Rosetta Stone.

'I can't believe it, Father. The man was a saint, and so meek. Hardly a word, unless you spoke to him.'

Between them they composed a succinct biography. Hendrie had been a parishioner for a year, had attended the eleven o'clock Mass each Sunday and special feast days. His obvious strength and practical skills had been utilised during the several months when there had been

188

no caretaker, until the arrival of young Joe Smith. He'd fixed the boiler, rewired the school office and fixed leaking drainpipes.

Ward held the picture of the youngster in boxing gloves: 'You can see the likeness now, of course. But this must have been taken forty years ago.'

'The children loved him,' said Aitken. 'He painted the hopscotch out for them and put up the netball post.'

'Family?' asked Brooke.

'I think he said he was a widower, but he sent money home, I know, for his children.'

Ward seemed close to tears. 'Colm — a wonderful name. I asked him what it meant. It's for the dove. A sign of peace. And now look at his sins.' He shook his head. 'Where will it end?'

Brooke was holding the missal when the photograph fell out.

A passport-sized shot of a woman: faded, foxed, with an odd rosy tint added to the cheeks. She'd been set on a high-backed wooden chair against a Gothic background of a ruined abbey. Brooke held the picture out to the priest and the housekeeper, but they shook their heads. Brooke was not surprised, because he knew who she was, and he doubted she'd ever been as far as Cambridge. On Saturday that would be rectified, for it was Mary Flynn, the mother of the murdered child.

32

Brooke stopped on Silver Street Bridge and looked down at the river, the ice now a single sheet of dull steel, the ducks in a row, in midstream, equidistant from the hazards of either bank: foxes, otters and rats. Beyond the open meadows which led to the Upper Town rose the central tower of the university library, a silhouette against the stars, a brutal landmark just a few years old, which always reminded Brooke of the podium at the Maifeld, where Hitler ranted to an audience of a million Berliners, faces upturned in the firelight of torches. The sudden weight of this image, and the thought of Luke camped out on the border, combined with the memory of Hendrie's shattered head, inspired a stab of despair.

He lit a Black Russian, studying the geometrical miracle, just downstream, that was the Mathematical Bridge. The hunt for Colm Hendrie's killer would be in full swing at the Spinning House, but he felt he'd earned himself a few moments of silent contemplation. He was sure now that he was engaged in attempting to solve one crime with two victims — so far. Hendrie had died with a picture of Mary Flynn in his treasured missal. It was the first link beyond circumstance and chance, although it asked more questions than it answered. If the boy was the target, why have a picture of his mother, not the five-year-old himself? The man giving out flags by 'The Homecoming' — surely the giant Hendrie — had been handicapped by *not* knowing which one of the children was the young Sean Flynn.

The heart of the mystery was the Flynn family itself, and Brooke was determined to unravel it. He'd return to London with Edison at the first opportunity and observe the house, then get both parents in for questioning, separately, and the belligerent brother. The genteel middle-class aspirations of that cold front room hid a darker tale. Today, they'd focus on Hendrie's brutal murder. Tomorrow they'd return to Shepherd's Bush.

Brooke, smoking, watched as dawn began to insinuate itself into the eastern sky, revealing a hoar frost which had turned the riverbank trees white, the water meadows crisp. When the sun rose it would catch the balls of mistletoe in the bare trees, chandeliers of ice, and the river would smoke, clouds of condensation rising in the sunbeams. Revitalised by this prospect of the hour to come, Brooke walked on briskly towards the Spinning House, at the last minute cutting into Market Hill, enticed by the prospect of crisply fried bacon.

'Well well, you've just missed your friends,' said Rose, automatically griddling some bacon. 'Young Jo was here, with a mysterious young man. She hid him over there in the shadows,' she added, nodding towards the distant row of market stalls. 'What's the big secret?'

Brooke shrugged, resetting his hat. For the

first time he wondered if Jo's penchant for living dangerously had returned. Was the new man married? Why hide his face from the benign Rose?

A bus rolled into the square and disgorged a crowd of grey shopworkers: Brooke couldn't decide if it was just the war, or winter, but suddenly colour seemed to be draining out of the world. Rose delivered his sandwich, the bacon protruding between two healthy slices of buttered bread.

She came round with a cup of tea of her own and joined him by the brazier. 'My last break before the rush,' she said.

When she'd finished her brew, she swilled the tea out of her cup and began to examine the leaves. It was a familiar performance, and Brooke put a brave face on being impressed, although he privately despised fortune telling. But Rose was a believer in her own gifts as well as local superstitions.

'Well?' asked Brooke despite himself, setting his empty mug on the counter. 'I must go, Rose. If you've occult news to impart, make it quick.'

It was pretty much the usual mumbo-jumbo. She saw whispering lips and a house of lies, a year of arrivals. There was a great circle, made of iron, issuing its last breath.

And finally, a letter arriving, or possibly a telegram.

She looked at Brooke, who'd taken off his glasses to massage the bridge of his nose. 'But not to worry, Brooke. It's good news. When it comes, expect to be blessed.'

33

Brooke's orders had ensured that by the time he reached the Spinning House 'the balloon had gone up', to quote the desk sergeant: the force's six radio cars were parked in the rear yard, the garage crowded with special constables drafted in to search the Upper Town, while Sergeant Edison was briefing all ranks in the mess room. The Honey Hill murder was every officer's number one priority. Door-to-door enquiries were planned for the rookery and the neighbouring streets. The dead man's workmates were to be individually interviewed at their current site — roadworks on the old A10, just north of the city boundary.

Finally, there was a note requiring Brooke's immediate presence in the top office. He found Chief Inspector Carnegie-Brown on the phone to Scotland Yard. When she'd finished she showed Brooke a cable from the Home Office demanding details of the Fenian murder. She asked Brooke to sit while she outlined the Borough's priorities: to prevent a second bomb attack, to apprehend the members of the IRA cell, to bring to justice the killers of Sean Flynn. If he needed assistance, the County force had been ordered directly by the Home Secretary to make manpower available. If he needed bureaucratic support, she made it clear he was to use her personal secretary.

'By the by,' she added. 'Any news on PC Collins?'

'Nothing. The house is certainly empty, and the family's relatives can't help. We're looking, but he may have gone AWOL. If he encountered the killer then we'd have to fear the worst, but we've no evidence for that presumption. And no body. So I think we must assume he has gone to ground.'

She dismissed him with a nod. Brooke promised swift results and melted away. The building echoed with frenzied activity. Edison, reporting to Brooke's office, made it clear all the necessary orders had been given and that operations were underway. Madingley Hall was sending down a liaison officer to discuss what was termed 'the wider situation' — presumably a reference to the possible existence of a second bomb. For half an hour they discussed the plan to interview and check the registrations of St Alban's regular parishioners at the Epiphany play. A squad of uniformed officers was to be on hand at the Great Bridge at six that evening.

'And there's this.' Edison handed over a note. 'The factory manager at Newton called in, wants to see you. A summons apparently, top secret too. He had to be persuaded to tell the desk sergeant as little as that.'

Brooke, gleeful at the prospect of getting out of the office, took the note and fled, after alerting Edison to the prospect of a trip to London in the Wasp the next morning.

'We're going to spy on the Flynn family,' explained Brooke. His detective sergeant beamed.

194

The towpath led Brooke through the city along the river. On the long stretch below the Great Bridge skaters were racing on a course marked out with barrels on the ice, the silver surface already scoured with a thousand lines, crossing and recrossing. It reminded Brooke that he'd promised Joy they'd skate by the house, re-enacting a childhood adventure.

Opposite Jesus Green a fire had been lit on the ice itself, in an iron cradle, and a man sold hot chestnuts.

Brooke crossed Newton's Bridge, trudging across the still snowy playing field where Ralph Milton-Forbes had illustrated the principles of RADAR as his pedigree hound inscribed frantic circles in pursuit of a ball. Its name? Brooke thought it had an Arthurian ring. Galahad perhaps.

Rafe Forbes was in his corner office, the dog stretched out on a mat. The plate glass metal-framed windows revealed a great curve of the frozen river embedded with houseboats and nar-rowboats.

'Inspector. Many thanks. Sorry about the call, but we've made an unwelcome discovery.'

Forbes was in the tweed suit, but Brooke noted the badge — the letter G on the lunar background — was missing. The silver hair had been slicked back with extra severity, exposing the angular famished face, which looked like it had been formed at speed. Despite the pedigree hound Forbes had something of the mongrel whippet about him.

'Let me show you,' he said.

They walked through two of the large

production line halls, the slight murmur of conversation fading away as Forbes strode down the central aisle. At the north end of the block was a set of wide doors marked GOODS IN — GOODS OUT.

A lorry was unloading packing cases.

Forbes, producing a penknife, ripped one open to reveal a stack of metal boxes, not in solid steel or aluminium, but perforated, like a child's Meccano set.

'We have these made at a factory in Birmingham. We install the electronics, the diodes, the valves, the circuits, the wiring. The box provides the framework. We track every one of these boxes from when they arrive. Each gets a number punched into the metal — here — see?' He walked to a bench where a series of the boxes was piled and showed Brooke the one he picked up: 6758b. 'The serial numbers are sequential and recorded at each stage of production through the factory. So, if we need to, we can trace any box and its journey through the factory. Foolproof really. Then — over here at 'goods out' — we hand over the finished box to the drivers from RAF Bawdsey. See?'

The finished electronics were encased within the Meccano shells, complete with serial numbers. A lorry, tailgate down, stood ready to take its shipment.

Forbes lit a cheroot. 'One's missing. It's only just come to light because it is only here, at 'goods out', that the boxes return to their serial order. It's the failsafe point, but it only comes at the end. Up to then each box takes its own

196

route, as I said, depending on whether they've been earmarked as receivers, transmitters, whatever. The technicalities are tedious. The fact is we've lost a transmitter, close to its final stage of production, and it is one of a new range with inbuilt anti-blocking. Top secret — a tired cliché I know, but there it is. Top secret, and bound for the frontline on the East Coast, and trials.'

'When was it taken?'

Forbes looked around. 'Wait here. I'll get the dog.'

He came back with the hound, the cigar still clamped between his lips, and they set out though the GOODS OUT doors and across the snowfield. Behind them steam rose from the factory's vents and piping.

'The unit was last recorded in situ the day before the bomb. First floor, the diode lab.'

'Is each lab locked?'

'Yes,' he said, shaking his bunch of keys. 'Same as the main doors. Three sets: Ridley, the managing director and mine. And there's no evidence of any locks being forced.'

He sucked the life out of his cheroot, ditching it in the snow.

'You think the bomb was a diversion?' asked Brooke.

'Possibly. But is a bunch of bog-trotting peasants up to this? The difference between the missing unit and a standard unit at this stage of production is not apparent. It would take me ten minutes to be sure. And the Air Ministry agrees. We have to 'entertain' — their word — entertain the notion that the IRA bombers have been

197

given help, possibly by German intelligence. Whitehall's ordered a stocktake, every nut, every bolt. That's two days of production gone. After that we'll have an RAF guard on the perimeter.'

He called the dog back from the distant veranda of the old sports pavilion, where it was tracking the ghosts of footballers past. It trotted up, a stick in its jaws.

'Sorry, old boy,' he said, patting the dog, looking up at Brooke. 'We live out on the downs near Newmarket. She gets plenty of room to run at home, as far as you can see. But we need to get back to the office now.' He slipped a lead through the collar. 'So that's the deal, Brooke,' he said, leading the way. 'Air Ministry will make the factory secure so this can't happen again. Your job, I'm told by the chief constable and the Home Office, is to find the transmitter before it is either spirited out of the country, or someone with the requisite knowledge picks it apart.'

34

Brooke was on the phone to Scotland Yard, attempting to set out his plans for securing the stolen RADAR unit — which were sketchy at best — when Edison appeared with a single sheet of paper which he placed on the blotter: YOUR WIFE — DUTY DESK. How long had he known his detective sergeant? Three months, possibly a week longer, but there was already a curious bond between them. Edison's personality spoke of experience, and a kind of common-sense grip on the ways of the world. The look in his eyes at this moment, an intensity of focus, told Brooke that he should cut short the call and descend the three flights of steps, two at a time. A second sense made him take his greatcoat, his cigarettes and his hat.

Claire stood back from the desk to make room for a woman who was trying to report the details of a burglary, her mouth obscured by a handkerchief. His wife held a letter, flat against her handbag. Brooke's eyes were damaged, in that he suffered from acute photophobia — a painful aversion to light — but his vision was excellent, 20:20 in fact, and so he saw immediately the capital typed letters of an official telegram. It was impossible not to think of Rose King and her ridiculous tea leaves, and the unreliable rider to her prediction: *It's good news.*

Brooke took Claire by the arm out into the street. There was very little need to speak because the situation, while long envisaged, was unique. Claire had never seen his office at the Spinning House, although he had called at the hospital many times. They had, until the recent alterations, used their secret place in the basement of the hospital. Since the outbreak of the war and the departure of the children, they'd gone there many times. He held a vision of her nurse's uniform draped over a boiler pipe. The Spinning House offered no such privacy or excitement. He couldn't recall a single occasion on which she'd been beyond the duty desk.

She would only visit the station in an emergency.

They walked out onto Parker's Piece. In daylight the great open park, on which the army was camped, had lost its magical night-time aura of chivalrous battle. After dusk, fires were allowed unless a siren wailed, so smoke drifted, and snatches of music were on the air. The scene now was bleaker. A listless line of soldiers waited in a queue for food from a mobile kitchen. A Bofors gun, set on a miniature hill of sandbags at one corner, was the focus of a training exercise, a platoon of attentive recruits watching a crew go through their split-second routine.

They found an empty bench under a tree festooned with balls of mistletoe.

'It's Ben,' she said, giving him the telegram.

The wave of relief left him giddy. He'd been keeping at bay the thought that it was Luke. An accident perhaps, his crushed body found under

200

a tank where he'd insisted on sleeping out of the snow and rain. Claire saw the confusion, and the sudden guilt, and understood the moment in its entirety.

'Sorry,' she said. 'Stupid of me.' She squeezed his hand.

He read the message:

ADMIRALTY BUILDING WHITEHALL
7 JANUARY 1940. 1400 HOURS
NORTH SEA/ARCTIC
CONVOY 18C

REGRET TO INFORM YOU LEADING SUB-MARINER BENJAMIN JONES MISSING AT SEA. HMS SILVERFISH UNACCOUNTED FOR 180 NAUTICAL MILES NNW NARVIK.

He read it three times as if some hidden meaning would rise up from the arid text.

'How's Joy?' he asked, finally.

'At the hospital on her shift. She thought it was best. I can't think of anything better. I'll join her later.'

He made himself hold on to the telegram.

'We'll have to wait,' he offered. 'Missing is missing, Claire. There's still hope.'

'This isn't part of the deal, Eden,' she said. There was something bitter in her voice which was so unexpected he felt his blood run cold. 'I have my two lives and they balance out. I look after people who are ill. I never stint. I use what talents I've got as best I can. It's not a crusade or anything, it's just the way I want to live my life.

201

When I come home there's a family. That's you, and Joy, and Luke — and it's Ben now too. And it's the child that's coming. They balance out, these lives. So this isn't allowed — is it?'

She smiled, but there was an uncharacteristic hint of cynicism. Unlike Brooke, Claire's faith in a God was unshakeable. It didn't express itself in the fabric of churches, or holy pictures, or ceremonies of any kind. But there was a God and he — or even she — was responsible for that balance between goodness and reward.

'I can try the Admiralty, through the Yard, if it helps?'

She nodded. 'Anything. If Ben's missing, then they're all missing. There must be a story, a narrative, a series of events. Anything would help. Anything would be better than this. It's so . . . insipid.'

She took the letter and put it in her bag.

For a few minutes they tried to concentrate on domestic issues: food and bills and shifts, and a planned outing to the theatre to see a comedy. Eventually the conversation died.

'Just tell me something about your day,' said Claire. 'Just something normal and common-place. Then I can pretend this hasn't happened.'

Out on Parker's Piece they were taking down some of the tents and a unit of soldiers was hauling railway sleepers into place along the outlines of what looked like a football field. Three men with wide brooms were shifting the snow from the grass and repainting the lines.

'Wembley for a day,' said Brooke, trying to put some light-heartedness into his voice. 'We're getting a royal visit from Prince Henry, the king's brother, Saturday. Apparently, he was a bit of a dud at school, but he's mad about football. They're laying on a match: Army v University. Security is down to us.

'It's Prince Henry's request that they play the game right there. On that spot. According to the record books, the first ever game of football using modern rules took place there in 1863. I've had all the details from Edison. Of course they'd been playing the game for centuries; hacking, fighting, brawling, but this was the first modern game of soccer.

'The sleepers are for the crowd to stand on. They're expecting a packed house. It's the last thing we need, but there it is. They're bussing in children too, so it'll be mayhem in its own way.' Brooke lit a cigarette.

'What about that poor child in the river?' said Claire.

He'd told her all about the violent death of Colm Hendrie, and his link to St Alban's and the dead boy's mother.

'I can't shake off the feeling that lies are being told,' he said. 'There's the Walshes — the head and his wife. He looks like a broken man, she looks like the Rose of Tralee. I can't be sure, but I think she's pregnant — the word 'bloom' falls well short of the reality. Then there's the priest: a good man, I think, but there's a secret there too. The priest and the housekeeper are a bit of cliché. They're close, of that there is no doubt, cooped up in the presbytery. A fine woman — that's her cliché. Then there's Smith the caretaker. Clean-cut, an athlete, a friend to the kids. Too good to be true?'

'I never had you down as a cynic, Eden.'

'I'm a sceptic.'

'Sounds like a nest of vipers to me,' said Claire.

They stood.

She ran a hand down one of his lapels. 'About the priest. There's an old saying, more popular with us girls I suspect. If you think two people are having an affair, they *are* having an affair. It's all in the body language. You've an eye for that, Eden. Trust yourself.'

Brooke kissed her. 'Tell Joy this: war is chaos. The *Silverfish* could be anywhere. Missing means just that, and no more. Tell her I'll try and find out some details. I'll see her at home. If she still wants to, we can skate on the ice.'

Claire retied a scarf at her throat. 'Did you like Ben?' she said, the voice again exhibiting that unfamiliar edge.

'He's not dead, Claire.'

She put a finger across his lips. 'I don't mean that. Did you like him when you met him?'

'I admired him. It's too early to say.'

They kissed again and parted.

35

Brooke took a back seat in the hall of St Alban's School, the place buzzing with excited voices, a crowd of possibly a hundred and fifty in place for an Epiphany play — *The Arrival of the Magi*. It was, he'd been assured by Father Ward, a mercifully short production, although he'd neglected to mention the sermon with which he greeted the audience of parishioners, evacuees, their temporary guardians and a handful of guests, including the local alderman, who'd felt motivated to leap to his feet to deliver a speech of his own in reply. The priest's address had actually been a model of its kind, its message that the Epiphany was a revelation, in this case of the newly born Christ to the wider world, represented by the gift-laden figures of Balthasar, Melchior and Caspar.

The hall had been created by rolling back wooden partitions between three classrooms. Windows ran down one side, neatly blanked out with blackout boards. The children's stage was hardboard, perched on milk bottle crates. On the floor sat the children, those in loco parentis on ranks of chairs, directly behind. Brooke nodded to Mr and Mrs Harper, dutifully sitting behind young John McQuillan.

Mrs Aitken played a piano as the audience joined in a rendition of 'A Boy Is Born in Bethlehem'. Brooke's musical talents were meagre, but he knew enough to recognise that the atonal accompaniment was down to the piano, not the pianist. His mind, despite the off-notes, was still focused on revelation, a concept which seemed almost palpable but just out of reach. Unbeknownst to the congregation a dozen uniformed officers were even now assembling on the Great Bridge, preparing to ascend Castle Hill. Once the play was over they would interview everyone. ID cards, papers and addresses would be recorded. The questions were obvious: many of these people, if not the vast majority, had known Colm Hendrie. Did he talk of friends, comrades, lovers? What of his family back in Ireland? Had he ever mentioned Mary Flynn? Edison had the woman's picture, retrieved from the missal. Did anyone recognise *her*? And what of politics, and the IRA? Did the Upper Town have its hidden revolutionaries?

The burden of the inquiry seemed suddenly crippling. Brooke took a deep breath and closed his eyes until a change in the music signalled the drama was about to begin. It was in the silence after the hymn as the three kings began to present their gifts to the doll in the manger that the siren, fixed atop the new Guildhall on Market Hill, let out its long, slow guttural wail, a note rising to a sustained pitch.

There was a groan from the audience, Mrs Aitken faltered at the piano and Father Ward took to the stage. 'The children know what to do now, so please follow them.' He raised a hand, said a line of prayer and set the drill in motion.

The young caretaker, Smith, led the way into the central corridor and then to the far end, where an open staircase twisted back and down to the basement. The heat here was dry and intense; a central corridor — exactly mirroring the one above — led away from the boiler room itself, where a coke oven fire door stood open, revealing the bright yellow-red glow of the coals. Beside it, a chair and cot bed marked the caretaker's billet. On a shelf was placed a small framed picture of a family of three on a wide, deserted beach. On a hook hung a heavy overcoat.

Off the central corridor there were half a dozen rooms, one or two given over to stores — wood, a coal bunker, various cans of oil and other hardware. The children were split into boys and girls and led into two of the rooms, where blankets and sacks were ready for makeshift beds if the alarm lasted. Candles were lit to supplement the occasional light bulbs. A general air of unbridled adventure had taken hold.

Father Ward waited at the foot of the stairs directing the operation. 'We've done the drill, of course,' he told Brooke. 'But this is the first time we've come down in anger, as it were. The sirens are rare by daylight so we don't get the chance. Everyone's a bit overexcited.'

A child, a girl of five or six, lingered beside the priest, holding on to his cassock.

'Can you tell the adults that we're going to take this opportunity to ask them some questions about the recent murder. No details, please. Just that.'

Ward nodded and fled. Brooke scuttled back

upstairs to collect the uniformed constables from the yard.

The adults had been asked to bring their stools down with them from the hall, and they sat now in groups in the other rooms, talking and drinking tea, leaving in ones and twos when their names were called by Edison to answer questions at a table set by the coke boiler. Vital information was recorded on clipboards.

The scene was strangely biblical. Brooke imagined the early Christians in their caves and tunnels below Rome. If Cambridge had catacombs, they'd be like this: ordered and geometric, with functional light bulbs and little signs on the doors for STORES, or POWER, or DRAINS. The dangers from which these Christians fled were very different — the long-feared air raids, rather than the horrors of the Coliseum — but there was a dim echo of a persecuted community, which added an edge of fear to the holiday mood.

Brooke checked Edison's list and said he'd interview the head teacher and his wife himself. He found them, alone, in a small room whose door bore the sign ACADEMIC SUPPLIES. Boxes of chalk, blackboards and exercise books were piled neatly on wooden shelves. They sat touchingly close, hand in hand.

Mrs Walsh was flushed, and Brooke's arrival seemed to prompt a crisis, because she turned to her husband with an imploring look.

The head sprang to his feet. 'One moment,' he said to Brooke. 'I need to get Kathleen a glass of water. There's a child coming.'

'Not tonight!' said Mrs Walsh, laughing. 'I just

feel faint. A glass, Liam, that's all.'

They shared a knowing look, recognising a nervous, over-attentive father.

'We can talk tomorrow,' offered Brooke.

She shook her head. 'It's fine. I'm fine. Ah — ' Walsh was back with water.

Brooke had brought his own stool and took a moment to settle. He offered again to postpone the interview, but the Walshes had recovered themselves.

'You recall Hendrie,' said Brooke. 'What kind of man was he?'

'I knew him well,' said Mrs Walsh simply.

Her husband nodded in agreement.

'A huge man, but very gentle. He'd stand at the back for midday Mass on a Sunday, and I thought — you know — a lost soul.' She shook her head. 'I made sure he got a cup of tea afterwards. He said he had children himself, back in Ireland.'

'Where?' asked Brooke.

She looked at her husband, as if the answer lay there, then at Brooke. 'Galway? I think it was Galway. A boy and a girl, I certainly remember that. And so I asked if he'd help at sports day in the summer and he said he would. We don't have the space here, the playground's tiny as you know and all that glass . . . So we go out onto Parker's Piece.' She'd got lost in the recollection, but now the reality of Hendrie's death seemed to over-whelm her and she held both hands to her lips.

'Did he seem to know anyone else in the congregation?'

'No. He was interested in the papers. Wasn't he, Liam?'

The head teacher was nodding. 'The diocese pays for the *Catholic Herald* and the *Irish Times*. I bind the copies up for Father Ward and he was always there, Colm, after the service, reading away.'

'Did he talk about politics, about the Republicans? You teach the children some Gaelic, is that right? Did he take an interest?'

'Never.'

'Perhaps he had the language already,' offered Brooke. The labourer's private interests seemed far removed from the world of the navvy. Had he provided the educated hand required to leave the Fenian slogan at the site of the bomb blast?

Walsh shook his head. 'Seemed more interested in the sport. Gaelic football. And the rugby, I think he said he'd played. In the scrum of course. A one-man scrum himself.'

'Did he support a club?' pressed Brooke.

'We didn't pry,' said Walsh primly.

Mrs Walsh plucked at a memory, her hand fluttering. 'Yes. I know. You should talk to Joe. He's sports mad too and they always had their heads together. And' — Mrs Walsh held up her hand, taken away with the excitement of the enquiry — 'he had a car — a van, I think.'

'You saw it?'

'No, no. He said if we ever needed anything shifted he could help. So a van. I said in the spring we always took the children to the coast, to Suffolk, on the train, and he said if I hired a charabanc he could drive it because he had the licence.'

The idea of Hendrie behind the wheel was

difficult to dislodge. Had he driven to the river, thrown the child into the water, on the night of the murder?

'This van, did he ever say where he kept it? There's nothing outside his rooms on Honey Hill.'

'No, but he mentioned it several times.'

'Is the mother coming to see the poor child's body?' asked Walsh. 'And to the school?'

'We don't know. She's here Saturday. And the father, I hope. I'll let you know as soon as we do.'

Walsh set his hands on his knees, nodding, as if assessing the responsibilities this entailed.

Distantly they heard the all-clear sound above. The children, disappointed, were roused and herded to the stairs. Smith, the caretaker, appeared through a door at the end of the corridor, switching off the lights; but beyond, fleetingly, Brooke had seen that the corridor ran on, under the church, illuminated by a series of light bulbs. Smith locked the door behind him.

Brooke saw it then in his mind's eye: the church's parquet floor, the brass grilles set in a line, the heat rising. He'd been stupid to push the thought aside. How was St Alban's kept so warm without a cellar? Ward had insisted there was no crypt: the parish was too poor. Or had Brooke become disorientated below ground? Did the corridor run under the presbytery, not the church? He stood back, watching a crocodile of children press past, trying to map in his head the plan of the basement to the building above.

Smith hung his keys by the boiler and helped shepherd the children up the stairs, leading the

211

way. Something about the caretakers hidden world: the fire, the cot, the single picture, made Brooke decide on action. He borrowed Edison's torch, helped himself to the keys and set off down the central corridor. Looking back, he saw that the caretaker had returned for his coat, which he shrugged on, before carrying a small child up the stairs and out of sight.

A heavy iron key — the fifth Brooke tried — opened the door.

Beyond, the lights were out but the torch revealed the corridor. If Brooke's mental map was correctly aligned, then he was standing below the altar of the church. In plain terms the priest had told the truth; there was no crypt, or even a simple cellar, just this narrow corridor along the walls of which ran heavy iron pipes — too hot to touch, pumping out the heat which rose to the ceiling, and the perforated iron grilles.

At the end of the corridor a set of brick steps rose up, so that he could touch the end grille above his head. There was light in the church above, a flickering candlelight warmth. Threading his fingers through the brass grille he pushed up, and the plate lifted without complaint, so that he was able to slide it across. He could get his head through the gap, but no more. A clear view of the altar revealed the glint of gold, the dull light outside making the stained glass just visible above. Three candles guttered in their holders by the door. The trestle tables and tea urn, set out for Brooke's incident room, lay in the shadows of the side aisle.

212

Was this the answer to the riddle? Had Sean been taken *down*? Was the half-opened window in the toilet a well-timed misdirection? The last pew, in which the boy had slept, was almost within reach. Here was another mystery. The child could have squeezed through the gap, but no adult abductor. Had he gone of his own free will?

It took Brooke less than a minute to get back to Smiths billet by the boiler. Not only was the caretaker's coat gone, but also the small framed photograph. Upstairs the children were being bundled into coats, the enactment of the Epiphany abandoned. Mr Walsh said the caretaker had gone outside to clear snow from the path to the gates. Brooke pushed the door open and walked out into the yard. The snow was thick, and a fresh fall had filled in most of the footprints, except the caretaker's, which led to the gate, where he'd neatly set aside the spade, and gone.

36

Brooke killed the light to his office and for a moment stood in the dark, noting the slatted moonlight which came in through the old blinds, catching the gilded paintwork on the Nile bed and the paperwork on his desk. The concept of an office job had always appalled him. As a student he'd dreamt of a career spent observing natural science; in Egypt during the Great War he'd hire a car to take him out into the desert, on the lookout for the fabled Barbary lion. There would have been laboratory work after the war, but even that held the excitement of discovery, the rewards of painstaking experiment. Notes to be taken, certainly, and records to keep, but not just pushing paper.

Joining the police, he'd envisaged days spent on the beat, or later, at the scenes of crime. The office was easily avoided. As his rank rose, his time at his desk had grown, but he'd discovered, by way of compensation, the power of the telephone and the intrinsic value of files and documents. In small doses this was exhilarating. The last hour had been a case in point. The sinews of the crime he was trying to solve now lay exposed, at least in part. Unless he moved quickly and surely, he thought it probable they'd never see Joe Smith again.

He shut his door, descending the Spinning House steps two at a time, and strode out into the night at pace. It was too late now for further calls, but progress had been rapid. Joe Smith had not only disappeared, he had apparently never truly existed. Aitken, distraught at the discovery she'd been harbouring a felon for six months, confirmed that the young caretaker had not eaten in the school canteen, so there had been no need for a ration book. It was clear she'd taken a motherly interest in the young man's welfare, and his flight had left her in tears.

Father Ward, equally appalled at the thought the young man he'd taken under his wing had been complicit in the kidnap and murder of a child, promptly handed over all the paperwork related to Smith's appointment, including his excellent references. There was also an ID card number and a previous address. Brooke rang the reference numbers provided. The first was a dockside haulier in Bermondsey, working late at his own desk, who recalled Smith and vouched for his work ethic and his honesty. The second was a bricklayer in Tottenham, a man who lived over his own builder's yard. The reference was again glowing, and Brooke was about to put down the phone when the brickie added, 'Joe was a good lad. They all are, the Irish boys. They know how to work.' Smith, it transpired, had exhibited a crisp, clear Ulster accent. His former boss thought he'd talked of Belfast.

Smith's disappearance and his contrived identity pointed clearly to the conclusion that he was a comrade of the butchered Hendrie, and the second of the three bombers seen by Dr Bodart. (Slim and dark?) He also bore a fleeting

215

resemblance to the killer Brooke had spotted on the rooftops of Honey Hill. The discovery of the narrow heating grille, and the access to it from the caretaker's basement billet, further suggested his involvement in the abduction and murder of Sean Flynn. But even the athletic Smith could not have inveigled himself through the narrow opening. Had he relied on an accomplice *inside* the church? Which left Brooke with the apparently blameless priest and his diligent housekeeper.

Catching Smith might solve all their problems. Brooke had alerted the railway station and set a constable on surveillance. Buses and trams had stopped for the night, but in the morning he'd have the depots covered. A school photograph of sports day on Parker's Piece had given them a decent image of the wanted man. Copies would be made, and enlarged, and sent to the ports — especially Liverpool, Glasgow and Holyhead. Brooke harboured two additional fears: first that Smith had access to Hendrie's mysterious vehicle, and second that he could lie low in the yet undiscovered bomb factory, wherever it was. And there was a sharper edge to Brooke's anxieties. The Ulsterman's ability to disguise his accent, to reinvent himself as an honest East Ender, eager to join the British in France, hinted at something more than a rough-and-ready revolutionary.

It was too early to even think of sleep, and there was no chance he could pick up the measured steps of the regime outlined by Aldiss. Instead of turning towards Newnham Croft and home, he slipped down an alleyway which decanted out onto Parker's Piece. A few fires smouldered between the serried ranks of army tents. Brooke showed his warrant card to a guard and zig-zagged across the encampment to the far edge, where a series of public shelters had been dug to offer safety in air raids. Each night the siren sounded hundreds took refuge here in the damp concrete cells. With every false alarm the numbers dropped, but Brooke knew that when the first bomb fell, and the city shook, thousands would head for Parker's Piece.

Grandcourt, Brooke's former batman from the desert campaign, was at his post outside Shelter 6. Like the rest it comprised a half-buried, reinforced concrete box, the entrance to which was through a pair of iron doors sunk in a long trench. Here the diminutive Grandcourt had constructed a perch, as he would have called it in Palestine, a seat, with a shelf for his pipe, a small fire burning in a neat brazier. He jumped down, and like many of those short in stature, seemed to diminish in height as a result.

'Time for a break, Grandcourt?' said Brooke.

The former corporal packed away his tobacco and stowed his gear in the shelter, locking the door.

When Brooke had been discharged from the sanatorium at Scarborough he'd discovered that Grandcourt, transferred to France after the victorious Fall of Jerusalem, had survived six months on the Western Front. The batman had returned home to find his job in the shipyards at Chatham had gone to a younger man. Brooke had secured him a post at the university's engineering department, running the stores. Grandcourt's extreme practicality and manic neatness had seen him flourish. His family had moved with him to a small house in Romsey Town, the working-class district half a mile north of Parker's Piece.

Grandcourt had volunteered for Civil Defence night work, guarding the shelters, but was always on hand for a drink in one of the many pubs clustered in the Kite, the maze-like district of terraced housing just north of the park, set between a parallelogram of roads. Brooke had quickly enlisted Grandcourt's company as a regular night-hawk, often relying on his practicality to help prise open a tricky case. Grandcourt was a touchstone of common sense and worldly know-how.

They cut down a tunnel between grand houses into the heart of the Kite, past a series of corner pubs, until they were able to slip into the public bar of the Elm Tree.

Grandcourt had just taken the first inch off his pint, wiping the head from his moustache, when Brooke placed the lump of golden wax he'd found in the attic above Hendrie's room on the table between them. The exact nature of the material had defied the combined expertise of Dr Comfort and the reliable Edison, not to mention the switchboard girls at the Spinning House.

Grandcourt smiled, and sniffed the gem, as Brooke called it. The pub was full, the general buzz of conversation providing a cloak for their own.

'It smells of cedar — am I right?' asked Brooke.

Grandcourt nodded. 'I've heard it called many things, Mr Brooke. One of the officers at Arras called it the 'tears of Chios' — but he was showing off. He said it was once worth its weight in gold. Chew it and it's a breath freshener, he reckoned. So good it was used in the sultan's harem. That got the boys laughing.' He sniffed it again. 'Used for incense, perfume, that sort of lark. It's a resin from a tree, out in Cairo they'd call it 'Arabic gum'. Not gum Arabic, mind, that's different.' Grandcourt set it down. 'I'd call it mastic. Mix it up right with some oil and it's the best glue in the world. Stick anything to anything. A kid in Cairo got some between his fingers and ended up losing a yard of skin.'

By way of illustration, Grandcourt put down his pint and interlocked the fingers of both hands, then struggled to pull them apart. 'Perfect bond.'

Brooke briefly told him where he'd found the golden teardrop and the news that Hendrie's killer could well have been the caretaker Smith, now on the run.

Grandcourt filled his pipe. 'Most bombs you place, Mr Brooke, concealed, if you will, even if it is in plain sight. A package left in a busy place. Or slipped under a bench. With mastic you can defy gravity, that's the trick of it.'

A brief discussion produced three possible generic targets: the underside of a car or lorry, a ceiling, or the underside of a bridge.

With the second pint Grandcourt, prompted by a question Claire always made him promise to ask, launched into a brief review of the current state of his family, a wife and three boys. Brooke, half-listening, found it impossible to forget the golden teardrop. The river was frozen now, offering access to each of the city's bridges. If a bomb, concealed beneath, went off at night casualties would be light — possibly zero — but the strategic impact might be considerable and the propaganda effect startling. A daylight explosion could kill dozens. The bridges needed to be surveyed at dawn and dusk each day. Another drain on the meagre resources of the Borough.

Outside the icy stillness had given way to a fresh blizzard, which cut visibility to fifty yards. Grandcourt's distant shelter was lost to sight, the air thick with feathery flakes. They parted company with a sharp handshake.

Walking towards town, Brooke watched the bulk of the city's grand hotel — the University Arms — loom out of the falling snow, its Moorish lead-green turrets dusted now with icing sugar. Inside, Brooke recalled, from a childhood memory, a soaring octagonal reception hall, the plasterwork astounding even to a six-year-old. His mother had taken him there to meet a friend, the wife of another academic. It was the clearest picture he had of her. She'd died the nest year of some whispered disease. He recalled red lipstick on a cigarette filter, and a cocktail glass with ice.

The memory made him think of the child he'd been, and the child Sean Flynn had been. What was the reality of the boy's life at home? His new-found friend had painted a picture of a boisterous, headstrong lad who loved football and could turn his hand to petty theft. It was a picture which jarred badly with the neat front room at 36 Askew Road, Shepherd's Bush. To this was now added the photograph found in Hendrie's pocket of the boy's mother. Hendrie's death and Smith's flight had revealed much, but Brooke still felt the key to the mystery was the child, and the home he had left behind in Shepherd's Bush.

37

They left the car in an anonymous side street a mile west of Shepherd's Bush. The Wasp was the only vehicle in sight. Mr Gerald Flynn's place of work was the London Underground pay office at Paddington, where the murdered boy's father was a senior clerk — according to the form neatly filled in and signed that had accompanied his son to Cambridge.

Edison, reluctantly abandoning the Wasp, set out for Paddington by train. The plan was a simple one: the detective sergeant would take a statement from Mr Flynn while Brooke tackled his wife. Then they could compare notes. Brooke found a cafe at the corner of Askew Road, from the front window of which he could see the gate of number 36. He planned to knock once the teenage son had left for his early shift, having checked his clocking-on time with the railway depot by phone the night before. He wished to interview Mrs Flynn alone, without the baleful support of young Bobbie.

Most of the snow had thawed in London, leaving slush in the gutters and the occasional sheet of trickling ice. He was smearing a slice of bread around the rim of his plate when he saw Mrs Flynn stepping out smartly down the short path to her front gate. Which wasn't in the plan, and so he had to move fast, leaving too much change on the table and dashing out into the cold sunlight, falling in twenty yards in her wake.

The wicker shopping basket swung at her hip as she made her way north, down Bassein Park Road into Uxbridge Road, a major thoroughfare heading west towards the centre of Shepherd's Bush. Something about Mrs Flynn's focused energy made Brooke hold back from catching her up. Despite the chaos of the city street she seemed on a mission. Trams clanked past, a horse-drawn dray negotiated the corner and the pavements were crowded. The area was what Claire would have called 'a cut above': swept gutters, thriving shops and even a tea house, with gilded signwriting on the window advertising *Patisserie*. Mrs Flynn did not linger, heading east, past the shops: a butcher's festooned with plucked fowl, a sprawling greengrocer's, a hardware store occupying a corner site, boasting *Six Floors of Essentials*. Mrs Flynn bowled serenely onwards, hardly glancing at the goods on trestles set out on the pavement.

As Brooke followed, he considered the questions he'd ask. There had to be something in the family's past to explain the boy's death. Were they involved in the IRA bomb plot? Had the child seen too much at home? What family — what mother or father — would kill to silence their own child? Edison had suggested on the long drive south that the parents might know who had killed the child but were too scared to talk. Were they victims too?

After twenty minutes Brooke could see ahead the wide expanse of a green, the snow still on the ground here, across the lawns. A horse, coat steaming, drank at a stone trough. The neighbourhood was a poor one, the shops grimy with soot, the gutters full of refuse and slush. Mrs Flynn entered the park through a gate and sat, very still, at a bench, watching dusty pigeons fluttering over a handful of crumbs tossed down by an old man leaning on a stick. She seemed able to combine sitting silently with extreme agitation, constantly checking a purse in her bag, a handkerchief in her coat, tugging at the fingertips of a worn pair of leather gloves. Brooke could have sat beside her and asked his questions then, but something held him back, a sense that this brisk early morning walk was somehow part of a greater design.

After ten minutes she sprang to her feet, straightening her coat, as if some decision — finally taken — had unlocked the spell which held her in the park. Initially retracing her steps, she turned off the high road down a narrow street cluttered with market stalls. At the far end was a small parade of shops and she ducked quickly into a greengrocer's. There was no queue inside, so Brooke stood outside watching as she chose a cauliflower, carrots and what looked like a bunch of parsnips. The greengrocer, smiling, seemed to know her well.

A butcher's was next door and she ordered three chops and some sausages, and proffered a set of ration cards, which were stamped. Brooke, at the back of a short queue, thought he saw three cards, but he could not be sure. The idea that a simple case of petty fraud might lie at the root of the mystery dampened Brooke's mood,

224

and so he was a few yards behind her as she entered the next shop, a general grocer's. The goods on offer were not extravagant and there seemed little choice. She bought three eggs, a half-pound of butter, some lard, a pint of milk and a can of peaches. Again, the ration cards were handed over, neatly splayed.

The pounding of the official stamp was rhythmic, before the grocer handed them back with a cheerful: 'Good day, Mrs Walsh.' He touched the brim of a small straw hat.

She fled, head down, out into the street. Brooke waited a few seconds, making sure he'd heard the man clearly. But there was no doubt: it had been Mrs *Walsh* — not *Flynn*.

Brooke loitered until the shop was empty, showed his warrant card and asked for a moment. The grocer fetched a girl from the yard and told her to mind the counter, leading Brooke into a backroom where an elderly woman sat in front of a smouldering coal fire.

'She can't hear us,' said the grocer, touching her for reassurance on the shoulder. 'What's wrong?'

'You served a woman a few moments ago. You called her Mrs Walsh.'

He nodded, looking over Brooke's shoulder to check the shop.

'That's the name on the ration card?'

'It is. She shops here regular. Has done for years. Husband died, I think. She's in service now, the other ration cards are for a different name. Floyd? Something like that.'

'Flynn,' said Brooke.

225

'That's it. Twice a week, sometimes more. Is it the card? They say there's forgeries, but I'd have trusted her. Nice woman, a better class of Irish — no offence.'

Outside, standing in the street, Brooke noted a school opposite, a handful of children forming a single line, waiting to go in for the register. Two storeys in red brick, with a niche for a marble saint kneeling, a girl looking up at a painted Madonna. It reminded him of the same grotto, caught in stone in the corridor of St Alban's. Walking to the railing he found a noticeboard: the Church of Our Lady of Lourdes. He kept thinking of St Alban's, with its careworn head teacher Liam Walsh and his young wife. Walsh was as common an Irish name as Murphy or O'Brien. The death of Sean Flynn was still a mystery, but Brooke felt with absolute certainty that he'd edged closer to the truth at its heart.

38

The story, when finally laid bare, was a tale of the times: a family torn apart, its victims hidden by the confusions of war. Gerald Flynn, when confronted with the name in his 'wife's' ration book, had reluctantly told the truth: he was a widower, with two grown boys, living with a married woman who was not his wife, with a boy of her own, until they'd sent the child north, away from the threat of the bombs, to Cambridge.

They were not married, and she was certainly not divorced or the recipient of an annulment from the church. In order to 'live in sin', Mrs Walsh had simply abandoned her old neighbourhood of Shepherds Bush and moved — spatially and socially — upwards: up Uxbridge Road, in fact, to the widower's house. A marriage in Ireland was manufactured for the benefit of the neighbours and the Flynns' few local relatives in London.

Her real husband was Liam Walsh, a school teacher. A brief description pointed clearly to the startling conclusion: the same Liam Walsh was now head teacher of St Alban's, Upper Town, Cambridge. Why had he left his wife and son? In a series of tearful interviews at the police station, she mentioned the attentions of the widower Flynn, which were eventually discovered by her husband, a quiet, thoughtful man, a form teacher at Our Lady of Lourdes. In a whisper she'd offered the single damning truth: that she loved the widower, not her husband. There had been rows, and threats, and finally blows. Liam had left, first for a rented room in Hammersmith, then a new job. He'd promised letters, and visits to see the boy, but there'd been no news.

Three years of silence had passed, during which Mr and Mrs Flynn had — in Gerald Flynns words — simply 'carried off' their new position of husband and wife without the need of a ceremony of any kind. The ration card had presented a difficulty. She could have tried to bluff the authorities, but the process of application was bureaucratic, so she'd decided to avoid outright fraud. The local community was close. Hence Mary Flynn's long walk to the shops and her old neighbourhood, where she was still known as Mrs Walsh. The war and its confusion had simply aided their subterfuge.

Young Sean, never reminded of his real father, had seemed to forget him. Nervous, unhappy, he'd been the cuckoo in the nest. Gerald Flynn resented the boy and had pressed for him to be sent away, on the grounds that it would 'make a man of him'. His mother resisted until the diocese wrote and made it plain this would be his last chance to leave under their care.

Even then they'd hesitated. Sean disliked being separated from his mother for even a few hours. All they wanted to do, Mrs Flynn had pleaded, was to live the life of a family, because that was what they were. A loving family. She'd committed a sin, many sins, but she'd asked forgiveness every day at Our Lady of Lourdes. She'd ask every day of her life. In the end, even she had to admit the sensible thing was to send the boy safely away.

The Flynns denied any knowledge of the IRA S-Plan, Colm Hendrie or Joe Smith. Mrs Flynn had no idea why the butchered Hendrie should have her picture in his Catholic missal. The teenage Bobbie again professed no interest in uniting Ireland, dismissing the whole complex skein of Irish politics as a bitter dispute between peasants who put religion before the reality of working life. His father had got them out of the slums, and young Bobbie was going to work hard to get himself another rung up the social ladder. He had dreams of owning his own motorcar.

The child's body still needed to be formally identified. Saturday was confirmed as the date for the trip north. Mr Flynn would try to get the time off work, but the weekend had been set aside for a full company audit. Edison's verdict was suitably neat: 'Bit of a nobby clerk, our Gerald. More interested in moving up in the world with his pretty wife. Not a ghost of the Emerald Isle in *his* accent any more.'

They left the Flynns in their suburban villa and drove north. They had, after all, committed no crimes beyond some minor misdemeanours in sending Sean away under what was, in fact, a false name.

The crimes, as such, lay north, along the old Cambridge road.

The rest of the story, the flight of the cuckolded Liam Walsh, his bigamous marriage to the much-younger Kathleen and his impending fatherhood, they'd kept to themselves, saving such revelations for the Saturday visit.

First, they'd confront the head teacher at home.

Brooke broke the silence as they rattled out into the countryside.

'You can see the dilemma, Edison. Father Ward said they got a list of the evacuees a week before they arrived. Names and addresses. So, Walsh knew in advance that his whole life might be ruined, and everything lost. Wife, child and job — and house!'

Between them they tried to reassemble the tragedy.

God, it seemed, had played a cruel trick. The boy, sent north, might easily have recognised his real father. The boy's mother most certainly would have recognised her real husband if, and when, she'd visited her son. Walsh risked prison as a bigamist. How could he protect the world he'd built at St Alban's?

Could all this amount to a motive for murder? Could Liam Walsh have killed his own son? Or was Walsh in some way enmeshed with the IRA cell, with Hendrie and Smith? Did the boy's arrival, and the possible exposure of the teacher's crime, threaten them and their plans? The mild-mannered teacher seemed an unlikely firebrand, but then he was hardly a typical bigamist either. In Brooke's experience the bigamist was often charming, louche, deceptive. Walsh seemed duty-bound, stoical and loving.

'I don't believe he'd have anything to do with

killing the kiddie, sir,' said Edison, nosing the Wasp through a blizzard as they descended a hill on the old Roman road from the downs above Royston. A snow-flecked milestone promised CAMBRIDGE 15 MILES. Around them, in the dusk, pale hills glowed. Ahead they could just see the half-blinded tail lights of a lorry they'd been following since they'd left the grey outer suburbs of the capital.

Brooke lit a cigarette, using a glove to clear condensation from the windscreen.

'What if someone else did it, Edison? Hendrie or Smith, perhaps. Either on Walsh's command, or to save him from the inevitable reckoning and the arrival of the police at St Alban's. Did they all fear discovery?'

Edison was silent for twenty minutes as they reached the city, creeping past the Spinning House, still on the same Roman road. 'He could have got away with it,' he said, negotiating an army lorry parked outside the Round Church. 'He could have kept his head down, he could have been ill when the mother visited. It's risky, but it's better than — '

'Filicide,' said Brooke. 'Somehow that sounds worse, doesn't it? But the child, Edison. What if *he'd* recognised his father? What if Walsh feared that moment above all else. He'd have had the boy in his class. He'd have had to teach him. See him every day. Put a plaster on his bloodied knee. Feel his forehead for a fever.'

The salt lorries had cleared the city's streets but stopped short of Castle Hill, so Edison put the Wasp into first gear and crawled up the

231

incline and in through the gates of St Alban's School. The playground was deserted, the snow still unswept.

Brooke hauled himself out of the car, stretching his legs.

'The moment of truth, Edison. Liam Walsh has got some explaining to do. I wonder how much of the truth he's told his young wife.'

The head teacher's cottage, a terraced house, was in a nearby street. Edison locked the Wasp and they set out, although Brooke cast a glance back, noting a light burning in the church, a weak echo of candlelight behind a stained-glass window, which depicted, in shadowy colours, the death of the eponymous St Alban: the martyrs severed head lying bloodied on the green grass, the Roman executioner standing back in silvered armour, a crowd of citizens shocked by the martyrdom. He imagined Father Ward, inside, bent in prayer before the altar.

39

Kathleen Walsh answered the door, standing back to let them into the cottage's front room. The conflict of emotions in her face was remarkable, and — Brooke felt — exhibited an extraordinary honesty. The shy smile of a welcome was almost obliterated by an acute anxiety. Her dark good looks were animated by the flames of a fire in the grate, which gave to her hair a sheen to match the kettle set on the hearth.

Edison, frozen after the long drive, succumbed to the lure of the fire and placed himself four-square in front of the flickering light.

'Is Mr Walsh in?' asked Brooke, aware of the particular metallic tick of the mantelpiece clock. Only later, looking back, would he recall the passing seconds it marked.

'He's in the church, Inspector. A prayer — it's a habit. He won't be a moment. He locks up for Father Ward.'

'He has keys?'

'Yes.' She said it so quickly and lightly that Brooke was almost sure she was innocent of what they'd discovered in London: innocent of the knowledge that her husband was not her husband, and the child that was coming would have had a half-brother.

'Do you mind if we wait?' asked Brooke.

'Not at all. Please — sit.'

On one of the deep, battered chairs a nest of knitting lay on the arm, a baby's shawl in white, almost complete. Brooke sat, lifting a thread of wool away as he subsided into the cushions. He was acutely aware that he had the power, in a single sentence, to destroy this woman's entire world, to reset all its principal certainties and replace them with uncertainties. A fallen woman, with a child, would have to leave her home. All Brooke had to do was to tell her the truth.

'How is your husband?' asked Brooke.

She looked puzzled by the question. 'Liam carries other people's troubles as well as his own. He worries for the child that's to come. Then this poor boy is taken from us, which he takes as a personal failure, when it is a simple act of evil. But that is how he feels: guilty. And these men — the bombers — he has sympathy for their ideals, but not for violence.' She laughed. 'He has sympathy for all ideals, I think — which is generous, isn't it? He is a generous man. And there's a school to run, the evacuees to accommodate. It's a burden, but one he sought out, as he always reminds me. He was a senior teacher; no one made him apply for the head's post, although everyone knew he'd be wonderful. And he is — in a quiet way. So the evening prayer helps. And I have my moment of silent privacy too.' She smiled again, tidying up the knitting into a basket. 'He'll be a minute, no more.'

Brooke looked at the clock: ten past eight.

Edison took up the conversation, asking about the degree to which the diocese, the bishop in

234

particular, interfered with the running of the school.

Brooke examined the clock face: tin-white, with Roman numerals, and marked with the makers name and the scroll-like motif *Riley & Sons, Galway City*. As a child he'd been fascinated by the indiscernible progress of clocks. Often, filling the hours between the end of school and the serving of dinner at home, he'd wander the city and note the clocks, watching trance-like in the hope of seeing a minute hand actually move. The silvered dials on the octagonal tower of Foster's Bank were a favourite. His father had once left him outside as he conducted business within, beneath a stunning dome of glazed tiles. Brooke had passed the time in the churchyard opposite, trying to catch the sudden stutter forward of the clock hands. It had become a lifetime's habit. Foster's clock, a finely tuned machine, had won, creeping forward to the chiming of the quarter hour undetected.

In contrast the Galway clock juddered, each minute leaping past.

Brooke asked the usual biographical questions. She had answered an advert in the *Catholic Herald* two years previously for a junior school teacher at St Alban's and left her family home in Connemara for the three-day journey. The ferry, caught in the middle of the Irish Sea, had spent twelve hours riding out a storm in the lee of the Isle of Man.

'Purgatory,' she said, smiling at the memory. 'We're going back to visit in the summer.' Brooke imagined a buffeting clifftop wind, the oddly penetrating light of the Atlantic and a winding lane.

Liam Walsh had been on the staff. A year after her arrival he'd replaced the old head teacher, an aged priest, and proposed on the same day. His first wife had died of a stomach tumour. There had been no children. He had seemed, to her, a troubled man, but a kind and generous one. They'd been married in St Alban's on a baking June day, the children providing an enthusiastic choir, Father Ward — himself newly arrived — the celebrant.

'We had the marriage breakfast in the play-ground,' she said, offering Brooke the photograph, which showed a single line of trestle tables, the adults standing, Aitken just behind the priest, Liam Walsh with his arm around his bride's narrow waist. Even in the sunshine the play-ground seemed hedged in by shadows, inky black at the foot of the church.

The old clock advanced to eight twenty-five. Mrs Walsh had started asking questions, about the missing caretaker and the hunt for young Sean's killer, and Edison was providing colour-less answers. Brooke felt she'd very quickly stopped listening to the answers.

Finally, she stood to add coke to the fire.

The clock ticked. Brooke's patience snapped. 'Stay by the fire,' he told them. 'I'll be a moment.'

Outside, the icy air was a shock. His footsteps echoed in the street as he climbed back up to the playground, with its three dull-brick guardians: the church, the school, the presbytery.

As he opened the door to the church he heard footsteps behind him and turned to see Mrs Walsh, wrapped in a coat, bustling to follow, with Edison in her wake.

Brooke waited in the porch. Edison, breathless, caught them up. 'Mrs Walsh says she's worried about her husband, more worried than she said.'

'What's wrong?' she asked.

Brooke pushed the door open and stepped inside. The scene was immediately clear: a row of candles, now fluttering wildly in the sudden draught, illuminated the nave. A gilded statue on the distant altar caught the light. But before them, in silhouette, the body of man hung by what looked like a belt round his neck, attached to a light fitting fixed to one of the brick pillars. A chair, toppled, had been kicked aside.

'My God,' said Edison.

'Liam?' said Mrs Walsh, the inflection suggesting the first ghost of a question.

There were no screams.

Brooke ran to the body, his metal Blakeys striking the tiled floor. Gathering up the chair, he called back, 'Get a knife.'

Mrs Walsh fled. Edison dragged over a table used for hymn books and, standing on it, together they struggled with the knotted belt, unclipping a heavy bunch of keys which was tangled with the buckle. Free at last, the body fell into their arms.

Mrs Walsh arrived too late with the knife, followed by Father Ward, and then, in his shadow, Mrs Aitken, in a nightdress. When she saw the body splayed on the brick floor she cried out to God and clutched the priest, burying her face against his chest.

40

Liam Walsh was alive, but his unwanted life hung by a thread. Brooke travelled in the ambulance beside a young nurse, who held the teacher's hand and told him not to worry but to sleep, sensing perhaps that his apparent unconsciousness was a screen, a protection against questions. On the other side of the patient sat his wife, occasionally leaning forward to lift a scrap of thin red hair away from the forehead. The nurse had cut away the collar of his shirt to reveal the neck, scarred by the vivid blue-red shadow of the noose.

The old ambulance crept down the streets on the ice, all four wheels sliding as they edged round the corner onto Trinity Street. On King's Parade a group of students stood back, allowing the ambulance to trundle past. Walsh's eyelids fidgeted. Brooke thought he could see colour creeping back into the face, and at the last moment, as the driver swung into the forecourt at Addenbrooke's, the head teacher opened his eyes.

'Sleep, Liam,' said his wife, leaning in close. He looked at her, but without a flicker of recognition.

They sat by the bed for an hour until a constable from the Spinning House arrived, despatched by Edison, whom he'd left in charge at St Alban's. In the corridor outside her husband's room, Brooke sat Kathleen Walsh down and told her what they'd discovered in London, for she had a right to know, as it was the truth and helped explain her husband's attempt to take his own life. The fact that the man she loved had come so close to death seemed to put the news into some kind of brutal perspective. Her reaction was stoic, and she thanked Brooke earnestly before going back to maintain a vigil by the bedside. Had he even detected a sense of relief in her eyes? What, Brooke thought, had she imagined?

On Sunshine Ward the curtains were drawn around a bed, muffled voices deep in debate, and Brooke heard Claire's patient, calm tones, so he withdrew, and tripping down the stairs almost ran straight into Joy, her uniform splashed with blood. She looked flustered, and then guilty. 'Sorry,' she said. 'It's the blackout. Another crash — the driver's in a bad way. I'm doing a double-shift to help them cope. We kill more people on the roads than we save from bombs. You look awful, Dad. Go home.'

He put a hand behind her neck and held her cheek to his. Then she was gone.

Out in the snow, which blew around in chaotic gusts, home was the last place Brooke wanted to be. The big house, with its draughty rooms, was haunted by the people who weren't there. He thought he might sleep if he found somewhere warm, so he set out for Frank Edwardes' house. Walking north he stopped outside the Scott Polar Research Institute to inspect the bust of the great explorer. Rarely could it have looked so convincing; snow drifts ran up to the graceful facade of the building, icicles hung from the whaling gun on its concrete plinth. Scott's head, the hair and hood iced, stared out with the kind of belligerent determination his real face had never held. Brooke felt he was one of those men whose personalities seemed to be fluid. Which reminded him of Walsh: what was *his* true nature?

The cricket ground at Fenner's was a sheet of paper. The night light burnt in the upper storey bedroom window of the house at the end of the road. The door opened on the latch, and Brooke trudged up three flights to find Edwardes awake, reading with a magnifying glass, his bank of radios humming with a bass note.

Brooke took a chair and told his former chief inspector what he'd told Kathleen Walsh, a story that amounted to a startling motive for murder, even if the mild-mannered head teacher seemed an unlikely monster. Walsh's motive for suicide was clearer. The previous evening, at the Epiphany play, Brooke had told Walsh the boy's mother was coming to identify the body and visit the school. Walsh must have feared certain exposure.

'Then there's the priest, Father Ward. There's something not right there. Aitken, the house-keeper, is emotionally close, if no more. She's always on hand. I'm passing no judgements, Frank, but I'm pretty sure they've a secret to hide.' Brooke settled deeper in the armchair.

'Any sign of the caretaker?' asked Edwardes.

'None. And it's not the only thing that's

241

missing. Hendrie's van is still unaccounted for. There must be a garage somewhere close, so maybe that's where Smith's gone to ground. It might double up as a bomb factory, too. Not an enticing prospect, is it: explosives, transport, motive, opportunity. All Smith needs is a decent target. If he's still in the country, that is.'

One of the radios emitted a staccato burst of Morse code, which Edwardes expertly transcribed to the pad on his lap. Finished, he reread the message, shook his head and tossed the paper aside. There was always plenty of what Edwardes called traffic — signals flying between amateur radio hams, traces of military signals from France and the Low Countries, but no sign so far of the telltale outgoing response from one of the much-heralded Nazi spies, the dreaded Fifth Column.

Edwardes sipped a glass of milk. 'You've thought of blackmail, of course. A slippery crime.'

Brooke sat up. Downstairs they could hear Kat rattling a kettle.

'You've got Walsh and Ward — both with secrets, one's a bigamist, the other a parish priest involved with a widow under the church's own roof. Both vulnerable, both at hand, with Hendrie in the congregation and Smith in his caretaker's billet in the cellar. Blackmail, Eden. All the hallmarks are there.' He fumbled in the bedside drawer. 'Open the window, will you?'

The old man lit a cigarette. 'Doc says I have to stop. So does Kat. I doubt I'm fooling anyone.' He tapped ash into a silver dish they'd given him at the Spinning House to mark his promotion in 1931. 'Your real problem is Smith. The rest can wait. You say the pattern is two bombs, and they've only set one so far. That's right?'

'That's certainly the blueprint: two blasts, then the cell dissolves. So, yes, there's one more to plant, and we know he's got the gear, the explosives, because we can't find the bomb factory. And he's got the mastic, maybe Hendrie had that; apparently, it's standard kit on building sites. Maybe he didn't want to hand it over. Perhaps the next target's more ambitious. If Smith has access to Hendrie's van, he could just leave it in the town centre and set a timer.'

Edwardes outlined what he'd do: cut all leave, get uniformed branch out on the streets by day, search lock-ups and garages in the Upper Town, work their way through the wharfside warehouses at the foot of Castle Hill.

'Find this van, you'll find the bomb,' he said.

Brooke sighed, then closed his eyes, but sleep seemed very far away. 'Trouble is we don't really know what we're looking for, Frank. Hendrie told everyone at St Alban's that he had a vehicle, but they never saw it. A description would have made the task a lot easier.'

'One thing you've got going for you,' offered Edwardes. 'Confront Walsh as soon as you can — and the priest for that matter. If you know their secrets, they're not secrets any more. If blackmail was the game, that's your big chance. They've got nothing left to lose.'

41

Brooke, back at the house, followed Aldiss's regime for sleep: he ate what was left of a shepherd s pie which had been left in the oven and was still warm, took a bath in the attic and lay down in the dark bedroom, the window open. Ice held the river still, so there was no sound from the weir or the lock downstream. The last thing he heard was an owl on the water meadows, which he imagined swooping between the old gas lamps, set to light the way for the skaters. But there were no skaters now. He'd let Joy down on a skating trip, which he must put right if they had the chance. He heard a clock strike three and fell asleep.

He woke up to hear a particular sound, the trembling of glass, the globes and teardrops which hung in a wire circlet in the front room; the old villas only surviving chandelier. Outside a dog had replaced the owl, and other dogs replied across the city. He turned the light on and reached for the glass of water on the bedside table, noting the concentric ripples on the surface. Sitting on the bed his hand rested on the white, worn linen sheet, and found there a gritty dust which must have fallen from the old ceiling.

He heard what sounded like an explosion as he stood up, about to step to the open window. A distinct *crump* of folding metal followed by the dull thud of the sound wave nudging the old villa on its foundations. The house was empty, so he simply got into his clothes and ran down the stairs. The fanlight over the door was white glass, frosted, and had gained a crack from top to bottom.

He locked the door and started to run. Snow had fallen, and was falling still, so his footholds were secure. There was no sign of flames or smoke nearby. The explosion itself must have been distant, but of great power for its reverberations to be felt here, on a far-flung stretch of the river.

Crossing Coe Fen he saw a police radio car on a road in the distance heading south towards the railway station. What had Jo Ashmore said when he'd visited her rooftop Observation Post? *A munitions train, imagine that.*

At Speaker's Corner, a group stood in the middle of the crossroads: three ARP wardens, a constable and two guards in army uniform from Parker's Piece. The consensus was two explosions from an area north of the station, a swathe of land set aside for marshalling yards. Brooke marched the constable to a police box and got him to ring the station. The duty sergeant at the Spinning House had a more precise location: the duty officer at Madingley Hall had rung to ask for assistance at Abbey Depot, a complex of rail sheds and sidings on the northern, fen edge of the city. Brooke knew it well: in the years after the Great War, petty thieves had raided the yards on an almost nightly basis, in search of anything they could sell, or anything they could eat. In the end they'd put a constable on a regular beat round the yards.

While snow still fell the wind had dropped, so Brooke stood quietly with the constable by the police box and smoked a cigarette, a habit he'd developed in the desert when an important decision was required. Sometimes it had been a matter of life or death: whether to advance or retreat, make camp or march at night. His men would stand and wait while he tried to distance himself from the moment, considering his options with any logic he could muster. He felt he owed them that at least, rather than the usual half-baked order, often inspired not by military intelligence but by an overwhelming need to assume command and avoid embarrassment.

'Who knows what's really happened,' he said at last, his breath a cloud of white condensation. 'I'll go to the spot. When I've got a good idea what's happened I'll ring the Spinning House from a signal box. In the meantime, you go back to the station, tell the desk to alert the hospital — they need to stand by. For now, the radio cars can wait on major routes out of the city. Stop all cars and search them, check papers. They could ring the Observer Corps too — there's a post on Kew's Mill by the station. They may know more.' He checked his watch. It was nearly five o'clock. 'Got it?'

The constable nodded.

'Then go,' said Brooke. 'And don't run.' Rule number one for constables: never run unless there is a clear opportunity to save life. The sight of a running policeman simply invites public panic.

Brooke, in plain clothes, was under no such

embargo. He ran over the railway bridge to Romsey Town, heading north, zigzagging, until a bleak common opened up, the river in the distance. The access lane into the rail yards had an iron gate, but it was open, an armoured car parked across the way. Brooke showed his warrant card. The army driver had heard the blasts and driven his CO to the spot. Brooke ran on, past rail sheds and cranes, heading for a signal box, where a light showed.

Climbing the steps, he looked out over the yards. The rails glittered, but there were no flames, and only a small amount of drifting smoke. The snowfield appeared untouched. In the distance he could see the tail lights of a goods wagon, and beyond it a whole train, stretching away into the dark.

Inside the box an army captain was on a telephone line, while the signalman was setting out a ground plan of the yards on a map table. Overhead they heard a plane executing a low fly-past. The captain, slamming down the phone, nodded at Brooke's warrant card and told everyone to stand by, before he switched off the interior light, plunging them all into the dark.

'Patience, gentlemen, I've ordered up some celestial light,' he said, and they saw a match flare as he lit himself a cigarette. 'Maybe best outside,' he added, pushing open a far door onto an observation platform above the main line.

A minute passed during which they could hear a great deal of activity, lit by handheld torches, as groups of men picked their way across the yard below.

The first searchlight came on with a bass-note *thrum*.

Soon three lights revealed the scene, each one operating from the back of an army truck. Brooke's eye went first to a stricken steam locomotive, two hundred tons of brass and steel and iron, lying on its side less than fifty yards from the signal box, not on the mainline, but to one side. Steam leaked from fractured pipes. It lay in a round pit, a turntable used to reverse the direction of engines or switch them from the north — south lines to the east — west. The central swing bridge, from which the train had toppled, was a mangled wreck of steel at its pivotal point. From the train cab a man waved a cap. For the first time they saw a flicker of flame, possibly from the trains own firebox.

A man in a well-cut overcoat with a fur collar joined them, introducing himself to the captain as the district engineer for the GER, the Great Eastern Railway.

'Christ,' he said, surveying the scene. 'They knew what they were up to. A bomb?'

'Yes,' replied the captain. 'Laid in the pit at the pivotal point. Wouldn't have had to be that big, but the timing was perfect. The loco was on the bridge. Second bang was her falling off. Question is — do we have to fix it? Second question — if we do, how long will it take?'

'Any casualties?' asked Brooke.

The captain shook his head.

Back inside the signal box it took the engineer ten minutes to answer the captain's questions. The turntable had to be fixed. Cambridge had

248

no other means of efficiently controlling the munitions trains which were ferrying arms to the East Coast ports. There was no Y junction allowing a train to execute a three-point turn, there was no balloon loop allowing a stately circular turn, although there was one twenty miles north at Ely. To use that would add hours to timetables, but it was the only quick fix. The turntable needed reconstructing. It might be done in three months.

Brooke had heard enough.

'You said the blast was perfectly timed. That could only be done by eye?'

The captain nodded, looking at Brooke for the first time. 'Yes — line of sight. You're right, of course. Unless they were just plain lucky. But it doesn't look lucky, does it? It looks like someone smart worked it out.'

Brooke heard dogs barking. 'They're searching the yards?' he asked.

'Yes. They keep dogs to check the trains. Who knows if they can pick up a trail.'

Brooke followed the sound of the hounds. A path led under the mainline, through a damp tunnel, and out into the fields beyond. The dogs were ahead, a pack of half a dozen, glimmering against the snow, pulling the handlers ahead. The concerted baying suggested a scent had been found.

The ground rose to the north to a line of trees, in the lee of which stood a little church his father had always called the Leper Chapel, a perfect Norman jewel swathed in a sand dune of snow so that its roofline was almost lost from sight.

Once it had been a refuge for outcasts; now the dogs were on the heels of another.

Brooke tried to run in the snow, his boots sliding left and right so that he had to study the rutted path left by the men. When he looked up he was surprised to see them coming back, led by a large man in a railway guard's uniform, a shirt open at the throat as if out with his dogs on a summer's evening.

Brooke showed his warrant card.

'Nothing to see,' said the guard. 'Footprints run out down by the road. Then there's tyre marks. He'd have needed wheels to haul the bomb this close. It was a hell of a blast. Even then, he can't be a weakling.'

Brooke thanked them and walked on. The path led to the road, perfectly covered in a shroud of snow, except for the tyre marks. But the guard had missed one crucial detail. The geometry of tracks was too complex to decipher, but twenty yards up the lane the pattern was clear. There were six crisp lines, three coming in, three going out, and no double-tracks where rear wheels ran over front wheels. The narrow axle length confirmed Brooke's diagnosis: a three-wheeled van. Not unique, but difficult to hide.

42

Brooke headed for the Nile cot in his office. The couch was designated as a daybed, but while he collapsed on it when he felt his body struggling with wakefulness, it rarely rewarded him with sleep. If he really wanted oblivion he took a cell below, but tonight the whole building was a hive. Officers came and went. The chief constable had made an unprecedented second appearance, a *Cambridge News* photographer in tow. Brooke had spotted several military cars in the station yard below. So he'd retreated to the third floor and hid behind the slatted blinds, feet up. Top-level discussions were taking place in Carnegie-Brown's office. Before he threw himself into the fray Brooke needed rest: ten minutes, a half-hour, anything. And for once the gift of sleep was his. The walk over the snowfields to the Leper Chapel had left him chilled, cold to the bone, so that the sudden institutional warmth of the Spinning House felled him like a tree.

Edison woke him with a cup of tea. Dawn was visible through the blinds.

The sergeant theatrically dropped a bunch of heavy keys onto Brooke's desk as he sipped from his own cup.

'Walsh's, the ones we got off his belt. I decided to take them into protective custody last night when you left for the hospital. It took a while, but I whittled them down quick enough: keys for the church, the school, the cottage. Which left this.' Edison held out his hand to reveal an old iron key with a crude block blade. 'The wife had left the cottage open, so I had a nose around.'

Edison coughed, the closest he would ever get to admitting a breach of regulation, let alone the law. 'Sure enough, there was a door under the stairs to a small cellar. Key worked smoothly enough, in fact it had been well oiled. Not much downstairs but a square of concrete, swept clean, and some sacks, almost empty, containing a dry, caustic powder. County's got a man they use from the university, he'll give us chapter and verse, but I took a handful down to a chemist I know with a shop in Chettisham. He was a bit sleepy, but he'd no doubt: potassium chloride. If we're talking Paxo, this stuff is the sage to go with the onion and the salt. A lethal combination.'

Edison sat down with a satisfied sigh.

'And its all gone?' asked Brooke.

'But for a few grains. I reckon the rest went to blow this locomotive off its rails. That'll be Smith's work.'

'Walsh was an accomplice,' said Brooke, shaking his head. 'Hardly your desperate Fenian hero, is he?'

'Takes all sorts.'

Brooke told Edison to rest, while he fetched fresh tea from the canteen. In an eloquent gesture of commendation, he added biscuits.

The repercussions of the discovery were clear to them both, but Brooke, on his feet at the window, spelt them out nonetheless.

'So Walsh is part of the cell — either by free choice or, more likely, coercion. The bomb factory's in his cellar, which begs the question: how much did the wife know? Or suspect. The arrival of young Sean threatens to expose Walsh, which puts them all at risk at a vital moment, not least in that it would wipe out their hold over Walsh. The child dies. How? That, we still don't know. Walsh will talk, when he can, because there's nothing left to hide. But he may not know it all.'

Edison fled to the sergeants' room to check on the hunt for Joe Smith. Brooke checked with Addenbrooke's by phone on the condition of the head teacher. Liam Walsh had been sedated and would be asleep or unconscious for at least six hours, possibly more. There was concern about the strength of his heart. When Brooke got off the line the girl on switchboard informed him that the detective chief inspector wished to see him in her office. The exact phrase was one of Carnegie-Brown's most chilling: *At your earliest convenience.*

She greeted him with a nod to the empty chair in front of her impressive desk. She'd spent an hour with the chief constable, a former military officer and a newly ennobled peer, and there was an air of suppressed irritation in her manner.

'Smoke if you wish,' she said, producing a silver box, neatly filled with her chosen brand, and a tartan lighter.

'To some extent we can relax,' she added, after a lungful of nicotine. 'It's the judgement of the military at Madingley, but most importantly Scotland Yard, that our bomber will have moved on. So far in this campaign each cell has delivered a *maximum* of two explosions. The bad news is this second bomb is conspicuously more sophisticated than its predecessors. The Home Office have issued a D-notice, so it won't make the papers, not this year at least. There will be a sweep of known IRA sympathisers in Liverpool, Birmingham, West London, Glasgow. There is a — '

She slipped on a pair of glasses and checked a note on her blotter.

'There is a 'total determination' to limit the S-Plan's effectiveness. But as I say, the caravan has moved on, largely in pursuit of Smith. We are left with the job of clearing up the local cell — and making sure Smith is not still in the city. Which, frankly, is extremely unlikely. Especially if, as you report, he has access to a vehicle. This man Walsh sounds like a local recruit. So he won't know anything of any real import.'

'He may know who killed the child.'

'Indeed. But the priority is Smith, Brooke. He may be a senior figure in the S-Plan, despite his age. Or because of it. So if we can find him we must. This vehicle?'

Brooke filled her in on the three-wheeler.

'It's too conspicuous parked on the street,' said Brooke. 'So there's a garage somewhere. We're on to it now, ma'am.'

'I see. Keep me up to date. Then we need to move on.'

She flipped a file closed and opened another.

'Which brings us to the royal visit. Downing Street were reviewing the schedule, but I suspect there will be a determination not to be intimidated. If the railway bomb stays out of the papers, off the radio, why cancel a VIP visit to our fair city? You can see the logic. So liaise with County Brooke. We need the security to be watertight. I'm told a thaw is coming too, so the football match is very much the highlight of the day. The prince is apparently looking forward to the game keenly. His safety is our duty. I'm sure I can rely on you.'

43

Brooke spent a day at his desk, largely putting in place the final details for the visit of HRH Prince Henry, as directed, and liaising with the Home Office on border checks for the runaway caretaker. A package containing Smith's mug-shot was to be shipped to officials on the Isle of Man, to complement those circulated to the ports. All the major rail companies were asked to keep watch at main stations, especially at terminals in London and Glasgow.

Brooke made regular calls to Addenbrooke's, but Walsh was still too ill, or drugged, to speak. His wife had not left his side. If they couldn't tackle Walsh soon, and the dutiful Kathleen, they'd have to get answers elsewhere. What did the parish priest and his housekeeper know of Walsh's secret, and Smith's for that matter? Had they been reluctant accomplices? Brooke placed a radio car at the church to keep a round-the-clock watch on the scene. He didn't want another bird to fly.

He caught up with Edison at the counter of the British Restaurant, a government-run canteen round the corner, which served up hearty meals. Over their heads, largely unseen by the workers eating below, stretched a fine plaster ceiling depicting pincers and compasses in trompe l'oeil, evidence of the building's former life as a Masonic hall. The setting gave the menu a slight lift. Over meat (unspecified) and two veg (examined by Edison with all the dignity of a veteran of the allotment), they discussed the chances of tracking down Smith's three-wheeler.

Edison had not been idle. The maintenance of three-wheelers was in some respects a specialist task. The engine, and its fuel mix of petrol and oil, were essentially those of a motorcycle. There were six garages in the town which offered the expertise, although any petrol pump could be used for fuel as long as the garage could provide two-stroke oil for the mixture in the tank, although some drivers carried their own supply.

They split the list of a dozen in half and went their separate ways.

Outside it was cold, but not bitter. Carnegie-Brown was right, a cool thaw was in the air, a tonic after hours in the fetid office. The first garage owner recalled no three-wheelers at all. The popular 'handyman's van' required little maintenance, Brooke was told, which was why it was used by several small businesses in town. Most owners were motorbike enthusiasts who could undertake maintenance work in-house at much reduced costs. In fact, such was the fascination with the two-stroke engine, most preferred to do it themselves.

'Frankly, it's more difficult to stop the sodding engine than start it. They're bloody marvellous,' said the first garage owner. 'So we don't see hide nor hair, 'cept for fuel.'

Brooke strode on, an early sunset leaving the roadside snowdrifts splashed with orange and gold. The second garage operator had two or three regular customers, but none had an Irish accent or an East End accent. Ditto garages three, four and five.

The Crossways Garage stood on the old coast road a mile north of the Upper Town. A bleak stretch of single carriageway ran into the distance towards the Fens. The owner offered Brooke tea, as he said he looked tired and desperate, and his own son was a constable in London, although he'd be called up soon enough. He had four three-wheeler owners on his regular books, but none of them fitted any aspect of the description Brooke offered, and were otherwise forgettable.

'You get the odd one-off customer, a course,' he added. 'I had one a month ago, less. Thought he was a Yank and I said so and he just laughed. You see 'em about a lot now — you noticed? Pilots I reckon, checking out the air bases. If it kicks off perhaps they'll come to the rescue, eh?

'He came in the once, as I say. The brake cables had gone and that's a terrible job, 'cause they rust inside the plastic coating. You have to drag 'em out. So I did. He helped, actually. So we had a bit of a chat. Nice bloke. Don't recall anything about the van — sorry.' He shrugged. 'He never came back.'

Brooke gazed into the small stove. Outside the light was almost gone.

The owner lit a pipe. 'I *saw* him again, mind. Least I think I did. It's a small town. I was down by the Old Ferry, you know it?'

Brooke nodded. It was the inn at the foot of Pound Hill, a hundred yards from Honey Hill.

258

'I saw him opposite on foot, coming out of a lane there that goes down to the river, the back of the colleges. I remember alright, because we passed in the street and he cut me dead, but he'd been as nice as you like when he wanted something done.'

It took Brooke twenty minutes to reach the spot.

The pub was open, with two great fires alight, and working men clustered round both at the end of the day.

He sat at a bay window with a half-pint watching the world go by. It was a busy street at going-home time, the pavements treacherous, slushy and wet, dusk falling. The lane opposite was a narrow alley, no wider than a standard car, snaking off between shops. Watching for twenty minutes, nobody left, nobody came.

After half an hour he crossed the road and walked down the little street. That day's fresh snowfall was soft. Meltwater gurgled in drain-pipes. At the bottom of the track there was a large medieval barn-like building, with carved stone lintels, and a once-grand arched doorway. Beyond it, across a meadow, was St John's College. A small slate sign had been etched with the address:

The School of Pythagoras

Up close, Brooke could see that the building was almost derelict, although the roof was sound. A set of double doors led into the 'barn' end, and these were held fast by a padlock and a heavy chain. Over this doorway was a small shelter, made of tin, which had been latched onto the old stonework, to offer some protection for the archway. Across the snow beneath ran the ghost of three parallel tyre marks.

44

Brooke set out at a striding pace for his old college, over the Great Bridge, and through Bridgetown beyond, where shop window lights were reflected in the icy street. Darkness was freezing the tentative thaw. Under the shadow of the tower of St John's he turned away into the old ghetto. Here the snow had gone from the narrow alleyways, but the damp stones were glassed with ice, so that his brogues skidded and skimmed, and he had to use both hands to brace himself between the narrowing walls. At Michaelhouse he didn't need to use his signet ring to deliver the coded knock, for the door stood open, students tumbling in, heading for open fires and dinner.

Doric, signing in a visitor, must have just come on duty, because he still wore the black coat and bowler hat provided by the college. Brooke stepped past and into the panelled room beyond without a word, until, out of sight, he took the seat within the chimney breast beside the glowing coals. This room, which he'd admired as an undergraduate, had the weathered, polished patina of a ship's cabin. The juxtaposition of the busy front counter and this hidden bolthole was deeply comforting.

The porter, free of visitors, joined him.

'Freezing, but the river's lost its ice,' said Doric, taking off the bowler and setting it delicately on a brass hook, but leaving on the greatcoat. Standing before the fire he executed a kind of stationary march, alternatively lifting his feet an inch or two and then setting them down again. Brooke imagined this habit had come from standing sentry in the dark cold nights in the Cape or the Transvaal.

'I need your help,' said Brooke. 'Do you know the night porter at St John's?'

Not only did he know him, he knew of the School of Pythagoras.

'They rent it out, Mr Brooke, and it's no end of trouble, that's what Griffiths says — he's my oppo. Always grumbling he is, because the tenants don't pay up one week, then they're off the next. Which is a shame, he says, because one of the fellows, a historian, insists it's the oldest house in the county — let alone the city. Older than the *university*, Mr Brooke.' Doric paused for effect. 'Never was a school neither, and nothing to do with this Pythagoras.'

Doric's fingers fluttered. 'He says the family that built it sold it to a college in Oxford of all places, and they sent students there as a retreat. Perhaps some of 'em were mathematicians, that might explain it.'

It was a long speech, and Doric seemed exhausted, so he shrugged off the coat and took a chair, set to one side, from which he could see the counter. Again, his feet began to shuffle, as if he was at the paddles of the college organ.

'It's the present tenant I'm after,' said Brooke. 'Do me a favour, Doric. Ring this Griffiths, tell him that a constable will call to pick up the keys.

262

I need to conduct a search and leave a watchman. Tell him to keep it all under his hat.'

In the end, Brooke went himself, unable to set aside his curiosity. The porter gave over the key with a brief nod, having been forewarned by a call from Doric. According to the records the current tenant was a farmer named Jackson, with an address in the Fens, near Chatteris. Brooke worked his way through the college's old courts, then over the Bridge of Sighs, to the Victorian buildings. Beyond that lay the old barn. It stood looking across a wide field upon which had been built several snowmen, two with college scarves, all of them frozen now, but slumped slightly, waiting for the thaw to begin again the next day.

The door was half a foot thick and opened on oiled hinges, the key turning with ease.

The interior was damp, the air heavy with the smell of petrol. A three-wheel van stood on straw, dripping melted snow and ice. The interior, viewed through a glass panel in the back door, was empty. Removing a glove, he touched the bonnet: stone cold. The building's medieval walls blocked out entirely the sounds of the city, but he could just hear the mice in the walls and possibly something larger in a pile of old sacks in one corner. He thought of PC Collins: had he discovered the tyre tracks at Silver Street Bridge and followed them here? Had Smith been lying in wait? Brooke searched the three ground-floor rooms but found no trace. At either end of the building, ladders rose up to lofts. One held firewood, the other was empty, except for a couple of horse blankets rolled up as a sleeping

263

bag. A single slate had been used as an ashtray, crowded with butts. Set against the wall was the black and white framed picture of the happy family on a windswept beach, which he'd seen hanging above Smith's cellar stove at St Alban's.

Brooke locked up. He'd have a watchman set in an unmarked car at the top of the lane. If Smith came back they'd have their man.

45

The sister on Liam Walsh's ward at Addenbrooke's Hospital told Brooke to come back the next day. 'The man's very poorly still, Inspector. His heart. The doctors are very worried. The wife's with him — she's sick to death.' They were standing outside the doors to the ward itself, and as they opened Brooke saw the ranks of bedsteads, the screens around one. Turning up in person made him feel like a vulture, but time was pressing.

'I wouldn't ask if it wasn't a matter of life and death,' he said. 'It may be he knows information which could prevent further outrages, Sister. You know as well as I what happened in Coventry. Five dead. We don't want that on the streets of the next place they choose. Norwich, Peterborough, Lynn. Who knows?'

The nurse sighed. 'I'll ring the station for you, how's that? As soon as he's strong enough. There's no point now. The man's out cold. Delirious too.'

Brooke knew the sister well. Her name was Heggarty, but he'd never noted her accent until now, softer than Belfast, softer even than Dublin, redolent of the far west of Ireland. But it had come to this, that now he *did* notice, and that was the shame of it. She ushered him gently towards the stairs and the exit. 'There's a constable by his bed. All's safe and sound. Mrs

Brooke's busy on her own ward, and your daughter's doing a fine job. You need to stop haunting the place. Go home.'

Instead, Brooke walked back to the Spinning House.

Uniformed branch had placed a constable in a car outside the School of Pythagoras. A twenty-four-hour rota had been agreed. The duty sergeant had a note for Brooke, newly delivered by a bicycle messenger. The handwriting was neat and controlled, instantly recognisable as that of his former roommate and now constant scientist, Peter Aldiss. He read it quickly, lit a Black Russian and read it again. He'd asked him to find out what he could about the Galton Society, and he'd done a thorough job. The results were disturbing.

He found Edison in the mess room, quietly drinking tea from a spectacularly large tin mug that required both the sergeant's large fleshy hands to hold it to his lips. Starting, he put the bucket down. 'Sir. Yes — a vice. I've got a two-pint one at the shed and I find it warming. Mrs Edison says I should pack it in. She says tannic poisoning is a bad way to go.'

Brooke offered him a cigarette, and tentatively he took one.

'I'm a pipe man really, but I don't mind.' He leant forward and took a light, the gold ringlet of paper bubbling. They sat in silence for a minute.

'What next?' asked Edison, eventually.

'The priest,' said Brooke. 'Walsh is too ill. We can't just sit around and wait.'

'Now?'

'Yes. But I can go alone. Go home, see Mrs Edison. Before you do, one favour.'

Brooke produced the note from Aldiss. 'This is worrying me. The factory manager at Newton's is a man by the name of Rafe Forbes. A university man — mathematics, I think. He either inherited money or married it. Lives out at Newmarket. Anyway, when I met him at the factory, the day after the bomb blast, he was wearing a badge, a silver moon engraved with the letter G, in blue. It's a society; Cambridge is full of them, isn't it, as if it isn't an exclusive club in its own right. The Galton Society. I asked an old friend to find out more. Turns out it is a very unpleasant club indeed, Edison. At first it was just about science. But as the years have gone on, they've developed a very specific interest. They are obsessed with selective breeding.'

Edison expelled some cigarette smoke. 'Newmarket's a good place for that, sir. The studs. If he's smart with the maths perhaps he won his money at the bookmaker's. If he did he's one in a million.'

'Yes. Perhaps that's it. But this isn't just bloodstock, Edison. This isn't horses, it's people. They want to weed out the weak, the deformed, the simple-minded. They called it eugenics. Discredited here now, but Aldiss says there's a department in Berlin which practises this new 'science'.' He put as much irony into the last word as he could muster. 'The Nazis are impatient with natural selection, Edison. They're killing people, the retarded, the disabled, criminals, deviants — making the race purer. It's

267

been going on for years. It's sullied the reputation of the whole discipline here, as I say, but clearly the real enthusiasts are keeping the flame alive, right here, in Cambridge.

'It'll all be talk, but it's dangerous talk. It makes me wonder about Forbes, and about the bomb attack. Is it all it seems? And there's the missing RADAR unit. Has it really been whisked out of a locked building? I'll call on Forbes tomorrow. But as I say, a favour first.' Brooke started copying out a name. 'Apparently this man is the society secretary. He's at St Benet's. A don. If he's not there, there's a home address. Track him down, Edison. I want a list of the current members. All of them. Don't take no for an answer. If you have to put him on a charge and march him back to the cells, do it. I want that list.'

46

The church of St Alban's was icy cold. Clearly, the caretaker's flight had left nobody to man the boilers, and the few candles remaining were unable to lift the temperature, or the shadowy gloom. Three parishioners sat ready for the confessional box, while at the altar rail another mumbled penance, the gentle clack of the rosary beads the only noise. Mrs Aitken, on the priest's doorstep, had directed Brooke to the church. The confessional hour had only just begun, so the detective would have to wait.

'Any news?' she'd asked. 'We've not seen Kathleen at all. She must be at the hospital.'

She'd held the door open just a few inches, as if worried Brooke would glimpse some secret within. The corridor beyond looked institutional, with worn lino and a long coat rack. A framed photograph of the new pope — Pius XII — stared back at him from the depths of the shadows by the stairs.

Brooke relayed the latest bulletin on Walsh. The head teacher was still unconscious. There were concerns about his heart.

'He's in my prayers,' she said, closing the door.

Taking a pew in the church, Brooke watched the devotions of the penitents with detached curiosity. It wasn't that Brooke had no faith of his own, just that in his daily life he found the existence of a God of little practical help. He'd always suspected his father had been privately agnostic, a position which, for a scientist, meant the subject was of no practical concern. Professor Brooke had spent his life trying to find cures for childhood illnesses, a mission which had been spectacularly successful. They'd given him a Nobel Prize. To a limited extent his father was God.

In the flickering half-light he dispensed with his glasses.

A woman left the confessional box and knelt at the altar rail. Her replacement slipped into the shadow vacated, pulling across the worn black curtain.

Brooke was left to continue his own form of thought-prayer.

Joining the Borough, on his return from the desert, had offered an opportunity to tilt the world towards light, and away from the darkness, even by small fractions of a degree. And even then, in those early years, the darkness seemed to be edging closer and deepening. The modest ambit of the Borough embraced many crimes. He'd discovered that some of these crimes were on the statute book, and some were not. And now, Brooke had encountered a man — men — capable of the callous murder of a child, the reckless killing of innocent men and women on the street, the cowardly employment of the disembodied bomb. He still had little time for God, but he was beginning to realise that evil might prove a more tangible entity.

The last penitent left the confessional. Above

the box a red light continued to shine.

Brooke slipped past the curtain and into the shadowed cubicle. An embroidered screen revealed Father Ward's head in silhouette.

There was an awkward silence. 'Father,' said Brooke, speaking quickly. 'There's little time. I'm waiting to speak to Liam Walsh. Tonight perhaps, or tomorrow. Now I know his secret, he has nothing to fear in telling the truth.'

The priest's face edged closer to the screen, so that an eye caught the light.

'I know you can't reveal what he said in confession, Father. But that's a narrow restriction surely, in a community such as this. Keeping the truth from Mary Walsh must have been the result of a very fine moral calculation. She knows now, of course, that her husband has a wife in London, and that Sean was his child, and that in some way he connived at his murder.'

Ward set a splayed hand against the screen. 'He was innocent of the crime. I can say that from my heart.'

'But you knew his secret?'

Ward said nothing. The sour smell of human sweat filled the box, only partly disguised by polish.

'At some point, Father, we'll be having this conversation at the Spinning House. I'd think very carefully about what you can and can't say. I mean to find the killer and you'll not stand in my way.'

'I can't speak.'

'Is that because they knew your secret too? Is it still a scandal in this day and age — the

271

housekeeper? A blind eye was turned here, I'm sure. And the children are not to know. But what if the bishop was told?'

'Marie is a widow.'

'That carries the day with the bishop, does it?'

There was a sharp intake of breath on the far side of the patterned screen,

'Her husband died in the fighting in Belfast in 1921,' he said, the tone implying a long-rehearsed defence. 'Shot in the back. There was a boy, but he left home, so she's alone, Brooke. She came here to leave the memory behind. When the street fighting was over she went out to look for her husband, a good man, and found him in the gutter. He'd bled to death, and the blood had gone down the drain. She has to live with that every day of her life.'

'And Walsh, and Hendrie and Smith? How much of their story do you know?'

'Too much.'

Brooke heard the rustle of the priest's cassock as he shifted on his seat.

'Liam is a troubled man. Now you know why. The others had a hold on him. Perhaps they knew his secret, as they knew mine. The confessional gave them no relief, for they said not a word — certainly not a word about bombs and killing. They demanded silence, and we kept quiet. That was all.'

And there it was: an admission of guilt at last.

'Who will you confess that sin to, Father?'

In the silence they heard the church door bang open, and voices on the nearby pews.

'Liam was a reluctant recruit, Brooke,' said

Ward. 'A man who believed in his country. In Dublin he'd followed his calling, to teach. His subject was chemistry. A fascination with the way the world works. At the time of the Easter Rising they asked him to make explosives. To devise fuses. Men died — and women, and children. For that he made his confession. Then he fled to London and a new life, and fell in love, and was cheated upon, and so he came here. He found love again and took his chance. But they found him, Smith found him, and recruited Hendrie. The intellectuals lead, the peasants fight. Hendrie was the infantry, a willing soldier. Walsh, blackmailed into bomb-making. Smith was the High Command.' The priest put his hand to the screen. 'And, Brooke, you should know this: Smith has a gun. He'd polish it by the fire in the cellar. As an act of intimidation it was extraordinarily effective.'

Brooke sat in silence, thinking through the implications of their runaway killer being armed.

'And your sins, Father?' he said, finally.

Ward bowed his head.

'They had a hold over you. Was silence their only price? They spirited the child from the church, down into Smith's basement. Did they need help that night?'

'Never. No. How could you think such a thing? I slept that night. My hands are clean.'

'Do you know where he is?'

'No.'

Brooke stood. 'Tomorrow, Father. At the Spinning House this time. Nine o'clock.'

Brooke slipped out of the confessional,

273

nodding to a woman who had been waiting, and walked away, up the nave and out of the door, so that he never saw the look of surprise on her face that, despite such a lengthy confession, he'd escaped without the need for a single moment of penance.

47

A Borough radio car was parked in the darkness of the playground outside St Alban's. Liam Walsh had regained consciousness, according to the uniformed driver, and had asked to speak to Brooke, despite the advice of doctors to rest. The interview would go ahead, but a nurse must be present: Sister Heggarty would meet him at the doors of Addenbrooke's at ten o'clock. He had fifteen minutes with the patient, no more.

As they drove through the city, cloaked in a mist, Brooke forced himself to concentrate on the coming encounter. Ward's studied confession had thrown a new light on the little community that was St Alban's. The cell — Smith, Hendrie and the reluctant Walsh — had thrived in an atmosphere of secrets and thinly veiled blackmail. That much was plain.

So much was still hidden. Who had decided Sean must die — and why? Who had struck the fatal blow? Where was Smith, and the elusive bomb factory?

In the passenger seat, using the radio, Brooke got the latest from the Spinning House. There was still no definite news on Smith's whereabouts, although a man answering his description had been seen alighting from a train at March, a small fen town to the north, where he'd been picked up by a motor car. He had been carrying a suitcase. The thought that the caretaker, surely the likeliest suspect for the child's murder, had slipped away, and might even now be close to one of the Irish ferry ports, made Brooke feel a weary sickness.

There was a further bulletin from Carnegie-Brown. After a brief conversation with the Home Office, uniformed branch were to make a second search of St Alban's in the morning — the church and the school — for any sign of the missing RADAR unit from Newton's factory. Brooke sent a message back, suggesting they include the head teacher's cottage and the presbytery. It might all be in vain; the suspect spotted at March could have been carrying the stolen unit in his suitcase.

The car dropped him at the hospital, and Sister Heggarty escorted him up to the ward.

Liam Walsh was awake, the window ajar to admit the misty air and relieve the thudding heat maintained throughout the building's five floors. The patient was oddly upbeat, certainly in comparison to the shambling, uncertain figure he'd presented to Brooke in the schoolyard and the classroom. Drinking tea, he even summoned a shy smile. The burden of his secret, once crushing, had been lifted. The constable withdrew, but not before presenting — from his notebook — a list of visitors that day: Kathleen Walsh; Marie Aitken; one of the other teachers, an elderly man called Fisher; and Kathleen Walsh again.

The second visit by the wife seemed particularly significant. It suggested reconciliation at best, a retreat from outright rejection at worst. Perhaps, after several days of extreme stress, this explained Walsh's almost buoyant mood. Brooke hoped his heart would cope with the questions he must face, and answer.

Sister Heggarty took a seat, set back against the screen.

Brooke had prepared his opening line.

'Did you have anything to do with the murder of your son, Mr Walsh?'

He'd no doubt been expecting the blow, but Brooke could see the nervous jolt nevertheless. He reminded himself that this man had tied a length of rope around his own neck less than twelve hours ago. The livid marks were still visible, a purple noose of bruising. But Brooke had only fifteen minutes, and he could hear doctors whispering outside, hovering beyond the screen.

'No,' he said, but his voice was thin and tense.

Sister Heggarty shifted in her seat.

Walsh had no doubt prepared his story, and he told it well.

He'd fled to Cambridge when his marriage had collapsed. He missed his son, every single day, but he thought it had been best for the boy to be with his mother. His proposal to Kathleen was, in his words, an error of judgement. In the chaos of war, he had convinced himself that the family they planned would have been left to build a life of its own.

'I should have told her the truth,' he said. 'It was a betrayal, and a selfish one at that. I can't imagine how she's found it in herself to forgive me. But all I had to do was stay silent — do you

277

see? I wasn't strong enough to resist the temptation. I let time pass. I let us fall in love. I didn't speak up. I'm sorry. I'm sorry.'

He closed his eyes and they waited patiently.

Finally, he took up the story again.

'Lying is a terrible burden,' he said. 'In the end I had to tell others.'

St Alban's had become a refuge. In Colm Hendrie he found a friend, and the big Irishman was close to Smith, the young caretaker. Over midnight whiskies beside the cellar boiler they'd swapped secrets. They'd affirmed their sympathies with the Republican cause. Stupidly, he'd shared details of his former life in London, and — courting friendship perhaps — had revealed his role as a bomb-maker during the Easter Rising. They asked him to join their cell, talking of their determination to play their part in the IRA's S-Plan. His refusal was countered by a less than subtle hint that he had little choice, if he wished to preserve a life with Kathleen and their yet-to-be-born child. The trap was sprung.

'They said I'd to help. That it was for a just cause and there would be no deaths. None. They promised.'

His role was limited to chemistry: he had to store the chemicals, mix the explosive charge and set the fuse. The factory was in his basement, but Kathleen was often at school, following a strict timetable, and so the secret was easy to keep. His wife knew nothing.

The dates for the bomb attacks were fixed, along with further assurances that no casualties were planned, but the targets were a secret Smith kept alone. Then, with days to go before the first blast, the paperwork from the diocese in Shepherd's Bush showed that Sean Flynn would soon be a pupil at St Alban's.

'I told them I'd ride my luck,' said Walsh. 'I hadn't seen the boy for nearly three years. I wasn't even sure he knew I existed. When his mother visited, I could disappear. I said I'd deal with it. They said they'd deal with it. The boy would be taken somewhere safe until the targets had been hit.'

Walsh's eyes had flooded, and he leant over, throwing the window wider and watching the white streaks in the light, the wet snow falling.

Brooke shook his head. 'But when you found Sean had gone . . . When we found his body . . . '

Walsh held his head in both hands. 'I found Smith in the cellar. He said they'd planned to keep the boy safe, that there'd been an accident. But we were to keep to the plan. I still had a lot to lose,' he said. 'Kathleen, my job, the child to come. He said I'd to lie low. I couldn't bring him back to life, could I?' The blood had rushed to his face, and his hands were shaking violently.

Sister Heggarty stood, checking her fob watch.

'There's worse,' said Walsh. 'They knew I had a picture of Mary. I'd shown them once, by the fire in the cellar: the woman I'd left behind. They took it from me. Joe gave it to Colm and said it was 'insurance'. If she came to Cambridge they'd have to look after her too. Colm wouldn't have touched her. But Joe.' He shook his head. 'I couldn't *do* anything.'

Brooke met the plaintive tone with silence.

Sister Heggarty tapped her watch, catching Brooke's eye.

'The priest, the housekeeper, were they involved?'

'Not directly. Smith knew their secret. It was enough to buy their silence, nothing more.'

'We've found the van, but Smith is on the run,' said Brooke. 'Did he say where they'd hidden the RADAR unit they stole from Newton's? That's crucial, Liam: we must try and stop them getting it back to Ireland, or worse, to Germany.'

Walsh sat up, eyes wide. 'No, no. The factory bomb's not us, Brooke. No way. The turntable — that's a direct order from Dublin. That was to be the first. The second's still to come.'

They'd set a pitcher of water and some glasses beside the patient's bed. Brooke felt nauseous, as if the room was spinning. So he poured himself a drink, and let the cold water slip down his throat.

'The IRA left a slogan at the site of the bomb, Liam. It was a Republican bomb.'

'No — well not us, Brooke. Smith was adamant: Dublin runs the S-Plan and there was only one cell in the city. He said the factory bomb meant someone was covering their tracks, using us as a blind. He said it was perfect, a real lucky break, because nobody would be ready for the second attack.'

48

The news that the IRA had the potential to strike again in the city transformed the investigation. Despite the late hour Brooke briefed the chief constable and the superintendent by telephone. Until they had Smith under lock and key, all leave was cancelled, while the Boroughs meagre force was immediately supplemented by uniformed constables from County, marched down Castle Hill and detailed to guard key targets: Marshall's airfield fuel depot, the Great Bridge, King's College Chapel and several factories engaged in work for the War Office. Carnegie-Brown, whose flat was less than a minute's walk away, appeared promptly, only to be embroiled in tense conversations with Special Branch and the Home Office. The prime minister, it emerged, was being briefed on developments. At Abbey Depot the Royal Engineers had arrived in force to assist railway labourers in trying to remove the stricken engine and start work on the turntable beneath. Meanwhile, vital munitions trains were being rerouted via Ely. Discreet surveillance of the School of Pythagoras was allotted additional manpower. Brooke rang St James's Palace, with his superior's imprimatur, to make a final request for the royal visit to be postponed. He had little hope of success.

Just after midnight Brooke descended to the duty desk and checked for messages. Edison, leaving the Wasp, engine running, at the kerb outside, appeared with the promised full list of members of the Galton Society.

'The desk rang,' he said. 'Thought you'd want this as soon as . . . Besides, they need all hands.' He handed Brooke the slip of paper: 'Talk about getting blood out of a stone. I said I'd take the request to the master of Benet's unless I got the list — that did the trick. He swears that's the lot: all current members of the Galton Society. I'm off to relieve the radio car at the School of Pythagoras.' He executed a smart salute and fled.

Brooke read the list there and then. Twice. A single name, halfway down, caught his eye immediately. In five syllables it changed everything. The twists and turns in the current inquiry were Byzantine. Retrieving his cigarettes, he checked the station clock and went outside to smoke. It was the dead of night: what could he do? In the morning he'd make enquiries, set in motion an entirely new investigation. But for now, he was left with action. Personal action.

Back in his office he got out the file on the Newton factory bombing and made a note of the key witness's address. He set off north, down to the river, along the towpath. A brisk mile and a half took him past Jesus Lock, white with cascading water, over Newton's Bridge and then out to the watery fen edges of the city, where the river was wide. The thaw had unlocked the river, black water sweeping past towards the distant sea. The dead arctic air had given way to something greener and softer: the first hint of a real thaw, even a distant glimpse of spring.

The mooring was opposite Coldham's Common, the site of the city's once-great medieval fair. A fog drifted here over flooded water meadows. Posts, driven into the bank, marked a line of moorings, each with a wooden landing stage. Six were full, one boat still lit up, a man smoking, sitting in a chair on the low roof.

Berth number seven was empty.

'Can't sleep,' offered the boat owner, shaking his head.

'I'm looking for the narrowboat *Elsie*,' said Brooke. 'I'm with the Borough.'

'She left at dusk,' offered the lone smoker. 'I told her to wait for the light, but she's not a woman who takes advice. As soon as the ice broke up she was gone.'

49

Brooke sat in Rafe Forbes's office looking out at the distant river, a pale luminous presence in the still lingering mist of morning. The shadows of barges crossed in midstream. On the opposite bank the chimney of the waterworks at Barnwell belched steam into the sky, childish white puffs, until they began to discolour with the gritty purple-black of coal dust. In the distance he could hear — or even feel — the pounding of the great engines, the pistons driving, pumping water to the city's taps. By comparison the noises of the factory were delicate and discreet, a drill bit whirring somewhere, the gentle trundle of the production lines, the constant single-note hum on the air of electrical power.

Forbes had seemed startled to see the inspector, parking him in his office with the sleeping Great Dane, while he dealt with an urgent matter down on the shop floor. Brooke, smoking, was grateful for the moment of reflection. Scotland Yard and Downing Street had rung to inform the Borough that the planned visit by Prince Henry would proceed. A patrician civil servant had relayed a brief sense of the thinking behind the decision: 'The Cabinet feels that the machinations of Irish ingrates should not be allowed to unsettle, in any way, the smooth workings of the Court of St James.' Brooke took the civil servant's name, always an act of mild insubordination, and remarked that he hoped the Cabinet's decision would stand the test of time.

The prince's visit was tomorrow. Brooke couldn't shift the uncomfortable feeling that the inquiry was running out of time. And now it had taken an unpredictable turn.

Forbes came back, a cup and saucer in his hand, a clipboard under his arm.

'Sorry about that. Everyone's under pressure and there was a hitch on the main production line. It's sorted out now. Good news, because the boys at Bawdsey are keen to get on. Who knows when Jerry will come.'

He patted the dog's huge head under the desk.

Brooke explained the essence of Liam Walsh's confession. 'The implications are clear. The IRA didn't plant the bomb. The modest blast was a diversionary tactic which, it has to be said, worked very well. Their sole aim was to steal the RADAR unit and focus attention on the 'Republican' bomb. I think the chief suspect has to be German agents. German agents with a set of keys.'

Forbes looked shocked. 'I can assure — '

'The Galton Society,' Brooke said. 'You're a keen member?'

Forbes straightened his tie. 'Used to be. No time now, of course. As I said, mathematics was my subject, at Caius. But you know, I like to take an interest in the wider fields. And statistics play a role.'

'We're talking about eugenics?'

Forbes laughed. 'You'd find the average meeting pretty dull, Inspector. Eugenics was once the subject of the day. No longer. As you say, the debate's moved on. But just because there's a war on doesn't mean you can't tackle the big issues. Race. The purity of the nation.'

Forbes's jawline set defiantly.

Brooke put a piece of paper on his desk.

'What's that, Brooke? More surprises?'

'It's a list of the current membership of the Galton Society. You'll note the name circled.'

Forbes retrieved his glasses from his tweed jacket pocket.

He shrugged. 'Augustine Bodart?'

'You know the woman? A professor of natural sciences at Davison College. Keen interest in hereditary patterns. Eugenics for plants.'

'We have dinners, lectures. I may have talked to her.'

'May or *did*?'

'Why the hectoring tone, Inspector?'

The dog growled under the desk.

'Because she is the woman, walking idly on the riverbank, who spotted our Fenian bombers and raised the alarm. She lives in a houseboat half a mile to the north, and reports to the Spinning House twice a week. An Austrian citizen. Eugenics may be out of favour in this country, Mr Forbes, but it is pretty much state policy in Germany.'

Forbes sat, focused — Brooke felt — on some inner turmoil.

'What if,' said Brooke, 'what if she didn't see three Irishmen leaving the scene. What if she stole the RADAR unit and set a modest explosive charge to cover her tracks, after employing an educated hand to transcribe a Fenian slogan, so that we wouldn't miss the point. She had to cut through the wire to get in, but she needed time to get the unit away, so a diversion was key. And talking of keys, she'd need a set to get into the factory and leave no trace of a break-in. Not until it was too late.' Brooke looked out at the river. 'But it doesn't all go to plan. She sees that there's a police presence along the river. A constable is approaching. My guess is she was in a tight spot, with the RADAR unit hidden under the coat. She needed to think fast. The explosion was imminent. She'd already set the bait — the fake Irish slogan. So I think she hid the unit somewhere on the towpath and then made up her story, picking the unit back up when she was allowed to walk home.'

The dog whimpered, but Forbes stilled it with a kick.

'She was interested in the dogs, in the breeding, the family lines,' said Forbes, his voice flatter, dispirited.

'So you knew her well?'

Forbes opened his desk drawer, took out a bottle of whisky and poured some into a mug.

'We had a dinner at my house — not just Augustine, the members, the Society. We take it in turns to play host. She took us to her college for formal hall. All a bit tatty if you ask me. Not a patch on Trinity.'

'Your house, you say. Just dinner?' asked Brooke.

Forbes shrugged. 'What's to tell? We walked to one of the studs nearby. A short talk on the bloodstock. Fascinating stuff, actually. I showed her the kennels at our house on the way back while the rest had sherry. She was certainly keen. I explained how it all worked. She asked some intelligent questions, about the other breeders, how we keep in contact, how the records are verified. The costs too.'

'The kennels are out in the grounds I take it?' said Brooke. 'The dogs are valuable. So — locks? Did you have to unlock them that night? At any time was she alone with the keys? A moment would be enough to gain an impression in putty.'

Forbes set his keys on the desk. A fob — a brass ring — upon which hung the factory keys alongside with the rest. He held his head in his hands.

50

An hour later, forty miles north of the Great Bridge, the lock-keeper at Denver Sluice put down the phone and checked the note he'd made, outlining precisely Inspector Brooke's description of the narrowboat *Elsie*. The vessel and its owner, an Austrian national by the name of Bodart, were missing. The narrowboat had last been seen at its moorings the day before, at dusk. RAF reconnaissance aircraft were flying over rivers and tributaries. Flood banks were being checked by local police, gamekeepers and water bailiffs.

A wooden signal box gave the lock-keeper a clear view up- and downstream. To the north the river, a ribbon at low tide, swept towards the sea through black tidal marshes, beyond which lay the North Sea, or as it appeared on many of the older charts, the German Ocean. Denver — the Great Sluice — comprised a complex of locks and gates which held back the devastating tides on one side, as well as the 'new rivers' built by the Dutch to drain the Fens on the other. The locks and barriers comprised the mechanical heart of the Fens, beating with the tides, protecting the land from floods, but letting the rivers — and their laden boats — slip back and forth between the sea and the land.

The detective inspector's orders had been brutally clear. 'It may be the *Elsie* will try to get

289

something out of the country in broad daylight. It's small, heavy, a metal box, with electronics. There'll be a woman in the narrowboat, but she may meet others. We cannot allow the *Elsie* to pass to the sea or make contact with a sea-going vessel at the sluice. We need to be vigilant.'

The lock-keeper printed out a card giving the *Elsie*'s vital statistics — length, livery and engine — and added it to the down-traffic noticeboard, adding the explicit order in capital letters: DENY PASSAGE.

The river ice was nearly gone. The army unit camped out on the bank, keeping permanent watch on the Great Sluice, had posted extra guards. If the *Elsie* appeared they were on alert to take her into custody, along with her owner. The lock-keeper went out onto the observation deck as a line of barges came into sight from Cambridge, carrying coprolite and sugar beet. Taking off his jacket he began to engage the winches necessary to raise the doors on the Big Eye, the main lock. Frozen snow still lay over the tarpaulin decks of the approaching boat. A heron, angular and still, stood on the forrard wheelhouse.

The boat slipped past, the gates closed and the lock-keeper waved a farewell to the diminishing captain, who stood at the stern. Back inside, out of the cold, he found he could not rest. Brooke's final words had been a disturbing warning. 'If the *Elsie* appears she must be stopped at all costs.'

The keeper opened the locked box below the

observation sill. It contained a pistol and a shotgun. He broke the gun over his arm and slipped in two cartridges.

51

Claire's and Joy's shift patterns ran in tandem so that this evening marked the start of three days' joint leave. They'd shopped together on Market Hill, pooling the ration cards to buy a chicken, supplemented with winter vegetables from Edison's shed, still black and dusty from the peat. At Rose's tea hut they'd ordered 'Inspector Brooke's usual' — bacon sandwiches — while Joy had swapped tales with Rose's daughter, Dawn, of pregnancy, and exotic cravings, and fussing mothers. Finally, they'd got sausage meat from the local butcher to complete the feast.

The fire had been lit, one of his father's bottles of claret opened, and Joy had bought a record on Green Street which crackled before flooding the house with the Ink Spots' latest release. The slightly forced party atmosphere even managed to survive the lyrics of 'Address Unknown.'

There had been no more news of Ben or the missing *Silverfish*. The good humour in the house was brittle, sustained by the weary maxim that no news was good news. They'd requested updates from the Admiralty, and the families of two of Ben's crewmates had been in touch to ask if they'd heard any news. But there had been none. Joy had pointedly wedged a snapshot of Ben, on the beach at Gosport, waist deep in the water, against the clock on the mantelpiece, obscuring the ticking hands behind.

Brooke opened the door to smell the food and hear the music, and for a fleeting moment thought that Rose's prediction had come true at last: a letter had arrived, or a telegram, bearing good news. One look at Claire's face told a different story. Her wide smile didn't match the dull light in her eyes. They embraced but said nothing.

After the Ink Spots, Brooke chose Beethoven, the *Emperor*, the 78 scratched and pitted but nevertheless delivering its upbeat power.

'I thought we were boycotting the Germans,' said Joy, helping her mother bring through the food, setting the chicken to one side for Brooke to carve.

'Not all of them,' he said, expertly sharpening the knife as his father had done. Claire, sipping the wine, said she'd sleep for a week once her head hit the pillow.

They talked about the thaw while they ate, that the forecast on the radio predicted an end to the cold snap within days, and that they'd missed their chance to skate after all.

Then the phone rang.

Joy was out of her seat before the second ring, her chair falling to the carpet. In the hall they heard her identify herself, and then a series of 'Yes, I see,' and 'I understand.'

She came back, picked up the chair and drained a glass of wine, which Brooke refilled.

'No news. Not really. Just some detail,' she said, closing her eyes to concentrate on getting it right, a habit she'd developed as a ten-year-old. 'The *Silverfish* was seen two days ago, at dusk,

293

thirty-five miles off St Abb's Head, north of Berwick, heading east on the surface in rough seas. There was a storm that night, so the Admiralty says she'd almost certainly have submerged to avoid the swell. There was no radio message. The next day a frigate travelling north saw a sub on the surface fifty miles off the coast of Norway, near Narvik. It was too far away to positively say it was the *Silverfish*. The Germans, at Kiel, have responded to requests for information; apparently, we do the same. They say there've been no reports of a hostile engagement with a submarine for ten days. So it's a mystery.'

Brooke got the atlas from beside the fire and they cleared away the plates and were trying to plot the boat's course when there was a knock at the door.

Claire opened it to find Edison on the step.

'You're not too late for food. Your vegetables are a wonder.'

Brooke appeared at her side.

'Cottage out at Hornsea, sir. Man with a gun demanded food and clothes.'

294

52

By the time the Wasp was on the road Edison had remembered a few more details: the gun had been a 'pistol', the man in his twenties, lean and bony. The reed-cutter's wife, who'd run to the pub in the village to ring the Spinning House, had been certain the man was American, but that was a common mistake with Irish accents, or — given Smith's ability to affect a Cockney lilt — a handy further disguise, and one he'd used before with the garage when repairing the three-wheel van.

The village, which lay along a lane running down to a riverside wharf, led to a pub. A group of men, standing outside, directed them down a track to the cottage. One man, carrying a spade, seemed eager to take up the pursuit of the felon. 'We're waiting for torches,' he said. 'Milly reckoned he went off across the common.'

Brooke, getting out of the car, told them to calm down. 'If he's got a gun, carrying a torch makes you an easy target. It's dark and cold; go home to bed. We'll get him. It's our job. You'll need to be up early to do your own work.'

They left them grumbling and walked away down the shadowy lane. When the cottage came into view, by fleeting moonlight, it looked like a medieval hovel: a set of three cottages originally, and a set of outbuildings, forming a rough farmyard.

Milly, the reed-cutter's wife, met them with a lantern at the door. 'Have you caught him?' she said. 'We're too scared to sleep. He might have had a gun but it didn't stop him shaking.'

A man appeared at her shoulder and introduced himself as Ted Brandon, waterman. There was no invitation to step into the cottage, so they stood on the doorstep in the damp cold.

'I heard him in the old barn cos I went out for the privy. So I shouts out 'Who's there!' a coupla times. And out he comes with the gun in his hand. Said I shouldn't have interfered. I said it was our barn and he shouldn't be in it. He bundles me inside and makes Milly get him a bag of food, and a Guernsey, and a scarf, and socks. I was in the last lot. In the trenches. You get to know just by looking at a lad if he's got it in him to pull the trigger. Not many do, you know. Not even if their life depends on it. They freeze up, can't move. I've seen 'em dead too, in no man's land — stiff arm, with the gun still in the fingers, and all the bullets in the chamber. But this fella, he'd use it alright.'

'He had a bag?' asked Edison.

'A haversack, over his shoulder.'

'Heavy?' asked Brooke.

'You said it. He had to brace his legs to swing it on his back. I reckon he had it squirrelled away in the barn — whatever it was.'

Edison took a note of names and addresses. Then they searched the barn by torchlight, but found nothing more than frozen carrots and rotting hay. A hole in the roof revealed the moon, masked by rags of cloud.

They'd watched him walk away, they said, struggling under the weight of the bag, heading out of the farmyard towards the distant city, across a windswept wilderness of rough grass, running alongside the river.

'And you're sure you don't know this man?' asked Edison.

'I never said that,' said Brandon. 'Course I know him. We both do. A student, we reckoned, although he was that fit he should have been in a uniform. We see'd him most mornings. He's a runner. Like clockwork these last months, since the spring. About six-thirty. He gets as far as the church then turns round and goes back. Runs right through the yard. Coupla times we gave him a mug of tea. Ask me he was on a recce, spying out places. We won't see him again, you see. He's scot-free now.'

Brooke walked to the edge of the darkness, trying to see the bend in the river. The waterman was right. Smith was free, and the haversack might well contain the second bomb, prepared and primed by Walsh. Prince Henry, effectively second in line to the throne, would arrive in the city in less than twelve hours.

Edison arrived with two tin mugs of tea he'd inveigled out of the Brandons. Brooke took a cautious sip of the brew. 'I'm afraid this is going to be a trial, Edison. They say this Prince Henry's a keen soldier. He missed the Great War by a year, and he's spent most of this one being driven around in a staff car as far away from the action as they can get him. I wonder if he knows he's going into battle tomorrow.'

53

Later, in his bed at home next to Claire, wide awake, he'd found himself haunted by the image the reed-cutter had summoned up from the Western Front: the men who'd died unable to fire a gun, cold hands holding cold pistols. Brooke thought the detail was crucial: a *pistol*. A rifle, a machine gun, a ten-pounder, a grenade — all of them were indiscriminate, the target unseen and generic, the quarry unnamed. But firing a single shot from a pistol was always an act of personal annihilation. The bull's eye was no preparation for firing a gun in anger at another human being. Brooke had been a medal holder in his regiment, levelling his .45 to place a bullet at the heart of a cork target, or between the eyes of a straw man. At Alexandria, and later on the road to Gaza, he'd fired the pistol in anger, but only over the heads of a rebellious crowd at a railway halt, and again in a skirmish at night in which he'd filled and refilled the chamber, shooting blindly at lights and shadows.

Finally, Grandcourt had laid a hand on his shoulder. 'They've gone, sir. Order's out to cease fire.' The barrel of the pistol had been hot and smelt of cordite.

But could he fire a pistol at a man with a face he could see? Could he plant a bullet in the chest of a man whose name he knew? He'd shot at the Turk who'd captured him in the desert in the

Great War, but by then he'd been hit himself, and felt he would bleed to death if he didn't retaliate. Could he have fired *first*?

In his mind's eye he saw Joe Smith levelling a gun, taking aim at his heart. He tried to imagine the moment: taking aim himself, pulling the trigger, the recoil jolt in his arm. But however hard he tried there was always a split second of hesitation, and what was missing was the sensation of the bullet going home, the visceral thud relayed by some high energy telepathy. If he couldn't imagine doing it, what would happen if he found himself confronted with the reality?

Lying in bed now he was bathed in sweat, which was turning icy cold because the window was open. The sound of the river, unlocked, fell over the nearby weir. He turned on his pillow and in the half-light saw the folded green beige cloth on the bedside table. Inside was a standard-issue .45 Webley pistol, issued under Carnegie-Brown's signature from the County's armoury in the Castle less than an hour earlier. Six firearms had been logged out for the security operation surrounding Prince Henry, four to constables, one to Edison, one to Brooke. Smith had, however, a distinct advantage. He'd killed before, and in the coldest of blood.

54

Brooke and Edison were on the platform at Cambridge Station to meet the train from Liverpool Street. Mrs Mary Flynn looked oddly insubstantial, as if she was, in reality, only half there. She didn't speak when Brooke shook her hand but clutched her husband's arm tightly. Mr Gerald Flynn was older by a decade, with a neat moustache, and a smart suit and trilby. There was something of the stuffed shirt about his manner, which was pompous and irritated, as if the trip north had been a mild inconvenience which needed to be swiftly brushed aside.

Outside, beyond the graceful arches of the station facade, the Wasp idled on the taxi rank, newly cleaned, and Edison opened the rear doors for the Flynns.

Brooke spoke through the open window once they were comfortable. 'My sergeant here will take you to the Bull Hotel. We've booked you a room, and everything's paid for. I'll need to talk to you both later, possibly tomorrow. Your appointment with Dr Comfort, the pathologist, is at two o'clock today. I realise this is a dreadful burden, but we do need a positive identification from the next of kin. Sergeant Edison here will be able to answer any questions you have. A visit to the school or the church at this time isn't possible. I think you've been told about the situation by Shepherd's Bush?'

They both nodded.

'Mr Walsh is still in hospital,' said Brooke.

'Will he live?' asked the woman who had been, and still was, his wife.

'Yes. But there's concern about his heart.'

'Did he kill our boy?' she asked. Again, the grey eyes looked dead, like beach pebbles.

Brooke touched his hat. 'Inquiries are underway. As I say, we must speak later. It's a fast-moving inquiry. I'm sure we will have answers to all your questions. But we have to move cautiously. Today, I'm afraid, we have a royal visit, by Prince Henry of Gloucester. I hope you understand. I must oversee security in person. Sergeant Edison will stay with you and take you to your appointment.'

Mr Flynn looked mildly placated, while his wife looked blank, no doubt steeling herself for the ordeal ahead.

Brooke tapped his signet ring on the roof of the car and Edison pulled gracefully away, down Station Road, to the distant buoyant figure of 'The Homecoming'.

The radio car took Brooke home to change in preparation for his ceremonial duties. Claire, off shift, was sweeping slush from the path, a chore she'd invented to take her mind off the fact there was no news of Ben. She abandoned it freely to help her husband choose a shirt and tie to match his best suit. Black brogues were polished to a shine. Finally, he stood before the full-length mirror in the attic room, beside the bath.

'You look like your father in that painting in the hall,' said Claire, trying to enjoy the moment.

Brooke, absurdly pleased, turned his head to mimic his father's stance in the photograph. It was an official portrait standing beside the King of Norway, on the day he received his Nobel Prize in Oslo. He'd always thought that if you didn't know the two by sight you'd think Professor Brooke was royalty. A sense of ease, and even mild amusement, radiated from the otherwise stern face.

'Joy?' asked Brooke, tightening the knot at his throat. It was his battalion campaign tie from Palestine and he'd rarely worn it, but had decided it might be appropriate to greet the Unknown Soldier.

'She's walking out to Coton to see Grace. Some other friends, too. Everyone's rallying round. The longer we hear nothing, the worse it gets.'

Brooke met her eyes in the mirror. 'Until we hear, we won't know. But another twenty-four hours and I'd say we need to think the worst, even if we keep it to ourselves.'

At the door she edged the coat back onto his shoulders. 'What about Ben's parents? There's a brother too?' he asked.

'They called last night. Joy spoke to his father. They thought it sounded like engine failure and that the *Silverfish* would limp into port sometime soon. He was very upbeat. I don't think Joy likes him. She thought he treated her like a child. She's a nurse, she's got as good a grip on reality as a retired naval officer. Better.'

Claire snapped his hat into place and pushed him lightly off the step and on his way.

The radio car took Brooke to the grand gate of Trinity College. A small crowd had gathered, held back by a handful of uniformed constables. Brooke took his place in the line-up, ready to welcome the prince, a situation not unlike the format of a wedding, what Claire liked to call 'the wall of death'. Brooke was sandwiched between the lord lieutenant, and the master of the college. A line of students in academic gowns had been dragooned into a matching opposite line, forming a guard of honour.

A convoy of black cars rumbled its way down the cobbles of the street. Brooke had rerouted the royal convoy to avoid the Great Bridge, which had added a few minutes to their schedule, so they were late. This had given time for a healthy crowd to assemble.

As the prince stepped out there was a round of polite applause, even a solitary cheer.

Brooke heard the stilted conversation as Prince Henry worked his way along the line of dignitaries. The royal voice was squeaky and breathy, and totally ill-suited to the large, jovial man producing the words. As Brooke waited, his eye roved the crowd, noting the regular uniformed constables, and, on a rooftop above, a soldier with a rifle, and another in a first-floor window above a bookshop. He wondered if Jo Ashmore had company in her unseen Observation Post.

The college, at least all of the relevant rooms, had been thoroughly searched that morning. The Borough's bloodhound had toured the grounds. Avoiding a bomb was, in fact, not that testing a mission, as long as they made sure the prince deviated at all times, and all places, from the published schedule of events. If it was a line-of-sight explosive device, operated by Smith, the dangers were magnified, but not recklessly. They had to keep the prince on the move and remain vigilant.

Then, abruptly, Prince Henry was pumping his hand. The man had a mouth tangled with bad teeth, but an open face and a practical, straightforward manner. His uniform was unadorned with medals or sashes but was otherwise immaculate. The buttons caught the weak winter light. He could have been a farmer, or a gregarious butcher. Brooke liked him immediately.

'Ah. Professor Brooke's son? I saw him a few times you know — on Bang's Parade. Famous then. Nobody took any blind notice of me — or my good-for-nothing brother. I lasted a year. Academic life's not me.'

Brooke wasn't sure if a question had been asked, but he felt he could speak. 'How was France? My son's in the BEF, somewhere south of the Luxembourg border. The letters don't say much, but it seems pretty quiet.'

'It'll stay that way.' The prince stepped closer, and Brooke saw that his eyes were slightly hazy, his skin marked with tiny broken blood vessels. There was a hint of genuine empathy in the steady stare. A plane came down near the border two days ago. There was a messenger aboard with military plans. Looks like Berlin's banking on the same route as last time, across the Belgian border, so your boy will be safe enough for now.

Tell his mother. It'll help for a while.'

Prince Henry rearranged his polished shoes on the cobbles. 'I'm told I can see a football match, Inspector, despite the close attentions of the Fenians. Thank you.'

Brooke gave him a nod. 'It was on the schedule, but we've tampered with the timings, so it's fine. And I put a watch on the pitch overnight. We just have to make sure you're never exactly where you should be.'

'Situation bloody normal,' said the prince, smiling. 'Standard military planning, in fact.'

'I can't vouch for the quality of play.'

The prince's eyes narrowed astutely to focus on Brooke's tie. 'Allenby's lot, eh? Did you see the Great Man?'

'Lawrence or Allenby?'

The prince laughed.

'I saw Lawrence from a distance, once or twice. Over a Bedouin fire, one night. But the legend went before him. He was everywhere in that sense. That's the essence of legends, they're insubstantial by nature.'

Prince Henry nodded slowly. 'Bit flashy too, if you ask me. They call me the Unknown Soldier, Brooke. Not sure what that makes him.' He shook Brooke's hand again. 'I have every confidence my life is in good hands, Inspector.'

55

Prince Henry disappeared from view into Trinity College, the gate above adorned with a rather wretched statue of his distant ancestor, Henry VIII, the college benefactor. The applause died away, as did the crowd. A detective inspector from County was closeted within the college, where the precise venue for lunch had been switched from the Great Hall to the master's lodge. The head porter, informed of the possible dangers inherent in the visit, had ordered the cellars searched for explosives, fearing a repeat of the attempt to murder another of the prince's ancestors, James I, but there was no trace of a latter-day Guy Fawkes.

Inside the college the prince would take a short rest and then an early lunch. Later, the planned car journey to Parker's Piece had been replaced by a zigzag walk, which would no doubt draw impromptu crowds. The royal visitor would ride back by open army staff car, change for dinner and then walk to Queens' College. A final check on security in the Great Hall at Queens' would be made at dusk. Before dinner there would be drinks in the new Fisher Building, which the prince was due to open officially, during a brief ceremony. If interrupted by an air raid warning the royal visitor would walk to the cellars of the new Guildhall, on Market Hill. Brooke's role was to stand by for the unexpected and be on hand to take personal control of the royal prince should an emergency arise.

Alone now, on the street corner, his charge safely inside the college walls, Brooke saw a constable heading his way. 'Sir. Police box in St Andrew's Passage. There's a call.' The blue box was almost hidden down a side alley. The caller was the duty sergeant at the Spinning House: a water bailiff at Upware, ten miles north of the city, had spotted the *Elsie*, moored two miles off the main river on Reach Lode. He'd got close enough to confirm the boat's identity, then fled back to a riverside pub with a phone. He awaited instructions.

Brooke checked his watch. He had two hours before the prince emerged for his next engagement. Deprived of Edison and use of the Wasp, he ran down to the river at the Great Bridge where the County force had stationed its patrol launch, on call for the duration of the princes visit. He waved his warrant card, effected a requisition, and ordered it north along the river at speed. They left a wake, passing through the locks at Jesus and Baits Bite, then the fen-edge villages. To the east of the river lay the Lode Country, an area of fenland bisected by straight cuts, which had once allowed boats to ferry goods from higher ground to the main river. The draining of the Fens had seen the soil shrink back, leaving the lodes high above the landscape they drained, each perched on Mississippi levees. It was a wilderness, even by fen standards. Bodart, if she'd decided to abandon the boat and slip away, could not have found a more desolate spot. Or was she still on board?

Upware, a collection of a few houses around a thatched pub, called the Five Miles From Anywhere, stood on the river beside the lock entrance to Reach Lode. The water bailiff, a squat, bustling man with a bedraggled coat, took Brooke on by foot, picking up the path beside the lode, high on the bank. The water itself was sluggish and stank of rotting peat. On the far side wild horses stood, heads down, chewing grass revealed by the melting snow. In summer the boats crowded the banks here, but in winter only the hardy remained — the locals called them river gypsies. A few were dotted along the path, before even they petered out. Then, in the far distance, around a subtle deviation in the arrow-straight flight of the channel, they saw the *Elsie*.

Brooke held back, fifty yards distant. The boat was neatly moored, a series of wooden planks protecting its paintwork from the wooden dock. She was a forty-footer, in black and gold. From the stovepipe smoke drifted, revealing a fire within. At the stern, the cockpit and entrance door were neat and tidy, newly painted, shipshape. A bilge pump patiently throbbed, spilling water out by the rudder, creating a current which must, Brooke realised, have helped keep the boat ice-free in the cold snap.

Brooke, short of time, decided to act. Recovering the RADAR unit was a priority. Was it on board? He called out a catch-all 'Hallo!', then approached, stepping aboard, and felt the subtle stomach-turning gulp of the boat shifting in its watery bed. Kneeling, he looked inside. The saloon contained a series of bookcases, a small desk, cabinets for papers. The stove was in the Bavarian style, with blue tiles and a wedding-cake design of layers, tapering by steps to a finial. A remarkable object, imported, no doubt. A cat made him jump, appearing on the sill inside, pressing its fur flat against the thick glass.

The water bailiff produced a jemmy and they sprung the lock on the cabin door. Methodically, starting at the prow, Brooke searched the boat, making sure to check the two sets of bilges. One of Rafe Forbes's RADAR units was not an easy item to conceal. Twenty minutes later he was pretty certain that Bodart had fled with her prize.

Climbing back onto dry land he found the bailiff smoking, an old dog at his heels, which must have been trailing them on arthritic legs. The cat sat on the roof of the boat.

'Cat's a pedigree,' said the waterman. 'Siamese. In his day the dog would have had her like that.' He snapped his fingers.

'Thanks for the call,' said Brooke. 'We could have missed her for months.' It was true. The narrow channel was a mile from the main river at this point, and the slight dogleg meant the boat was hidden, despite the open country.

'It's me job,' said the bailiff bluntly. 'Boats coming upriver reckon they're searching every vessel at Denver. That right? What they after?'

'Who said that?' asked Brooke.

'Every skipper you talk to. Downriver too, they

reckon. One story says there's a spy trying to get out to sea. Armed too, and dangerous. This his boat, is it?'

'Gossip's a wonderful thing,' said Brooke. 'Best stick to facts. We're looking for a woman, middle-aged, solid, a German accent certainly — but she's Austrian. Keep your eyes open for us. Can you put out the word — north and south?'

The bailiff nodded.

Brooke was fifty yards from the boat on his way back when the obvious question struck him: why leave the stove alight? It created smoke, and made it look as if someone was on board.

Walking back, he used a metal toolset on the small grate to swing open the stove door. Inside, smouldering, was a thick book of maps and a folded set of charts. Brooke got the embers out into a metal bucket and then laid them in a line on a damp tarpaulin on the bank. Various German hieroglyphs dotted a series of Ordnance Survey maps of the upper river, the Wash and the north Norfolk coast. The charts covered the German Ocean.

Brooke adjusted his hat and tried to put himself in Bodart's shoes. She would have taken care to pick up the river talk. If she'd heard the way ahead was blocked it would explain her decision to lay up the *Elsie*. Burning her maps seemed to signal a desperate change of plan. But where had she gone? Back downriver to the city perhaps, rather than risking open country? It was a ten-mile hike, but she could have done it under cover of night. Desperate, thwarted, friendless — did she have any hope left?

56

An hour later Brooke was on the touchline watching football on Parker's Piece, on a field cleared of snow and on a mat of straw and mud. According to the porter at Trinity, 'a light lunch' had involved several rounds of Brandy Alexander, an officers' mess concoction of brandy, champagne and sugar cubes, which was the prince's favourite. He'd then enjoyed a boisterous walk through town, cheered on, and now stood smoking a large cigar as the game unfolded in a series of crunching tackles and barely controlled mob violence. The precise position of the ball appeared to be of passing relevance to the tactics.

Brooke, who'd taken up position on the opposite side of the pitch to his charge, learnt that the teams represented the university on one hand, the London Regiment on the other, and that the royal visitor had indicated that both teams would be treated to tea at Trinity after the final whistle. Brooke suspected that this was another euphemism for a bout of hard liquor. An air of a public holiday hung over the field, as most of the thousand-strong crowd were in uniform and had been given leave to visit the local pubs before kick-off. A hundred children — all boys — watched from behind one of the goals, waving flags and cheering wildly.

Brooke observed the prince. It was difficult to

avoid the conclusion that he was happier surrounded by soldiers than academics, or his entourage: a dour group of men in long coats who stamped their feet in the slush and smoked, passing silver cigarette cases up and down the line. The Boroughs tallest constable had been assigned to act as a nominal royal bodyguard and stood at the prince's shoulder.

The game had become a mud bath, the teams indistinguishable; a delighted prince, abandoning strict neutrality, urged on the soldiers. The final whistle brought a huge cheer and both teams were dragged into lines to meet the guest of honour, who was then escorted to his car, having duly invited the players back for refreshments. Brooke set off across the grass, leading both teams in a long, straggling line of steaming athletes. The players, no doubt anticipating the warmth, food and drink, sang in the narrow streets. The celebratory tone was infectious. A crowd, which had reappeared at the college gates, cheered them out of sight through the gate.

They had beaten the royal car back to Trinity by five minutes, as it executed a roundabout route dictated by security, again avoiding the obvious bridges. The open staff car eventually crept down the cobbled street and the prince slipped from view, leaving a trail of rich cigar smoke on the air. Brooke checked his watch: it was four o'clock precisely. A hint of dusk was in the sky, and the lights of the porters' lodge were bright and welcoming. Prince Henry was due to walk out for dinner at Queens' at six.

Brooke lit a cigarette and sat on the wall as the crowd dispersed. To one side of the great gate a bay window extended from an upstairs room. This, by legend, had been Isaac Newton's room, and below on the lawn stood an apple tree grown from a seed from the one in his country garden, from which the fruit had fallen and begotten the law of gravity, and much else. Brooke's father had been rather sniffy about this story, pointing out that there were other trees — notably in the city's Botanic Garden — which had been grown from a graft of the roots of the original. These trees were exact replicas of the original, biological twins rather than hybrids. It struck Brooke that it was in the nature of science that one day, somewhere, someone, would try to do the same with an animal — a sheep perhaps, or a guinea pig. It was a disturbing vision.

Which made him think of Augustine Bodart and her sweet peas. He'd left further instructions with the Spinning House to widen the search for the fugitive. In particular he'd ordered south-bound trains searched before they left for London. Davison College had provided a picture of Bodart from the files. Brooke was determined to stop the Austrian reaching anyone who might be able to spirit the RADAR unit out of the country. Might she know how to contact other agents in the capital?

He found it hard to feel sympathy for her plight. No doubt her commitment to eugenics went back to her student days at Heidelberg. The sophistication of her undercover work in Cambridge hinted at considerable preparation.

She'd been at Davison for nearly three years. She was undoubtedly an agent of the Abwehr, the German intelligence service. But for the river gossip they'd have nabbed her at Denver Sluice.

The clocks chimed the hour and he saw Edison, half running down Trinity Street.

Breathless, he bent once at the waist and then straightened. 'Sir. The child in the morgue, it isn't Sean Flynn.'

'It has to be,' said Brooke, standing. A murder of crows clattered out of the trees by the gatehouse and wheeled overhead in the evening sky.

'Mother's certain. She fainted first time, so we had to wait. But she's had a second look, and then the husband, too. No doubts.'

Brooke tried to calculate the repercussions of the news. If the body wasn't Sean Flynn's, whose was it? He saw the faces of children, their suitcases and labels, and Father Ward, distraught that one of the evacuees was missing.

'They're both pretty shocked,' said Edison. 'They've gone back to their room at the Bull. I said we'd find their boy, but where do we start?'

Brooke, calculating, thought he already had part of the answer: he knew where to find Sean Flynn. And he knew he was alive. What remained elusive was the motive behind the subterfuge.

'We need to get everyone together at St Alban's,' he said. 'All the evacuees, the staff, everyone. The priest too, and the housekeeper. Tomorrow, if we can. Get a message to the school, Edison, and the church.'

He stood, quickly lighting a fresh cigarette.

'For now, let's get Prince Henry safely over the city boundary and off our manor. Then we can concentrate on the child.'

'And a call from Brandon, sir. The reed-cutter at Hornsea rang the station to say he's lost his boat. Moored down by the towpath he says. A rowboat. Looks like our man Smith is a planner alright. Oars were stashed in the barn, and they've gone too, so it looks like he had it all worked out. Now he's got the bomb, and a boat.'

57

Brooke and Edison stood together in the gathering shadows of the great gate. They were still deep in conversation on the subject of Smith's possible targets when one of Prince Henry's equerries, half running from the porters' lodge, tripped on the cobbles, spilling a suitcase of clothes across the flagstones. Out it all came, the regalia of a collegiate formal dinner: black tie, dinner jacket, polished shoes, a cummerbund and a pair of daring braces in gold and blue, the royal soldier's regimental colours.

Brooke helped him repack and showed his warrant. 'Change of plan?'

'His Royal Highness likes to call it 'the element of surprise',' said the man, in obvious exasperation. 'They've all had a few drinks. The soldiers have gone, of course, back to barracks. But the students are in their cups. Did I say a few drinks? Well, a few *more* drinks. Someone's suggested a steeplechase along the riverbank, over the meadows, over the styles, to Queens'. Prince Henry's borrowed some kit and they're setting off, it's like the Berkshire Hunt. They want to catch the light before it goes. One of the students has got a horn. Another one's volunteered to be the fox. I've to tell the porter at Queens' they'll arrive by the back way, over the wooden bridge. I'd better go.'

He set off, and as if on cue they heard a

hunting horn on the breeze. Even if they ran the long way round via the water meadows, the hunt would be over the bridge in twenty minutes, possibly less. There was no catching them now.

Brooke thought of the child in the sack floating downriver to its death, sweeping under the Mathematical Bridge. He didn't like the sense that fate was contriving a circular narrative, a story that was being drawn back to its beginning.

'Go with him, Edison,' said Brooke, pointing at the retreating equerry. 'Try and get a message down to the bridge. If they can reroute them over Silver Street, do it. There's no real risk — it's out of the blue, Smith couldn't have known. But let's play it safe.'

Edison ran, gaining on the fleeing equerry with admirable pace.

Brooke heard the hunting horn a second time, the sound floating over the college roofs from the meadows beyond; the yells of the runners, a mimic adding the raucous bark of a beagle, an impersonation greeted by laughter, and cheers, and shouts quickly taken up: *To the bridge!* Then the sound of the pursuit faded quickly, lost beyond the college buildings and the riverside willows.

A plan, which arrived fully formed in Brooke's mind, propelled him along the street, then down Garret Hostel Lane to the river. He still had the key to the Michaelhouse college punt, donated by Doric. The wharf lay at the end, beyond a locked door, to which he also had the key because it was from this secret place that he swam on summer nights. The door lock turned smoothly, but the padlock on the boat was still stubborn, and as he applied force he heard the hunting horn again, very close, and in the dusk on the west bank he saw them for the first time, white shirts in the shadows, a bedraggled line, heading south, appearing, then reappearing, as they measured a line of poplars. The joker's fake bark had been taken up by the mob, a perfect counterpoint to the horn.

Freeing the iron lock at last, Brooke used a foot on the stone wharf to propel the punt out into the stream. While his body steered the fragile craft, his mind sought reassurance. It was impossible for Smith to have anticipated the change of route. But the anxiety would not abate: something, some small detail, had eluded Brooke's calculations.

Ice nudged the boat, but the downstream current was limp, so he made good headway, standing in the bow, using the pole, grounding it in the gravel, pushing upstream. The long, slow bend of the river unfurled and the Mathematical Bridge came into sight. A crowd, no doubt alerted by telephone by friends at Trinity, had gathered, bunched at either end of the graceful curve, but lining the rail as well so that the runners would have to squeeze through as they ran over the water. At this point the bank to the west was no higher than a foot, giving Brooke a clear view of the hunting party, twenty men wearing shorts in pursuit of a student with a red sash. They were approaching the bridge at speed.

Ahead, upriver, a man sat in a rowing boat in

midstream, fifty yards from the bridge, his back to Brooke. This single image transformed the scene. Time ticked slowly, as if the world was winding down. In his left hand the man held a loop of wire, which dropped into the water and was gone. His right hand was furiously at work at some mechanism unseen in the boat. His build, the neat bullet-like head, but especially the easy languid strength, told Brooke it was Joe Smith. Brooke hadn't known the prince would run this way; how had Smith?

He heard hunting cries on the wind. The approaching front runner — the fox — was fifty yards from the bridge.

Kneeling in his boat, Smith had set aside the wire and now worked at something with dexterity, not power. The tension in the shoulders, the stooped head, was electric.

The red-sashed student clattered over the bridge to the cheer of the crowd. The following group set up a volley of cries, their pace slackened, embroiled in a melee of back-slapping, until they came to a halt, pushing forward to cross the river. Brooke thought he caught sight of the prince, in a cluster at the tail.

Smith stood in the boat, expertly rebalancing himself as it rocked, the wire trailing from his left hand. In the half-second he had left to make a decision Brooke saw a second thin wire, this one dropping from the bridge into the bankside shallows.

The picture was complete. The fleeting doubt, *How did he know?*, was brushed aside.

The steeplechasers began to jog over the bridge.

If he shouted, Smith might detonate the bomb.

Brooke levelled the pistol, steadied his right hand with his left, took aim and shot him in the back; and there it was: the fleshy lethal thud of the bullet going home.

58

The act of killing a man in cold blood had left Brooke in a state of subliminal shock, in that he was able to deal efficiently with the duties of the next two hours, but only as an observer of his own actions: an out-of-body experience occasioned by death, but not his own. One persistent thought disturbed him even in this odd, dispassionate state: that he would one day know Joe Smith's story, his real name, his place of birth, the events which had made him a violent rebel. Fleetingly, it occurred to Brooke that there might be a sweetheart, or even a wife. The thought of children was not allowed to impinge.

Smith's body had dropped where he stood and lay in the boat looking up into the sky as Brooke brought the punt alongside. This moment might have proved to be a fulcrum of his life: had he shot the right man? Anxiety made his eyes swim, and for a second, he didn't recognise the face, but then death acts instantly to wipe away the life in the eyes, the tautness of the skin, the set of the jaw. It *was* Smith, but his spirit had fled. On his back he exhibited the exit wound of the pistol shot, in his chest, slightly left of centre.

On the Mathematical Bridge a crowd watched in absolute silence, while distantly the sound came of a police whistle, and then a radio car bell. Edison arrived on the left bank with the college porter. Brooke, his ears ringing from the single shot, tested the man's pulse and found perhaps a slight echo of the moving, pulsing blood, then it too was gone.

Standing on the platform of the punt he cupped his hands at his mouth and addressed the watching students. 'Clear the bridge. Do it slowly. A bomb has been planted and will still be live.' The figures melted away to the east and the west. The bridge stood revealed in all its geometric beauty, a graceful arc comprised of brutally straight lines. Now, up close, Brooke could see the package, secured to the wooden beams below by the tears of Chios. An electric fuse wire had been thrown clear by the dead man in the second after the bullet had struck. The other end was still secured, falling into the brown, peaty water from the package of explosives.

Edison stood awaiting orders.

'Meet me at the Michaelhouse wharf,' called Brooke. 'Downriver, the east bank. The door's open.'

In the silence, and the soft air of dusk, he was astonished to hear the calm tone of his own voice.

Brooke attached the rowboat to his punt and let the current take them both downstream. Drifting, at an elegiac pace, it felt like a floating funeral cortège. The water-drawn hearse, slipping between the river's banks, edged round the slow bend to the wharf. A few minutes later Edison arrived with two constables, and they were able to get the body ashore.

Smith looked up into the evening sky: his eyes, open, registered a puzzled shock; the boots on his feet, robbed from the reed-cutter, hung loose despite the tied laces, and round his neck was knotted an old woollen scarf in blue and white hoops, the embroidered badge representing a pouncing lion, its paws wide and splayed like a kitten playing. The image struck a chord, but Brooke brushed the idea aside.

An ambulance arrived and the medics, in an unhurried but well-choreographed ritual, gently lifted the corpse onto a stretcher. The university anatomy building and Dr Comfort's cold morgue was less than half a mile away. Quickly, before he was taken away, Brooke checked the dead man's pockets, retrieving a pistol, a wallet containing nearly £50 in one-pound and five-pound notes and an ignition key — possibly to the three-wheeler parked in the School of Pythagoras.

Edison went with the body while Brooke walked to the porters' lodge at Queens', commandeering the phone line in the back office to ring the Spinning House. It took five calls to track down an ordnance expert at the RAF base at Witch-ford, north of Cambridge. He could be on-site within an hour. Meanwhile, Brooke rang the Conservators, stopping all vessels on the Cam, and set uniform branch to block the river with boats at Mill Pond and the Great Bridge. The range of buildings overlooking the river beside the Mathematical Bridge was evacuated. The dinner of welcome for Prince Henry would go ahead an hour later than planned, in the Great Hall, which lay two courts away to the east.

Putting the phone down, Brooke heard a voice call his name from the outer office. Here he

323

found Prince Henry, still in mud-spattered kit, sitting by a small coke fire, cradling a large glass of what looked like whisky. He had a second glass on the hearth, warming, and he offered it to Brooke and indicated the spare chair.

The porter hovered.

'I think I mentioned that I felt my life was in good hands,' Prince Henry said, the lightly toned voice again jarring with the barrel chest. 'I owe you an apology. The change of plan, the game of horse and hounds, was childish. Frankly, I underestimated the enemy. It's a deep-rooted systemic prejudice, Brooke. We respect uniforms and history, chivalry and the agreements of gentlemen — the rules of engagement. Why should I, a member of the imperial royal family, worry about a peasant skulking in the shadows.'

He raised his glass and they both drank.

'We're fine,' said the prince, dismissing the porter from his own lodge. 'What I don't understand is how the devil did he know I was going to run over the bridge? *I* didn't know until half an hour before I set out with the rest.'

Brooke let the whisky hit the back of his throat. A malt, certainly, of fine quality.

'I've just discovered the answer to that myself. There's a large map of the college buildings hanging in the back office. The Fisher Building, which you are due to officially open tonight, is on the far side of the river. So you see, you would have had to cross the bridge. He was in place early, and then he saw the students gathering to form a guard of honour, no doubt loudly proclaiming the change of plan. So he took his chance.'

'Had he killed before?' asked the prince.

'I think so, possibly to keep his identity secret until he was able to carry out his mission. A child, I'm afraid. It's a complicated case, and not entirely resolved. There has been an unexpected development.'

Prince Henry stared into the coals. 'It's an uncomfortable thought, Brooke, but coming so close to death is an invigorating experience if you survive. I always wanted to be a soldier, but they won't let me near the front line, although I try to fob them off. So all this is oddly exhilarating. But history will not record the moment, I'm afraid. My people have been on the phone too. Downing Street's view is that the attack demonstrates that the IRA have improved their capabilities and widened their ambitions. The Republicans would love the headlines, and they'd know the Germans would read them with interest. So a D-notice has been slapped on the entire episode. It never happened.'

Brooke shrugged. A sudden memory of the gunshot made his hand jump.

Prince Henry looked away. 'Doesn't mean there won't be credit where credit's due. You saved my life. I'll mention it to my brother when I see him. It's a good story, no doubt it will even grow in the telling. There may be a medal, Brooke. But then you've got one of those already.'

He threw the whisky back, stood up and shook Brooke's hand.

At the door he turned back. 'And thank you for letting the football go ahead. It was terrific fun. The soldiers won, you know, which I greatly enjoyed. Goodbye, Brooke.'

The image of the muddied players on Parker's Piece seemed to meld into that of Smith, lying dead in the rowboat, the blue and white scarf around his neck. Looking into the crinkling coke fire, Brooke sensed a revelation. He let his mind float free. The pale hand of the dead child had haunted him, but now he recalled slitting open the hessian sack, and the light catching the cheap tin lapel badge of the golden cannon on the red background. And then there was the victim's new-found friend John McQuillan, a scruffy child, his hands disfigured by ink blots, but just above the frayed cuff an expertly rendered motif in filigree lettering: *QPR*.

A thrill of enlightenment made Brooke smile.

He finished the malt and went back out into the office to use the phone. He caught Edison passing the duty desk at the Spinning House. Brooke told him the hunt for Sean Flynn was progressing well. He would meet Mr and Mrs Flynn at nine o'clock the next morning by the main door of St Alban's Church, Upper Town.

But first, immediate business called. His detective sergeant was required at the morgue.

59

Brooke walked to the Galen Anatomy Building
and took the steps steadily to the fifth floor. His
body was exhausted, even if his mind felt oddly
clear. Dr Comfort's morgue was cold, the
windows open on three sides. Outside, across the
city, night was rising. Joe Smith lay naked on one
of the steel tables; the bloody wound in his chest
had darkened to a deep ruby brown, in contrast
to the young man's skin, which had taken on the
translucent tone of lard.

'Fine specimen,' said Comfort. 'An athlete,
certainly.'

The pathologist's servants hovered at the far
end of the room, ready to help him manhandle
the body and wield the tools of his trade, the
bone saws and the drills.

The dying light outside and the electric light
inside were playing tricks with the shadows.
Smith's body seemed to shimmer, as if fidgeting
on its cold metallic couch. The young man's
extraordinary vitality in life seemed to have
secured him a strange afterlife, an impatience for
the grave.

'I can't witness the autopsy,' said Brooke,
looking out the window. 'Given I fired the fatal
shot. I've asked Edison to attend, he's on his
way. I'll leave this too.' He placed his pistol on
an empty dissection table. 'One bullet fired. I'll
be placing a written statement on the chief

constable's desk overnight.'

Comfort nodded, cradling a cup of tea. 'I don't think there'll be much doubt here, do you, Brooke? There were fifty witnesses on the bridge. The bomb was in place, stuck to the underside of the bridge with some kind of adhesive. And the fuse line was attached. County's organising the chemistry on the explosives. No doubt the Home Office will want chapter and verse.'

Brooke walked back to Smith's body.

'The cause of death is pretty clear, Brooke.' He put a hand on Brooke's shoulder. 'You did the right thing, Eden. Go home, rest if you can't sleep. Talk to Claire.'

'I didn't warn him,' said Brooke.

'You couldn't take the chance. Imagine if it wasn't his body on that table, but the prince's. And you with a full chamber of bullets in your pistol.'

Edison's heavy footsteps announced his ascent of the stairs.

He pushed open the double doors but didn't bother taking a further step.

'Sir. Call from a police box by the Great Bridge. Someone turned up at the School of Pythagoras half an hour ago — with a key. She's still inside too. Looks like she's waiting.'

Brooke grabbed his hat. '*She?*'

60

For one hour they waited outside in the radio car parked at the turn in the lane, the old building visible in the half-light. Frost began to make patterns on the narrow windows of the School of Pythagoras as night took hold. A lingering drift of snow, caught in the shadows between the building's cold buttresses, had frozen into a glassy slope. The woman, whoever she was, must be sitting in the dark waiting. Was a meeting planned, of accomplices, or fellow travellers? Candlelight bloomed at one of the arrow-slit windows, flickering, which only made the old building look bleaker and colder.

On the stroke of eight Brooke lost patience, left the sentry in the lane and approached with Edison. The distant traffic must have masked their footfall because, once they'd pushed the double doors open, she looked startled, rising from a bench where she'd been wrapped in a shawl. The candle, in a jam jar on a high shelf, cast her in sharp contrast, her face half-lost.

It was Marie Aitken. Her eyes flitted beyond them, as if looking for someone else. Then her shoulders slumped, and she sat, gathering the shawl again about her shoulders. The animation of her face, of her manner, which had made her look younger than her years, fled now, and she looked beaten and defeated. The red hair was captive to a headscarf. One corner of her mouth

329

hung down as if afflicted with palsy. Her eyes, normally green and bright, looked bloodshot and oddly blank.

'I thought that if I waited he'd come,' she said. 'He wanted money, clothes, and I said no. Then I thought: who else can he turn to? So I came back.'

'Mrs Aitken . . . ' said Brooke.

'He's fled, hasn't he? I won't see him again. That's what he threatened when I said I wouldn't help, that he'd go north, that they'd get him a boat across the sea. He'll be gone then, a new man, with a name I'll never know.'

Brooke sat beside her. 'Why did he ask *you* for help? Was it blackmail?'

She shook her head. 'He asked for help, demanded help, because I'm his mother,' she said.

It seemed that St Alban's held many secrets. Brooke wondered if there were more waiting to be discovered even now. It was a kindness, he would tell himself later, that he didn't tell her then that her son was lying naked, broken, in the morgue. That Brooke had put a bullet in his back.

Edison found several candles, all in jars, and began to light them methodically. Brooke took off his overcoat and swung it round her shoulders, and sent his sergeant to get the Wasp, which they'd left up at the school.

She needed warmth, food.

'Joe Smith was your son?' he asked finally.

'Yes. My only son.' She clasped Brooke's overcoat to her shoulders. 'And it's come to this . . . '

She wept then, fat tears washing down her face.

After a minute she seemed to recover herself. 'He was two when his father died. That's not an excuse, it's a fact. We lived in Belfast. The mobs were out. The mobs were always out, cos it's a way of life. The south was fighting for independence. The north must fight too. My Declan was a patriot, but never a fighter. I don't know why he went out that day. The violence, the hate, and the drink of course — it never appealed. He was a gentle man who loved his books, and the Gaelic.'

She hauled air into her lungs. 'Shot in the back,' she said, almost spitting it out. 'A soldier's bullet, perhaps. But a soldier from which side? We never knew. He bled to death in the gutter and left me with the boy.'

Brooke's mouth ran dry at the appalling symmetry of the moment: *Shot in the back.*

She held her hand against her lips, the coloured bangles on her arm catching the light.

'So we left for London, and my sister. That's where Joe grew up. I wanted away from it all. A new start for the boy.'

After a minute, in which she seemed lost in a reverie, Brooke broke the silence. 'But Joe didn't stay in London?'

'No. We'd be there now, but for Declan's brother. Rory came with us, you see. Rory was full of stories, and he liked to tell them. Rory was all talk. Made out Declan was a hero, fighting for the cause, struck down by the hated British.

'I'd kept the truth from Joe. So that's my mistake. And a lie took its place. But there we are, he had a right to his own history. He missed

331

Declan, even though he never knew him. A boy needs a father. I should have given him a new one. So that's my second mistake.

'Look where it's led. Rory was with the IRA from the start. He recruited Joe: a godsend of course, an Irishman with no accent. And he gave him a story to follow, in which he had a hero's role, just like his father. Most of all Rory taught him to hate, and to enjoy the hate. That's a touch of evil.

'They took him to Dublin. Then to the far west, to train with a gun. The plan was that he'd go to London and stay with me, help when the bombing began. But I didn't want any of it. I'd done housekeeping for the church, in Poplar and Mile End. So I got the job here.

'He found me. He found my secret. I'd lost one man, I thought I had a right to find another. It's not my fault if he's a priest.

'Joe said it was perfect. He needed a place, a niche, a base. Ireland called, Ireland expected. He talked like that, brainwashed I'd say. I was to keep my mouth shut and help where I could. Joe said that he was in deep, that if I didn't help he'd end up on the end of a rope. He didn't want to be a martyr. Not yet.'

She shook her head.

Brooke found an edge to his voice. 'He killed the child?'

'We both . . . ' Her voice broke and she pressed her hands to her lips. 'We *all* killed the child. They were going to get him on the way from the station, get him away for a day — maybe two — hide him in the cellar, and

332

then, when they'd done what they had to with the bombs, they'd put him back on the doorstep. Good as new. But Colm couldn't get to the boy, there was such a crowd. So I put some laudanum in his drink that night, sent him off to sleep. When I handed him down to Joe, through the grille, he was fast away.

'Joe said he left him asleep in the cellar while he went and told Colm to get the van. They were going to keep him here. But when he went back to the cellar there was no sign of the boy. The cellar was locked, so he knew he was hiding. There's a bottle store, and that's where he found him, but he made a bolt for it, and Joe had a wrench to frighten him. One blow, and he went down. Joe said he'd seen dead men, and he knew it when he saw it. It wasn't cold-blooded. That's what he said.'

She glared at Brooke. 'He was lying. I know that. He killed him alright. Is that what I gave him at birth? Cold blood? Joe said he died in action. That he was a little martyr.' She buried her head, weeping. 'Colm said he'd put him in the river quick. So they used the van. Joe went too.'

They heard the Wasp creeping down the alley over the ice and snow.

She shook her head. 'I can't forgive him. To think the child was still alive . . . He's flesh and blood, but I can't forgive him. He's not his father's son. He's dead to me now.'

Brooke saw the white naked body of Joe Smith laid out on the morgue table.

'I'm sorry. There's something you need to know.'

61

Brooke's house, one of two villas, stood in a grove of willows and beneath the perennial green cover of a great cedar tree. He paused at his back gate, listening to the dripping of ice from the branches, enjoying the promise of the warmth that would soon be his: there had been no siren and the lights burnt in the garden room, glimpsed through a gap in the old curtains. Smoke, white and lively, rose from the chimney pot. A fire had been set. He could hear the sound of falling water at the weir, and — just — the sound of jazz playing inside the house.

Putting the key in the lock, he threw open the front door.

His wife appeared from the kitchen. Brooke knew immediately it was, as Rose had predicted, good news after all. She had a telegram in her hand.

'Eden, it's Ben. He's been captured. He's alive.'

Joy was a few steps behind her mother. Saying nothing, she hugged her father. They all embraced, and Brooke felt the guilt dissipate, the knowledge that he'd killed a man set firmly in a wider perspective, of light and darkness, good and evil.

The facts, contained in the telegram and augmented by a call to the Admiralty, were sparse. A German submarine — U-541 — had surfaced at an unspecified spot north of Heligoland, off the north German coast. A life raft had been spotted

containing eight men. There had been a fire
aboard the *Silverfish*. The boat had three inflat-
able rafts. But they had abandoned ship at night,
when the blaze had threatened to reach the maga-
zine, and had not seen the other rafts since. The
men had been taken aboard and landed at Bremen.
They were being held at a camp near Hamburg.
The Red Cross had been asked to verify the
details and report on their condition. The Admiralty advice was to await developments. Contact
had been made with the Kriegsmarine, and there
were hopes a repatriation might be negotiated,
although Berlin would have to be consulted.

Claire and Joy held hands.

'We should celebrate,' said Brooke.

'I could cook,' said Claire. 'There must be
something left in the cellar to drink.'

Brooke rebuttoned his coat. 'I said *celebrate*.
Get your coats.'

Ten minutes later they were arm in arm,
Brooke in the middle, crossing Coe Fen towards
the colleges. Opposite Trinity a small restaurant,
which catered for students in need of well-
cooked English food, had become a family
favourite. The menu, unencumbered by rationing, boasted duck and pheasant, ice cream and
sponge pudding. Over a glass of sherry Brooke
told them what had happened at Queens'. He
didn't want to overshadow the celebration, but it
seemed indecent to remain silent.

Joy, matter of fact, told him what he wanted to
hear. 'You did the right thing, Dad. Thank God
you were there.'

'You should take a day off, Eden,' said Claire.

'Do something, anything but go back to work.'

Brooke raised his glass. 'Ben's not home yet. But now we know he will be.'

They went to the Boar's Head for a drink and then, promptly countermanding Claire's advice, to the Spinning House. Brooke checked on the prisoners while they waited outside on the street. Marie Aitken was in cell six and had refused food. Father Ward was in cell one and had eaten well. In the morning Aitken would have to identify the body in the morgue. Of all the punishments which awaited her, this seemed to Brooke the cruellest. The duty sergeant reported that Mr and Mrs Flynn had confirmed that they would be at St Alban's in the morning at nine.

A typed note from Edison had been left for Brooke.

Sir. So that you know. Dr Bramley at Caius tested the package attached by mastic to the Mathematical Bridge. It contained a chemical mixture very close to the Home Office's prediction. It's Paxo, the IRA's preferred explosive. A fuse wire was attached and would have been detonated by electrical impulse. They dredged the river and snared the wire. A line-of-sight detonator was found mid-river, close to the spot where the witnesses place our man. Copies on your desk. E.

On the doorstep Brooke almost bumped into PC Collins, the constable he'd sent to check out Silver Street Bridge while he searched the river for the lost child. Here he was in a civilian suit,

336

hair cut brutally short. He could have passed for sixteen, or even younger.

'Sir,' he said, executing a salute, which made Joy and Claire giggle as they stood by on the pavement.

'Collins, we've missed you.'

The young man coloured violently, his cheeks turning bright red. He lifted his hat to Joy and Claire, and they clutched each other before turning away, laughing.

'Too much wine taken,' said Brooke.

'Sir.' The young man seemed tongue-tied.

'You disappeared,' offered Brooke. 'Remember?'

'I'm due at the army muster next week. Cambridge Station. I've been called up. The chief inspector thought I'd best take the time I was away as leave, seeing as how I'd gone anyway. She said I was on a charge, sir, and it's on my record, but I was best just to return the uniform.'

He had a package under his arm wrapped in brown paper.

'Sorry I let everyone down, sir. I want to serve. In France. I think I let my imagination get the better of me. I want to do what's right. I just needed to think.'

'Where did you disappear to?'

'Old friend from school, up the road in Peterborough. Not far. He talked some sense into me.' Collins was nodding all the time, as if agreeing with his own version of events.

'When you checked out the bridge for me that night, the night the child was seen in the river,

337

what did you find?'

Collins shook his head, his eyes flitting to the door, eager to escape. 'Not a soul, sir.'

'Car tracks? Footsteps?'

Collins shook his head, but Brooke could see it in his eyes: he hadn't looked. If he'd done his duty then, at the right time, the whole affair might have been very different.

'Good luck,' said Brooke, and turned to go, ignoring a proffered handshake.

They walked back via Parker's Piece. The normal domestic peace of the tented barracks had clearly been disturbed. A large crowd had gathered in the square's furthest corner. Grandcourt appeared, clutching a tin mug of coffee. Claire made a fuss of him, asking after his wife, the two girls, the house in Romsey Town.

'What's up here?' asked Brooke eventually.

'Shelter four reckon they've found a body inside. Sirens last night so they was all packed out. Could be anybody. All that excitement, and no air, maybe their heart gave out.'

Brooke left them and pushed his way through to a military cordon, showing the guard his warrant card, and ducking underneath a plank on oil drums set up as a barrier. The shelter was identical to Grandcourt's, a concrete bunker sunk in the earth.

At the iron door he met a young army doctor coming out. 'Ah. Police? Good. Definitely for you, if not military intelligence. Nasty, but not much doubt. Dead twenty-four hours, possibly more.'

The bunker had three chambers, each one as

338

long as a train carriage, but about twice as wide. Benches ran down each side, and the floors had been cleared of belongings and food and rubbish left during the previous night's raid. Light was provided by overhead bulbs but was still weak. The concrete floor was gritty, the air damp.

Brooke tied his scarf tighter at his throat and followed the doctor into the last chamber.

'Here,' he said, turning on a torch. The body lay in a foetal ball, wrapped in a large fur-lined coat, the head tucked in under the bench.

Brooke knelt, and the glare of the torch revealed the face. It was Augustine Bodart. The expression was hard to determine, but Brooke saw pain, and possibly a fleeting triumph. Her pillow was a suitcase, covered in a blanket. Together they edged her body away from the wall. The limbs, stiff and tightened, reduced her instantly to an object. Brooke used a penknife to crack the flimsy lock on the suitcase and flipped the lid. Inside was one of Rafe Forbes's precious RADAR units, its wires and valves reminiscent of the mechanism for a bomb.

'Here's the devil,' said the doctor. He'd slipped on a suede glove, with which he inched the dead woman's upper lip higher, revealing a glint of metal caught between two of the back teeth. 'I'm no expert,' he said, sniffing the air. 'But if that's the smell of almonds I'd say that was a cyanide pill. You can detect the same aroma on her right hand, on the fingers. There's something in her other hand,' he added.

Brooke gently prised the fingers away from the palm to reveal a curious collection of woodland objects: the fragile helicopter seed of a sycamore, a conker and a very small intricate tree cone. Despite the fierce grip she'd been careful not to crush the treasures.

'What can that mean?' Brooke asked. At the moment of death, she'd chosen to hold these tightly instead of another human hand. He didn't think they'd ever know truth.

He searched her pockets and found a train ticket for London. Had she gone to the station only to discover the constables searching the carriages? A purse held a single ten-bob note and a few coins. Brooke thought it was a curiously affecting idea: that Bodart had chosen a bunker crammed with humanity, parents and children, grandchildren and grandparents, sons and daughters, for this lonely death.

For a moment he imagined the despair which had driven her to suicide: alone, in a foreign country, thwarted in her plan to go home, to do — at least by her own lights — her duty. Had she, fleetingly, been jealous of these people? Or did she, at heart and at the end, think she was better than them, a member of a superior race? Brooke had no answers but one: death always looked the same.

62

Brooke sat alone in a pew at St Alban's, dazed by a three-hour bout of deep sleep at home in bed, which had left him curiously elated. He'd woken reborn, saddened only by the realisation that he'd forgotten this simple act of awakening, fresh and remade. Claire lay beside him, their shared sheets twisted together. For the first time in recent memory sunlight lay across the bed, a level, clear light which shone through a thinning mist beyond the window. It was only after a minute of timeless expectation that he remembered firing the shot, and sensing the impact as the bullet found its mark.

Now he sat in the church, the same sun shining through St Alban's modest stained-glass windows, gaudy with colour. At any moment five-year-old John McQuillan would enter by the side door which led into the playground. The case, as such, was closed but for this one small, tragic act. He regretted the undoubted fear which the boy would feel at the summons. But the child had brought it on himself, even if his motives — like his friend's — had been almost wholly innocent.

Childhood was a time for games, and that is what they would discuss. The games that children play on long train journeys. The games that desperate men play were now history: Liam Walsh's bigamous marriage, the IRA bomb cell, the brutal murder of a small boy. Did Joe Smith and Colm Hendrie know the boy was still alive when they hauled the sack over the parapet of Silver Street Bridge? That truth would never be certain, but Brooke was sure of one thing: Joe Smith was a born killer. Once he'd killed, he'd killed again, and but for a bullet in the back he'd have murdered many more. His compatriot Hendrie had been despatched, disfigured, butchered, all to protect the patriotic mission. With the first bomb Smith had struck at the heart of the nation's transport system. With the second he'd planned a political assassination, a rallying cry against the dominion of the British Crown. The irony was that his own father, the hero who had supposedly inspired his deeds, would have almost certainly hated him for what he'd done.

The door opened, and John McQuillan hesitated, half in the light, half in shadow.

'They said to come,' he said.

'Come in, John,' called Brooke. 'Nothing to worry about.'

The boy looked no better, pale and strained.

Brooke had chosen a pew-end, so that he could face out into the aisle, and he gestured for the boy to take a seat opposite.

The boy worked a blue cap anxiously in his hands.

'Show me again,' said Brooke, touching his own sleeve.

The boy pulled back a jumper and stiff shirt cuff to reveal the skin, decorated with the elegant tendrils of the blue-stained letters *QPR*, set on its flag.

'Looks as good as new.'

'I use a pen every day. Keep it clear.' He wouldn't look at Brooke, his eyes on his arm, then his shoes.

'The man who killed Sean, your friend Sean, he wore a football scarf. It was blue and white, John. And he lived with his uncle who was a docker in London. So what was his team?'

'Millwall — the Lions,' said the boy, brightening, bouncing slightly despite the hard, wooden seat.

'Right. And that made me think how we come to support the teams we do. Me — Cambridge Town, and they're not even in the League. And there's Sean. When I saw his body, he had a badge with a cannon on it: a red background, a gold cannon. Very smart. So what was his team?'

'Arsenal,' he said, but only in a whisper.

'That's right, John. Except it's not right, is it? Because Sean came from Shepherd's Bush, and that's where QPR play, at Loftus Road. It made me think, John. I reread your file too, the form the school got from your mum. And you're from Archway, right? And that's in north London. And we all know who plays there, don't we?'

The boy couldn't speak.

'And it all made me think of two things. It made me think how unhappy you've been since your new friend went missing, and about games on trains. You said you played jacks in the corridor, and I spy out the window.'

The boy's mouth hung open, revealing a fleshy throat, and milk teeth.

'But it gets boring, doesn't it, after a few miles.

343

So I think you decided to play a really good game, one that would fool all the grown-ups, and it wouldn't hurt anyone, and although you'd probably have to give it up, it wouldn't be the first day, or the first week. And when the truth was out everyone would know you'd fooled them. Not just the teachers, but the other kids too. Sounds like a great game, doesn't it?

'So you swapped the labels, didn't you? Names and addresses. Easy-peasy. You became John McQuillan, and he became Sean Flynn. It was a secret between new-found friends. Blood brothers. It's a bond, John — sorry, *Sean*. I don't suppose that's been a problem has it — answering to John. It's just the English for Sean.'

The boy nodded, and then the tears began to fall.

'And then, as the train pulled in, you had to give up on a game of hangman. The answer was *ARCHWAY* — Sean, John's home. It's alright. None of it's your fault,' said Brooke. 'None of it — don't let anyone say any different, Sean. Your mum and dad will be here soon.'

'Dad hates me,' said the boy, his lower lip hanging down, a sob beginning to wrack his frame. 'His boys are grown up, earning money. I'm a burden. I heard him say it. A burden. He wouldn't even call me Sean — he said John was better, he said it was a proper name. He says the family's got to move on. We're not in the gutter with the rest, that's what he says. We've got a house with a WC upstairs. I'd rather play in the street. I wanted to be someone else. But I miss Mum. It was scary when John disappeared. I

344

thought it was because of what we'd done. So I didn't tell.'

'Your mother loves you,' offered Brooke.

'She won't tell me about my real dad. They tell me I don't remember him, that I can't. But I do. He took me to the football. He stood on the terrace and I sat on his shoulders. I had Bovril. I do remember.'

'You should ask your mum again about your dad. There's a story to tell.'

'Have you met him?'

'Yes. He left home because he thought it was the best thing for you. He misses you every day. He said that to me. He's very sad now. I think he misses you a lot.'

Brooke stood, punched his hat into shape, and held out his hand. 'Come on. They're waiting. It's going to be quite a surprise.'

63

Later, at dusk, Brooke sat in his office at the Spinning House. Before him he had John McQuillan's file, which gave his parents as Fergus McQuillan (deceased) and Bernadette McQuillan, of Bedford Street, Archway. The mother's profession was given as cleaner. There were five children listed. It was now almost four o'clock on a Sunday afternoon, so if she'd gone to Mass it would have been that morning. They'd be at home, and there might have been a Sunday lunch. Given the ration books available it might even have involved meat. Brooke imagined a modest fire, Bernadette in an armchair with a cup of tea. They'd be missing young John, but possibly also savouring the peace and quiet. If Sean Flynn's character sketch of his new-found friend was accurate, he was a junior tearaway, and possibly a burden to his widowed mother. Maybe some of the boys were old enough to work, if they hadn't been called up, and there might be a bottle of beer or two. There was enough money because the form listed a phone number:

ARCHWAY 6787

Brooke finished a cigarette, picked up the phone and asked switchboard to get him the number. It rang in a faraway world of echoes, then — suddenly — loudly and close.

A woman's voice in a strong Irish accent said, 'Archway 6787,' the inflection polite, inviting enquiry.

64

Inevitably the thaw didn't last, so that the snow returned to Fenner's cricket pitch, while icicles hung from the elaborate iron gates as Edison parked the Wasp in front of Frank Edwardes' house. He'd polished the ruby-red paintwork, and a tartan rug had been neatly folded on the back seat. He fussed with the wheelchair in the boot as Brooke strode up the path to let himself in, finding his old senior officer ready and waiting, sitting on a bench in the hall, wrapped up in scarves and gloves.

Kat appeared from the kitchen, smiling broadly.

'He's been down here since six. He took the stairs on his backside. The doctor's given him a painkiller — an injection, so he'll be fine. But back by early afternoon, Brooke, please; and I'll need help getting him up to his room. Here,' she added, handing over a flask. 'It's pretty much neat whisky with a dash of black tea. But it does the trick.' Then she handed Brooke a picnic basket. 'Just a few things to help the party along,' she said.

'You aren't joining us?' asked Brooke.

She shook her head. 'Skating on the river was a treat when we were courting. But I've got the memory, I don't need to see it again. I'd find it sad, I think, just watching.'

'I'd like to see it one more time,' said Edwardes.

'I'm going to put my feet up in an empty house,' said Kat. 'It'll be bliss.'

They got Edwardes into the wheelchair and Edison pushed it down to the car, leaving tracks in the snow, which reminded Brooke of Smith's three-wheeler.

Once they were out of earshot Brooke took Kat's hand. 'What do they say?'

'The pain's bad so they've started giving him more morphine. That will kill him in the end. Probably in his sleep. Tonight, tomorrow, soon. So this is wonderful, Eden. I'll rest and sleep and then I can sit with him after dark.'

'I can help,' offered Brooke, readjusting his hat. 'We'll bring him safely back.'

As the Wasp crept away on the compact snow he glanced in the rear-view mirror and saw their passenger blowing his wife a kiss.

The sun was just up, the city streets in shadow, wedges of golden light touching rooftops and towers, domes and spires. Parker's Piece was dotted with snowmen.

The route to Newnham Croft and Brooke's house was simplicity itself, but Edison pulled into Regent's Street and headed instead for the city centre, so that they could pass the Spinning House. On the pavement, in a neat line, stood the Borough's full complement. Brooke swung round in his seat. 'Look left, Frank. It wasn't my idea. The order came down from the chief constable.'

At the flash of the Wasp's headlights the line of constables came to attention and executed a smart salute. The Wasp swept past, Edwardes' face pressed against the cold glass.

At the house they'd got the French windows open to give a clear view of the water meadow where the floodwater had frozen to create a perfect skating rink. Grandcourt, who had insisted on helping, had turned up before dawn with a van and six empty barrels, which he'd arranged on the ice to mark a circuit and then swept the loose snow from the track. He stood now, surveying his work, his head obscured by a great cloud of pipe smoke.

The hoar frost clung to the riverside trees and the first light of day was numinous, a curious pink, edged with green and gold, the sunbeams in motion like celestial searchlights.

'Good day for a hanging,' said Edwardes as Brooke helped him into the wheelchair. 'Any news, Brooke?'

'The death warrants stipulated nine o'clock,' he said checking his watch. 'Within the hour, either way.'

'What a thought,' said Edwardes. 'I had to witness one in Bedford. I was the prosecuting officer back before the Great War. I had to stand underneath and wait for the body to fall. That's a memory I'd rather be without. Worst ten minutes of my life.'

Brooke tightened the scarf at his throat: 'Edison's going to check with the radio indoors. News will be on the hour. There's a crowd outside the prison gates. Apparently, they've been there all night. Ghouls.'

The Coventry bombers were due to hang at Winson Green Prison, Birmingham. But the general expectation was that the Home Secretary, Sir

John Anderson, would bow to pressure and sign a reprieve. The Irish government had pleaded for mercy, and there had been demonstrations on the streets of Dublin, while in parliament Anderson had been urged to ignore the inevitable bloodlust of the general public. There were larger issues in play. The government needed Irish men and Irish women to go on helping facilitate the smooth operation of the economy: labouring, cleaning, working in factories. They also wished to see them continue fighting in Her Majesty's Army. So there would be hope in the young Fenians' hearts this morning. Brooke imagined them on death row at that very moment, praying perhaps, or watching the dawn sky, expecting footsteps in the corridor heralding good news.

Brooke's prisoners from St Alban's were in the same prison. Father John Ward, Marie Aitken and Liam Walsh faced charges of murder too. Their fate was uncertain. If the two Coventry bombers cheated the rope the public outrage might turn on them. The shadow of the scaffold was a long one. Which would be an injustice, felt Brooke. All three had been, to some extent, blackmailed, and none had sought the death of the boy. Smith had masterminded the bombing, gaining control over gullible and weak patriots, torn by conflicting allegiances. Smith's ultimate fate was uncertain too. A felon's burial was planned in the grounds of Cambridge Gaol. But a small section of Irish public opinion pressed Dublin to demand the repatriation of a hero of the republic.

Brooke watched Joy and Claire skating, hand

351

in hand, picking up speed in the frosty distance, leaving a glittering silver line through the snow-covered ice. Laughing, they ensnared Grandcourt and towed him round the course. The idyllic scene helped erase the prospect of the week ahead. The body of John McQuillan had been released by the coroner at midnight and was now on its way to Highgate, and the great Victorian cemetery, where the boy would be buried with his father, Fergus. The funeral was tomorrow afternoon, and Brooke and Edison would represent the Borough at the graveside. If he got the chance he'd slip the Victoria 1899 penny that he'd collected in the desert arroyo into the boy's grave.

Joy and Claire, finally releasing Grandcourt, made a beeline for Brooke and stood by as he struggled into his father's old fen sliders.

'Look, it's Jo — and her new man,' said Claire, Brooke noting the peculiar joyful lilt to his wife's voice at the prospect of substantiating gossip.

He was introduced as Flight Lieutenant George Wentworth, currently an outpatient at the Royal Air Force Hospital at Ely.

'George flies Blenheims,' offered Jo, taking his arm.

Brooke knew what was wrong from first sight, because at the sanatorium in Scarborough, after the Great War, when *he'd* been the patient, there were others with facial disfigurements who'd adopted the same strategy. Wentworth stubbornly held his head to one side, as if mesmerised by the distant vision of skaters and the smoking icy river, so that only his profile was visible. But in the end, offered a mug of tea by Joy, he'd had to turn towards them to drink, revealing a livid burn, roughly covered now with a skin graft. One eye was slightly distorted, as if in mid-wink. And then Brooke understood: the missing mirror in Jo's hut avoided anxiety about reflections, while the thoughtful turning away to light a cigarette hid the sudden, blazing match.

'You skate, Jo,' said Wentworth, relaxing slightly and trying hard to make his lips construct a smile.

They watched as Joy, Jo and Claire formed a chain and began to circle in an accelerating blur.

'Jo grew up here, did she say?' said Brooke. 'That villa there. She's always been a breath of fresh air. Where did you two meet?'

'I feel a fraud,' said Wentworth. 'I'm grounded for good and the doctors have got their claws in me. Another year, longer. So I volunteered for the Observer Corps. I'm on the swing shift with Jo. She's saved my life,' he added, and gulped some tea.

'I very much expect you've saved hers,' said Brooke.

Wentworth was dragged away by Jo to meet Rose King, who'd left the tea hut to her daughters to join the party. Claire, quick to switch roles, served mugs of tea.

Someone touched Brooke's arm and he turned to find Peter Aldiss clutching a glass of whisky. He was so used to seeing him at night, in the pallid lights of the laboratory, monitoring his living experiments, that Brooke was taken aback.

'Bit early,' said Brooke, nodding at the stiff drink.

'Time's relative, Eden,' said Aldiss, his great lumpen head weighed down so that he seemed to be studying his own shoes. 'I've been up all night with the observations. But I thought I'd respond to your invitation. See some daylight for once. Feel the sun. I helped myself . . . '

He raised his glass. Then he fished in his overcoat pocket and produced a small paper envelope containing the handful of woodland seeds they'd found in Augustine Bodart's dead hand. For a moment Brooke could actually smell the fetid, damp public shelter.

'Alder, sycamore, oak, birch,' listed Aldiss, touching each. 'Odd, isn't it? We always assumed she was a spinster. I made some enquiries at the Old Schools.' Brooke raised his eyebrows.

The Old Schools was the university's administrative heart, and widely seen as a nest of bureaucratic intrigue. 'In the end they coughed up her file. The whole case has caused a stir in the colleges, as you can imagine. It was felt we should find out all we could. Turns out she was married to a German academic — Professor Karl Lewin, of Heidelberg. A communist, and not just a fellow traveller, but a paid-up party member. So out of favour, I'm afraid. In fact, they put him in camp at a place called Dachau, outside Munich. He's been there since 1937, which is when his wife took up the position in Cambridge at Davison College. So they had her in their power, you see, from the start.' He carefully folded the envelope away. 'He's a world expert on the propagation of trees. Was. News is, and there's no way of confirming this, but there's

354

a report he was shot a few days ago. Summary execution, tied to a post. How about that for evil, Eden? Using one human being to control another.'

Finally, Claire took Brooke's arm and they skated together, describing figures of eight around a distant pair of gas lamps. Brooke reminded himself of the *Rubáiyát of Omar Khayyám: Be happy for this moment. This moment is your life.*

After an hour on the ice Brooke subsided into a deckchair beside Edwardes.

'Any news on Joy's submariner?' asked the old man, taking one of Brooke's Black Russians.

'Not much. The Red Cross has been told they're all fit and well. Which doesn't help because repatriation would be easier if they needed medical care. So he's in the bag for the Duration, Frank. Let's hope it's a short war.'

'When's the big day?' asked Edwardes.

'The baby? 10th June. It's on the calendar. But you know, first child, might be late. We talk of little else. I'll be a grandfather, Frank. I'll need to take my responsibilities seriously.'

Slyly, he watched Edwardes out of the tail of his eye. He was drinking in the picture before him: the blue sky, the white ice, the distant pinnacles of the university. He wondered if he was remembering his days courting Kat, in the long, cold winters which ran up to the Great War.

Claire appeared with a tray of hot toddies she'd made with the expert help of Doric, who had turned up after all, despite an aversion to

355

sport of all kinds, but taken refuge in the old villa's kitchen. Brooke enjoyed two glasses before settling in a chair on his own, wrapped up in his greatcoat and scarf, on a stretch of the riverbank.

It was Edison who woke him up, gently shaking his shoulder. Brooke's eyes swam slightly, and the sudden blaze of light was painful. He sat up, shaking his head, laughing out loud that he'd stolen an unexpected nap.

Across the meadow Dr Comfort, who'd been invited but Brooke hadn't seen, was kneeling in the snow beside Frank Edwardes' chair.

Edison bent forwards slightly. 'I think Mr Edwardes has gone, sir. I don't think there's anything we can do.'

Brooke thought it was a memorable scene: a group beginning to collect around the old man, the sparkling snowfield, the sky above a confident unblemished blue.

'And the radio's just confirmed the news, sir,' added Edison. 'They hanged those men. Side by side. No reprieve. Just the file returned with the age-old instruction: *Let the law take its course.* Apparently, one of them made a speech on the scaffold. God Bless Ireland. So that will satisfy the bloodlust. Means our lot will live.'

'Yes,' said Brooke. 'Which is justice I think, don't you?'

Acknowledgements

I have again relied on the work of Mike Petty, Cambridge's own local historian, in fleshing out day-to-day life in the city in 1940. Anyone who wants to read further should go to www.mikepetty.org.uk. Bradley and Pevsner's *The Buildings of England — Cambridgeshire* has been an unbeatable guide, as has the excellent *111 Places in Cambridge That You Shouldn't Miss*, by Rosalind Horton and Sally Simmons. My special thanks must go to Professor Enda Delaney of Edinburgh University, for his help in setting out the status of the Irish in England between 1939–45. His book *Demography, State and Society: Irish Migration to Britain, 1921–1971* is a model of clarity on a complex subject. And finally, my thanks to the Conservators of the Cam, the navigation authority, who not only answered my questions but by wholeheartedly engaging with the book provided it with — for me — its trademark scene: the great draining of the river. I am also indebted to Steven Fielding's *Hanged at Birmingham*, David O'Donoghue's *The Devil's Deal: The IRA, Nazi Germany and the Double Life of Jim O'Donovan*, and Julie Summers' *When The Children Came Home*.

I must thank my publisher Susie Dunlop and the team at A&B; particularly my editor Kelly Smith, Ailsa Floyd in marketing, and my copy-editor Becca Allen. They are a class act. I am grateful to those who read the draft manuscript and offered invaluable criticism, encouragement and expertise. In order of reading they are my wife Midge Gillies — who also provided a constant source of support and ideas — Mick Sheehan, Chris Simms, and Lesley Hay, who proofread the final draft. My agent, Faith Evans, represents a constant call to meet the highest standards in storytelling for which I am often not as grateful as it may appear.

We do hope that you have enjoyed reading this large print book.

Did you know that all of our titles are available for purchase?

We publish a wide range of high quality large print books including:
Romances, Mysteries, Classics
General Fiction
Non Fiction and Westerns

Special interest titles available in large print are:
The Little Oxford Dictionary
Music Book
Song Book
Hymn Book
Service Book

Also available from us courtesy of Oxford University Press:
Young Readers' Dictionary
(large print edition)
Young Readers' Thesaurus
(large print edition)

For further information or a free brochure, please contact us at:
Ulverscroft Large Print Books Ltd.,
The Green, Bradgate Road, Anstey,
Leicester, LE7 7FU, England.
Tel: (00 44) 0116 236 4325
Fax: (00 44) 0116 234 0205

Other titles published by Ulverscroft:

THE GREAT DARKNESS

Jim Kelly

Cambridge, 1939: In the opening weeks of the Second World War, the first blackout — the Great Darkness — covers southern England, enveloping the city. Detective Inspector Eden Brooke, a wounded hero of the Great War, takes his nightly dip in the cool waters of the Cam. Though the night is full of alarms, in this Phoney War the enemy never comes. But daylight reveals a corpse on the riverside, the body torn apart by some unspeakable force. Brooke investigates, calling on the expertise and inspiration of a faithful group of fellow 'nighthawks' across the city, all condemned, like the detective himself, to a life lived away from the light. Within hours, the Great Darkness has claimed a second victim. War, it seems, has many casualties. But what links these crimes of the night?

DEATH TOLL

Jim Kelly

Bodies are being exhumed to higher ground at King's Lynn's cemetery to avoid flooding. But when the coffin of murdered pub landlady Nora Tilden is hauled up, the corpse of a young black man is revealed; killed by a billhook blow to the head and dumped in the grave when Nora was buried, twenty-eight years earlier. Was he the victim of a racist crime? When DI Peter Shaw and DS George Valentine investigate, they are led to The Flask, Nora's pub just along the riverbank, where her family hides more than one dark secret. It's soon clear that no one can be trusted. Can Shaw and Valentine discover the truth behind the murder before it's too late and ghosts from the past claim another victim?

DEATH WATCH

Jim Kelly

5 September, 1992. Fifteen-year-old Norma Jean Judd disappeared from her home, never to be seen again. 5 September, 2010. Exactly eighteen years later, Bryan Judd, Norma Jean's twin, is pulled from the searing heat of a hospital incinerator. When his charred remains are examined, the murder squad confirms that this was no accident. Could his death somehow be linked to his sister's disappearance? DI Peter Shaw and DS George Valentine begin their investigation into Bryan's life and uncover a secret world of criminal activity in Bryan's neighbourhood and at the hospital where he died. Can Shaw and Valentine solve Bryan's murder before any more lives are violently snatched away? And will they ever learn the truth about what happened to Norma Jean?